Once Burned

Catherine had been betrayed once by a faithless suitor—and vowed to guard forever against such a threat to her honor again. But now, late at night in her dim-lit library, she found herself not on guard but in danger.

The man who called himself John Smith smiled as he asked why she needed a book at this ungodly hour.

Catherine laughed shakily. "I am overtired. Have you ever been so fatigued you could not sleep?"

He leaned closer, and his voice was a silken whisper. "Fatigue is the furthest thing from my mind right now."

He grasped her shoulders and she was intensely aware of the warmth of his hands through the flimsy muslin of her gown. He was going to kiss her. The knowledge was a fire building inside her, and when he kissed her, and his kiss deepened, she heard a faint sound and realized to her horror it came from her own throat.

Catherine may have been burned once by love—but it had been nothing like this. Now as she responded to this man's lips, it was as if her very bones had turned to flame. . . .

A Dedicated Scoundrel

by

Anne Barbour

A SIGNET BOOK

SIGNET
Published by the Penguin Group
Penguin Books USA Inc., 375 Hudson Street,
New York, New York 10014, U.S.A.
Penguin Books Ltd, 27 Wrights Lane,
London W8 5TZ, England
Penguin Books Australia Ltd, Ringwood,
Victoria, Australia
Penguin Books Canada Ltd, 10 Alcorn Avenue,
Toronto, Ontario, Canada M4V 3B2
Penguin Books (N.Z.) Ltd, 182–190 Wairau Road,
Auckland 10, New Zealand

Penguin Books Ltd, Registered Offices:
Harmondsworth, Middlesex, England

First published by Signet, an imprint of Dutton Signet,
a division of Penguin Books USA Inc.

First Printing, June, 1997
10 9 8 7 6 5 4 3 2 1

*For Marie Shaffer—a special cousin
to whom I owe a debt of gratitude
for all her PR work on my behalf.
Every author should have such relatives!*

Prologue

Sweet Jesus, he hurt. All over. The pain seemed a living entity, writhing within him, ripping tissue, tearing muscle, and splintering his bones into jagged chunks.

For what seemed like hours, he drifted in and out of consciousness until at last he awoke and cautiously opened his eyes. It was dark. Where the devil was he? Someplace that smelled incredibly foul. He rather thought he must be lying in a pile of excrement—hopefully, not human. He moved his head tentatively, an action that brought a groan to his lips. Almost immediately a smooth hand reached to touch his forehead.

"Be easy, *querida*. You are with Yelena now. All is well." The whispered words, spoken in a guttural, peasant Spanish flowed over him like the caress of her fingers. Yelena. Did he know a Yelena? Perhaps. Lord, if he could only remember. He struggled to sit up, an action he regretted instantly.

"Who are you?" he gasped, falling back into his filthy mound of straw. "Where am I? Good God, what happened to me?"

The woman's only reply was a rich chuckle, but when he tried again to lift his head, she said quickly, "No, no. Better to stay as you are. I am Yelena Padilla; you are in my father's barn. I do not know what happened to you, *señor*, only that I found you here when I came in to see to the animals before bed. Here—" She slipped an arm beneath his head to place a wineskin to his lips. "Can you drink? It will help."

Greedily, he gulped the grappa. Raw and sharp, it burned all the way down his gullet, but, snorting and coughing, he managed to retain a few drops.

"*Gracias.*" God, it even hurt to breathe. His ribs must be broken in a dozen places. Who—what—? Sighing, he nestled into the woman's generous bosom. Well, every cloud . . . he mused muzzily. The next moment, his reverie was broken by a coarse, masculine shout.

"*Hola!* Yelena! Where are you, you lazy girl? What is this?" The voice lifted in surprise as the toe of a sturdy work boot nudged the injured man ungently.

"A stranger, Jorge. An Englishman, I think. He was here—scarcely alive—sprawled in the cow byre when I came in. He's been beaten."

"I can see that. For certain, this uniform is not of the French. Well, he is none of our concern. We had better notify the alcalde."

Mierda! The injured man lifted a hand to his head. It still felt like a receptacle for discarded musketry, but at the mention of the mayor, alarm bells screamed in his brain. Screwing his features into an expression of piteous supplication, he glanced upward.

Jorge snorted. "Like that, is it? You do not want *soldados* nosing around?"

There was a thoughtful pause, and the farmer bent over the injured man. Calloused fingers rummaged in the pockets of the tattered uniform, eventually drawing forth a pouch that clinked suggestively.

Jorge grunted. "Ah—this will buy you a few hours' silence, *soldado*. But—" He turned to the woman. "He must be out and away from here by sunrise tomorrow, Yelena. Otherwise, we risk our own necks, and there is not enough gold in here for that."

Rising, he tucked the pouch into his unsavory shirtfront and brushed his hands together, as though ridding himself of both the dust of the barn and responsibility for his unwanted guest. Turning, he stumped from the primitive little building.

The woman, too, made as though to rise, but the injured man grasped feebly at her hand. "No—my angel, do not leave me."

Yelena laughed softly. "You have a smooth tongue, English—to go with your pretty face. Do not fear, I shall return—with bandages, and perhaps I shall bring you some of the soup I have simmering on the stove in the house."

With a rustle of homespun skirts, she was gone, and the Englishman was left to contemplate his situation.

His mind, while still fuzzy with pain, had begun to clear. Lord, he thought he'd made a clean escape from the French encampment. By God, he was sure of it! The attack had come later—much later, and unless he was very much mistaken, it had come from his own side. What the devil was going on? Who had beat him nearly to death and left him broken and bleeding in a water-filled ditch? He should have drowned—it was God's own luck that he hadn't. It had taken every ounce of determination in him to make it to this meager shelter.

He turned his thoughts in a more pleasant direction. He was alive—that was the important thing, and he would be spending the evening with Yelena. Not his usual choice of companion, but no doubt a pleasant armful—although he was not sure he could manage even the most minimal dalliance. At any rate, he would recoup for a few hours, and find the strength to make his way back to Salamanca. And then—and then, he would discover the man responsible for his current predicament. A curious emptiness filled him. Dear Lord, could it really be—?

No matter. Whoever was responsible would pay—would pay dearly and long for what he had done.

He turned his face into the dubious comfort of his malodorous bed, and with a sigh, drifted into the healing darkness of sleep.

Chapter One

"Justin, this is all so incredible, I can hardly take it in." Charles Rutledge leaned forward, placing his elbows on the massive Kent desk that held pride of position in the center of his study. It was late, and the man who paced the floor opposite him threw grotesque shadows on hangings and walls in the light of the single candle that flickered fitfully on the desk.

"Incredible seems to be the *mot juste*, Charles," said the man dryly. Lord Justin Belforte flung his not inconsiderable length into a sturdy leather chair, and ran long fingers through hair as black as the night that hung in a thick curtain outside the room's single window. Justin was not a handsome man, nor was he particularly prepossessing in aspect, yet there was that about him that tended to arrest one's attention. His features were spare and arranged with precision, but his mouth, oddly, was full and mobile. It was at the moment, curved in a sour smile. "However," Justin continued, "I hope you have found my story believable."

Charles lifted his head at the faintly discordant note in Justin's tone.

"Of course, I do," he responded gruffly. "No one who knows you could believe the faradiddles that've been brayed to the world in the press over the last few days."

Justin exhaled a long breath. He had not allowed himself to consider the possibility that Charles would fail him. Someone had done so recently, to be sure, but that was another matter.

"But, who the devil *is* responsible?" continued Charles. "For it appears there's no doubt we have a traitor in our ranks."

"To say nothing of a would-be murderer."

"Incredible," repeated Charles. "And it was such a simple assignment, to begin with."

"Yes!" exclaimed Justin. "That's just it. I was commanded to ride to Huerta and order the Spanish officer in charge there to maintain troops on the bridge. Wellington was concerned that the French would use it as an escape route after Salamanca. A small task that should have been accomplished in a couple of days. Instead, I was captured, and someone was sent in my place to order the officer to abandon the bridge. Not only half the remaining French army scuttled to safety, but General Rivenchy escaped as well."

Charles sighed heavily. "And when you were captured—You believe that was a personal attempt against you?"

"I can think of no other explanation." Justin spoke sharply and rose again. "It was all too easy, Charles. The window left ajar—my horse left conveniently saddled in the stable. I was suspicious even at the time, but decided to chance it. I almost made it, too. In another five minutes I would have been in friendly territory. It was no accident that I was set upon just beyond British lines. Those bastards were waiting to ambush me in an area I couldn't avoid, and at least a couple of them were neither French nor Spanish. I could swear one of them muttered something in English. It was only God's mercy to the just and pure of heart that I didn't turn up my toes in that water-filled ditch. Every inch of me was battered to oblivion."

Charles grimaced.

"And you were attacked again just today? Who knows you are in England?"

"No one. After I contacted you, I crept into a snug little mouse hole in Limehouse. There's an abbess there who takes very good care of me, and I can depend on her discretion. I've spoken to no one else. Yet I was set upon last night on my way home from dinner at a nearby tavern. There were only two of them, luckily, and not very skilled at assassination."

Charles sighed again. "Perhaps you should not have returned to England."

"What the devil else could I have done? Wellington's staff was out for my blood in Salamanca. As far as they were concerned, it was I who was responsible for Rivenchy's escape. Not that I can blame them for their supposition. The whole scenario was beautifully arranged." Justin's eyes, an odd, gun-metal shade of gray, glittered darkly in his white face. "Charles, I have been branded traitor!"

"But, surely, my boy, not for long. Believe me, I will spare no effort in unmasking the real villain in the piece. For," said Charles heavily, "he must be found. Not only because he's almost ruined your reputation—"

Justin's laughter was a mirthless bark. "My God, yes, we can't have the pristine reputation of Lord Justin Belforte besmirched by such calumny."

Charles hesitated. "I was sorry to hear about the duke, lad. I wish I could go to him and—"

"And what? Tell him he was wrong to suspect his loving son? Lord, do you think he'd believe you? St. John is probably with him as we speak, commiserating with him, hovering at his bedside and telling him, yes, it's a wise father that knows his own son, and it was inevitable that I'd come to a bad end, and all the rest of the litany. My brother's perfectly right, of course, as usual. I just never thought I'd come to this particular bad end. Although," he concluded musingly, "I suppose, if one wants to go out with a flair, dancing at the end of a noose for treason certainly borders on the spectacular."

"That's not even remotely humorous, Justin," said Charles harshly. Justin made no reply beyond a sardonic quirk of his mobile brows. He began to pace the floor once more, and now his shadow leaped across the wall in a sinister fashion.

"Have you heard from Robbie?" he asked, his tone inconsequential. "When I left him in Spain, he said he had a spot of leave coming. Is he—?"

"Never mind Robbie," Charles spoke sharply. "You must not contact him. You mustn't speak to anyone."

"I fear it's a little late for that. It was Robbie who met me on my return to camp and told me of Rivenchy's escape—and my supposed part in it. He helped me sneak away from Salamanca and arranged my passage home from Spain."

Charles swore softly. "He'd have done you a greater service if he'd encouraged you to stay put and face down the accusation. But, what's done is done. Take yourself out of the city, Justin. Go to earth, and leave this to me."

Justin stiffened, but a lazy smile curved his lips. "Leave? And miss the fun?"

Charles rose from his desk and walked around to plant himself in front of his friend. "Now, listen to me, you young whelp. I don't want you galloping off in all directions at once. You're a wanted man—and when Scovell wants a man as badly as he wants you, he'll scour Spain to find you."

Charles referred to George Scovell, the man who had risen from the ranks by sheer wit and grit to become England's spymaster in the Peninsula. Wellington had often boasted that Napoleon's army did not make a move without his knowing of it, and Scovell and his men acted as his ears and eyes.

"And when he does find you," continued Charles, "he'll turn you over to the people at the Horse Guards. Wilkerson may not give you the opportunity to exonerate yourself. As you say, you've been well and truly screwed, my boy. Even should he wish to give you the benefit of the doubt, the fact is now that you have the journalists screaming for your blood, the politicians will not be far behind. After all, the escape of a French general, with the cooperation of a British officer, is bound to attract attention. Wellington may come under a great deal of pressure to hang you from the highest yardarm—at the earliest possible opportunity. In addition"—he hesitated—"I should not be telling you this, but we have reason to believe that a spy has been operating on the Top Floor for some time now."

"The Top Floor!" This was the designation given to the Depot of Military Intelligence at Whitehall, newly created, and dedicated solely to the gathering of intelligence. "My God! Have you any idea who—? How do you know of this?"

Charles lifted a hand impatiently. "Oh, missing dispatches. Incidents of the French obtaining information on planned attacks, troop movements, et cetera. And no, we have no idea who is behind it. I have been working on almost nothing else for the past several years for he almost cost us our victory at Salamanca. It was the element of surprise, as you know, that swung the tide for Wellington there. I have been virtually glued to my desk, putting off some journeys I should have made some time ago. At any rate, we have theorized that the man has a contact in the Peninsula."

Comprehension spread across Justin's features in a wave of anger. "And now I suppose I'm the prime suspect for that."

Charles said nothing, but squirmed uncomfortably.

"Pah!" muttered Justin. "Very well, then, I'll hie myself to Hertfordshire."

"Your father's place near—where is it—Barkway?" asked Charles doubtfully. "I'd think that would be one of the first places anyone would look for you, outside London. You've always had a fondness for it."

"Yes, but I want to stay within skulking distance of the city. I'll only stay at Longbarrow for a day or two. There's no one there except for old Bribbage, and he's closemouthed as a post. By the time my assorted ill-wishers realize I've flown our fair metropolis, I'll think of someplace else. I'll let you know when I alight more or less permanently."

"What do you mean, skulking?" Charles's voice sharpened again.

The mocking smile dropped from Justin's lips. "I can't just sit with my hands folded waiting for you to pull my groats from the fire, Charles. I know you will do your best, but I mean to uncover the truth of what happened as quickly as possible. You see," he finished, fixing the insouciant grin in place once more, "while I freely admit to being notably lacking in moral scruples, I don't fancy being

blamed for something I didn't do." He sat back in his chair, searching for another subject with which to distract Charles. He glanced
around the room and chuckled.

"How often have I sat in this chamber, old friend? In this chair.
Lord, I remember the first time I came to you here. I'd just been sent
down from Oxford with my tail between my legs with not a friend
in the world."

Charles lifted a hand in negation. "I was just pleased you thought
to seek refuge with me. Mary was, too."

He referred to his wife, who had passed away many years ago.

"God knows, I was headed for trouble." Justin shook his head,
glancing about once more with appreciation. "I've always liked this
room. You have a collector's eye, Charles. But—Isn't something
missing? Yes, that infernal clock. It used to hang above the mantel,
and its ticking drove me daft. And, by God, you've done away with
that statue of Venus or some other scantily clothed deity."

"The clock is out for repairs," replied Charles dryly, "and the
Venus has been removed to my drawing room. I created a grouping
of classical figures there, and I see what you are doing. I am not to
be diverted, Justin. I wish you will disappear for a while and leave
this business to me."

"You always were very free with your advice. I clearly recall—
once again sitting here in this chair—the times you upbraided me for
my wild ways. Not nearly so severly as did my father, but still, I always thought it a case of pots berating kettles, for you gamble yourself from time to time, do you not?"

"Yes," replied Charles austerely. "I admit I enjoy a little flutter
occasionally, but I never made it my life's work as you seemed to be
intent on doing. Now, if you can drag yourself once and for all from
your little journey into the past, I want you to listen to me."

"Charles!" exclaimed Justin, all bruised sensibility. "I always listen to you."

"Good," said Charles, unmoved. "Then hear this. Stay away from
London. Stay away from Robbie. Stay out of trouble. Do nothing
until you hear from me. Do I make myself clear?"

"Perfectly, my dear fellow." Justin smiled sunnily.

Some hours later, as dawn slanted through the streets of London,
a nondescript figure made its way out of London along the Huntingdon Road. Garbed in serviceable breeches, coat, and boots, he did
not look precisely disreputable, but no one, even on closer inspection, would take him for a gentleman, except for his horse. He rode a
magnificent stallion, a fine, ribbed-up hack, albeit rather oddly

shaped, and Justin sat him with a muscled elegance that belied the humble clothing. Justin had thought long and hard about bringing Caliban with him in his exile, for the animal rather tended to stand out in an inn stable. However, master and mount had been through a great deal, and the stallion's speed and stamina had saved Justin's bacon on more than one occasion. In addition, Caliban was possessed of a number of tricks that tended to come in handy now and then.

His thoughts as Caliban trotted at an easy pace were not pleasant. He marveled at the suddenness with which one's life could suddenly plunge into the sewer. He'd been in scrapes before—indeed, sometimes it seemed as though his whole life had been one, long horrific predicament. He had been accused of many wrongdoings before, up to and including felonies—often with good reason. There had been the time he had purloined an entire ship, after all. But it had seemed like a good idea at the time, and he had managed to squeak through the episode without serious inconvenience to himself.

However, this was treason, and somehow it carried a different ring. Treason could not be carried off as an excess of high spirits, or a necessary route to the accomplishment of a purpose one considered important. No, there were some depths to which even he would not sink, and treason was one of them.

And then there was the matter of the attack against him. Two attacks, if one counted the encounter with a pair of street thugs on a dark street in London—one of whom muttered his name. He recalled his interrogation by the French officer at Huerta. How had the good *capitán* come into possession of so many details of his life? It seemed certain that someone close to him was aware of his mission and had revealed that information to the nearest French garrison. A wave of nausea swept over him as he considered the one detail of the interrogation that loomed in his memory—the one detail he had omitted in his report to Charles. The officer had referred repeatedly to a file that lay on his desk, and on the top of the packet lay a sheet of paper, covered with a handwriting that was familiar to Justin.

Even now, the memory of the fleeting, upside-down glimpse he had caught of the paper brought the taste of bile to his mouth. Perhaps he should not have been surprised, but he was. The realization of the identity of the man—the man who may have contributed the information that almost caused his death—had come as an undeniable and appalling shock—one which he still could not bear to contemplate.

Just before he reached the village of Buntingford, Justin turned off the main highway into a leafy lane that circled the little hamlet. Soon, he turned again; this time into a barely discernible track. It was a byway that would cut several miles from his journey, and it served the additionally useful purpose of taking him out of the way of inquisitive fellow travelers. Justin had used it many times, even though it led through private land.

He returned to his painful musings. Lord knew there were enough scoundrels and miscreants among his acquaintances who might well have conspired to spirit General Rivenchy away from his stone prison near Salamanca, but who in Scovell's cadre of operatives would fill that description? The men he knew there were fanatically devoted to the British cause, risking their lives—many times to no good purpose that he could see—for God and country and all that other balderdash. He sometimes wondered how he had ever fallen in with such an idealistic lot.

Because of Charles, of course. Charles, who had scooped up a troubled, disillusioned boy, teetering on the brink of ruin. Justin had just been sent down from Oxford, and was very badly in need of a friend when he'd first met Charles. The Duke of Sheffield had recently washed his hands of his second son for the last time, and Justin had endured yet another lecture from St. John, starting with his evil nature and his ingratitude and proceeding through the whole tiresome list of his iniquities.

Charles had been the friend of one of his tutors, one of the few individuals at Oxford who regarded the young Lord Justin with anything warmer than the gravest disapproval. On reaching London, alone and friendless, Justin had approached Charles, who promptly lent him the money to purchase a commission in the army. It was not long afterward that Justin stumbled on Charles's true profession—that of intelligence agent for His Majesty's Army. To Justin, the news was almost too good to be true, and he begged Charles to let him join in the fun.

Justin grimaced. Yes, that was how he had envisioned the life of a spy—as a glorious adventure. And, for once, he would be on the right side of an adventure—risking life and limb for God and country. By God, he'd be a hero!

The reality, of course, had been a far cry from that exhilarating vision. He had plunged into a miasma of lies, deceit, and trickery from which, nowadays, he rarely emerged. Not that lies and deceit were beneath him, of course and, truth to tell, he enjoyed the occasional, masterful piece of trickery, but it had all grown tedious in the extreme.

And now this—slinking out of London with his tail between his legs, all because—

His attention was caught by a sound from a small, dilapidated shed set a few yards off the track. He did not slow, but he stiffened, every sense alert. The sound came again. It sounded like the cry of a woman, and—yes, tethered outside the shed was a dainty mare.

Justin shrugged and urged his mount forward. Rescuing damsels in distress was low on his list of priorities at the moment, and he had no desire to make his presence known in the vicinity. He wished to arrive at Longbarrow before nightfall. He had chosen his bolt hole well, he thought. It was one of his father's smaller estates and Justin had always loved it. It was currently in the care of an elderly couple who had known him since boyhood and who could be counted on to keep his presence a secret.

Justin glanced curiously at the shed as he drew abreast of it. The thought snaked through him that no female in her right mind should have so much as set foot in a hovel so obviously on the verge of collapse. Perhaps—A loud crack sounded, and before Justin's bemused gaze, one side of the little building slowly gave way. The other walls tilted accordingly, until one side of the roof sagged to the ground.

The woman inside the shed screamed again, and without thinking, Justin leaped to the ground. In seconds he had reached the doorway, now twisted and gaping.

"Hello!" he called. "Is someone here?"

"Oh!" The answering voice was melodious, but at the moment, high-pitched and trembling. "Thank God! I'm stuck, I'm afraid. Can you help?"

Gingerly, Justin forced his way inside the shed. Peering through the dust rising from the collapsed wall, he could see no one.

"Where are you?" Inhaling a bit of debris, he sneezed violently.

"I'm over here—near the hearth." The woman continued as Justin followed the sound of her voice. "I followed Silk—my dog—in here. I don't know what she was after, but she's stuck, too, I'm afraid. I think a table fell on her, and she yelped. When I began pulling it off, the whole place collapsed, and—"

By now, Justin had reached her side. The female appeared to be tall and slender, and she was attired in a plain riding habit. A quick glance served to apprise him of that she was indeed—stuck. She lay, or rather sat, crouched, under several timbers that had fallen directly across her legs. Other, smaller pieces of roof, were strewn across her shoulders.

"Are you hurt?" Justin asked, moving to tug at the largest of the timbers.

"No—only my pride. It was such a stupid thing to do, charging in here when I knew this old shack was on its last legs."

"You're right," snapped Justin. "It was. A stupid thing to do, that is." He ignored the sputtering protest that greeted this statement, and with great care, he removed the remainder of the timbers, releasing her from her temporary prison. Brushing the remainder of the debris from her person, he assisted her to her feet.

He had been right. She was a very tall woman.

"Oh, my goodness," she gasped. "Thank you so very much. Now, what about Silk?"

With a muttered exclamation of impatience, Justin directed his attention to the source of a flurry of growls and whimpers that emanated from a spot a few inches from where the woman had been trapped. Dropping to all fours, he reached under the collapsed table to grasp a furry backside that waggled indignantly under his fingers.

"Come along, you insufferable little mutt." He was by now growling rather impressively himself, which only caused the little dog to wedge herself farther into the pile of debris.

Cursing freely under his breath, Justin shifted position, and with both hands clutched at the little animal and gave a mighty heave. An ominous creaking sound filled the area, and at a warning cry from the woman, Justin looked up. Time slowed as he watched the roof crumple, and the last thing he saw was the swaying of the nearby chimney piece as the stones separated and seemed to reach toward him.

He did not know how much time elapsed before he woke. His head ached abominably, and as he struggled to sit up, cool fingers pressed against his forehead. For a moment he thought he must still be in that Spanish cow byre. However, he was enveloped in the fragrance of clean white sheets, and a fresh breeze from a window bathed him in a sunny warmth.

Cow byre? The memory was oddly fragmented, and he was unable to grasp it again.

"Mariah, I believe he is regaining consciousness. Oh, thank God. Sir, you must not sit up. Please, just rest."

He glanced about the room in which he found himself. It was large and elegantly furnished, if rather feminine in atmosphere. He was lying in a tester bed, beneath a light comforter. A wardrobe, commode, and dressing table were set along the walls of the chamber, and a small writing desk had been placed under one window. Some rather fragile chairs completed the complement of furniture, and on one of these, pulled up to the bedside, sat a young woman.

No, not a young woman. She must be, he judged, coming up on thirty. But, well preserved. Yes, indeed, for despite the sensible cap that covered a mane of thick, lustrous hair of an unusual shade of honey-gold, she possessed the figure of a girl. Her most startling feature, however, was a pair of wide-set eyes of a deep, pure green—which, at the moment were fastened anxiously on his face.

Another woman moved into view. She, too, wore a cap and looked to be a comfortable sort, with short, curly brown hair and brown eyes. She was neat and plump and moved with brisk efficiency as she placed a basin of water on the bedside table. Having done so, she turned to survey the patient.

"Well, he looks none the worse for wear, at any rate," she said. The glance she ran over his supine form was tinged with suspicion, and he wondered what he had done to warrant such wariness.

He uttered a faint moan, not so much because he was in pain—although he was still suffering some residual aches from whatever had befallen him—but because he had learned long ago that it was never wise to pass up an opportunity to gain a little sympathy. One never knew when it might come in handy.

"Oh, dear," said Green Eyes. She dipped a cloth in the water basin and began to lave his brow.

"Thank you," he whispered weakly. "Where am I? What happened?"

"You are in my home," she replied in a singularly musical voice that he thought he had heard before. "I am Miss Catherine Meade. You were injured when the shed roof fell in on you. When you went in after Silk. My dog?" At his increasingly blank stare, she stopped in confusion. "Do you remember anything of what happened?"

"No, I'm afraid not." He formed the words with the appearance of great effort.

"Oh, my. Well, I must tell you, sir, that you acted quite the hero."

The devil you say, he thought, startled.

"Yes, and I'm afraid your only reward so far has been a nasty bump on the head."

Well. He chuckled inwardly. We shall have to see if we can come up with something a little more substantial, won't we, my emerald-eyed poppet?

Perhaps something of his thoughts must have appeared in his eyes, for she shuttered her gaze and sent him a faint smile.

"Yes. Well, in the meantime, we must notify your family of your contretemps. What is your name, sir?"

Instinctively, he searched within himself for a false name. Somewhat to his surprise, nothing came to mind. He searched farther. Still nothing. A name hovered just on the edge of his consciousness, but refused to present itself.

He spoke at last in a labored croak.

"I'm sorry," he gasped, with perfect truth. "I cannot seem to remember my name."

Chapter Two

The man felt a cold sweat break out on his forehead in large, prickly beads. His name! What the devil was his name? How could he forget his by-God *name*? He was almost overwhelmed by a stabbing sense of panic. He was in danger—he had to get out of here!

But when he threw aside the comforter and bolted upright in bed, a wave of dizziness sent him plumeting back into his pillow.

"Sir?" Miss Green Eyes—what was her name?—Meade—bent over him. "What is it? Are you all right? You truly do not know who you are?"

He shook his head, then winced at the pain caused by the slight movement.

"Well, never mind. The doctor will be here soon, and I'm sure he will—"

"Doctor?" The word erupted harshly.

"Why, yes. We sent for Dr. Beech as soon as you were brought here. I'm afraid you were in the shed for some time, under all the rubble. I could not free you myself, and had to go for help."

She hesitated. "Perhaps you could tell us what you were doing there? That is, were you on your way to see us?"

"To see you?" he echoed blankly.

"Yes. I thought that, since you were on my land, you must have been on your way to visit."

"Visit," he repeated, wishing he did not sound so much like a demented parrot.

"Perhaps," interjected the second young woman, who was now occupied in brushing the dusty coat that hung on a nearby chair, "we'd better leave him to sleep it off until the doctor comes. Your grandmama will be wanting to know what's afoot."

"Of course." Miss Meade rose with a graceful rustle of skirts. "Please rest now, sir. We'll be back shortly, and if you need anything, you have but to call."

The next moment she was gone, leaving an unidentifiable but piquant fragrance in her wake.

He stared at the ceiling and gave himself up to furious thought. All to no avail. He could remember nothing about a shed—or a dog—or ever having seen Miss Catherine Meade before in his life. He did not remember what he might have been doing on her land. My God, he couldn't remember anything! Not who he was, or where he was from, or where he was going, or anything else about himself. It was as though he had been born just five minutes ago.

He swallowed the tide of panic that rose within him. He had to get out of here! Once again, he threw aside the covers, and this time he was able to put his feet on the floor. For all the good it did him. With a startled gasp, he toppled over. He swore, long and fluently. His foot was apparently broken—or at least, sprained.

Painfully, he crawled back into bed and, pulling the comforter up to his chin, awaited developments.

In her own bedchamber, Miss Catherine Meade turned to confront the woman who had followed her.

"Mariah, what would you have me do? Throw him out into the road? He is injured—and he does not know who he is?"

"Mmph," sniffed Mariah. "Says he doesn't know. That's two different things. I don't trust him, Cath. He dresses like a peddler, but he owns a horse that's worth three hundred guineas if he's worth a farthing."

Catherine stifled a snort of amusement. "Are you saying he's lying about losing his memory? That he stole his horse? You're making a great deal of the fact that he does not dress as well as he might. Don't forget, he ran into a collapsing building to rescue Silk—and me."

Mariah chuckled. "I don't suppose he expected that little shack could do any harm if somebody threw it at him. He just didn't reckon on the stone chimney piece. I'm not saying he's a thief—necessarily. I'm just saying, I—"

"You don't trust him," finished Catherine. "Well, to be frank, I'm not sure I do, either, but he's hurt and he's in our house. We'll see what Adam Beech has to say before we decide what to do with him."

Mariah brightened. "Indeed, the doctor will know what to do."

She bustled from the room, and Catherine began the task of removing her stained riding habit. There was certainly nothing about the stranger, she mused, to cause one to have misgivings about him. Upon catching sight of him in the shed, her impression had been one of latent strength. It was his eyes, however, that had arrested her attention. A peculiar shade of gray, they reminded her of the barrel of her father's favorite hunting rifle. She used to touch it as a child, attracted by the smooth sheen of the metal and the danger the weapon represented.

Later, when he was lying in bed, she sensed a sort of coiled tension about the man, as though he felt himself in some sort of danger.

She shook herself. Goodness, she was not ordinarily so fanciful. She wondered what Adam would have to say about the presence of this odd visitor in her house. She sighed. Quite a bit, she supposed. He always had a great deal to say regarding anything that could be remotely construed as a threat to her well-being.

She frowned. Adam was a good friend as well as a good doctor, and she had enjoyed his company and companionship over the sometimes lonely years of her exile, but she wished he were not quite so proprietary in his attentions toward her. She shrugged. Not that Adam would ever allow his actions to go beyond the bounds of convention, but he always made her feel so— so what? Guilty that she did not feel more for him than friendship? How absurd. One could not force affection on oneself any more than it could be forced on another.

After washing the dust from her person and combing the debris of her mishap from her hair, she donned a simple morning gown of pomona green. Hurrying from her room, she walked swiftly down the corridor and tapped gently on a door just a few steps from her own. At the faint response from within, she entered.

"Grandmama, I did not know you had risen from your nap." Catherine advanced into the room and stooped to embrace the old woman, who sat reading in a comfortable chair. The sitting room was, like the adjacent bedchamber, decorated in palest blue.

"Sit by me, child." The old woman patted the chair opposite hers. Lady Jane was a small woman, and spare. She dressed with a great deal of elegance, but modestly, withal. Her greatest pride was her hair. It had once been a glorious gold, as Catherine's was now, and, though it had turned a snow-white and had thinned considerably, still crowned her neat little head in spectacular coils.

"Mariah tells me you were in a bit of a bother," she said in a fragile voice. "Are you all right?"

"Quite all right, Grandmama. Did she also tell you of the mysterious stranger in our midst?"

"Yes, indeed. She seems to think he has come to do us some mischief. Tell me all about it," she commanded.

Catherine seated herself and related the circumstances of the morning's adventure.

"And he cannot remember his own name?" asked the old woman. "How extraordinary! What do you think of him, Catherine?"

"Think of him? Why, there is nothing to think of him, Grandmama. We have exchanged only a few words, and those were not of any consequence. He is simply a man who has suffered an injury—one that has somehow damaged his brain."

"Mmph. Where is he?"

"We put him in the green suite. I think—What is it, Grandmama?" she asked as the old woman rose slowly and with some effort.

"I want to see him, of course."

A second woman entered the room, and Catherine sent her a significant glance. The woman was large and stooped and nearly as old as Grandmama, and she had been Lady Jane's handmaiden since that lady had made her come-out, nearly seventy years before.

"You'll do nothing of the kind, my lady. You have not had your cordial yet. Besides, you didn't get much rest last night, and you agreed to stay to your room today."

Lady Jane swung on her. "You're an interfering old biddy, Hannah Riggins. I have no intention of cowering in my chamber like a frightened rabbit when there's something going on. Now, help me—"

"Grandmama," interposed Catherine hastily. "I'm not sure the, er, patient is up to receiving visitors. Why don't you—oh!" She paused in some relief, listening. "Someone is here. It must be Adam. Why don't you wait until Adam has seen the man and he can then give you a full report. Time enough then for you to descend on him."

She smiled, knowing well her grandmother's innate curiosity.

"Oh, very well," grumbled Lady Jane, subsiding once more into her chair.

Dropping a kiss on the old lady's hair, Catherine ran lightly from the room and down the stairs, intercepting the figure who had just entered the house.

"Adam!" She held out both hands in greeting. "I am so glad you are here. Thank you for coming so promptly."

The gentleman who grasped her hands was not tall, but compactly built, and muscular without appearing stocky. A shock of brown hair fell over a pair of brown eyes that sparkled with humor, and perhaps something warmer.

"Good Lord, Cath," he said, "from what your groom said, I expected to find the floors stained with the blood of a mysterious stranger sprawled at death's door on your best Persian rug."

"Nothing nearly so dramatic," Catherine replied with a laugh. Once again, as the two ascended the stairs, she recounted her adventure.

Adam stopped abruptly, subjecting Catherine to an intent scrutiny. "My God, the whole thing collapsed on you? My dear, are you all right?"

"As you see." She bobbed an impudent curtsy. "Actually, it was our mysterious stranger who caught the brunt of the damage. Adam—" Her expression sobered. "The poor man suffered a terrible blow to the head when the chimney piece fell on him, and he has lost his memory!"

"What!"

"Yes. I have heard of such cases, have not you?"

"Mmp. Yes, of course, but I've had no experience with them except for a time or two when it was faked for the patient's convenience."

The two had resumed their journey upward, and now stood before the injured man's door.

"Oh, I'm sure that's not the case here, Adam. The fellow seemed quite panic-stricken when I asked him his name. His mind had obviously gone blank."

"We'll see." The doctor opened the door, but when Catherine moved to follow him, he stayed her.

"You won't want to come in, of course, my dear."

"Oh, for heaven's sake, Adam. He may be in bed, but he's fully clothed."

"But I shall wish to examine him," replied Adam gently. "I'll call you when I'm through."

Irritated at his unnecessary devotion to the proprieties, Catherine would have continued her dispute, but Adam had already entered the chamber and closed the door behind him. She stumped away in some indignation.

Lord, did he think a woman nearing thirty would faint at the sight of a man stripped down to his drawers? Actually, she supposed many spinsters would, but surely Adam knew her better than that. Had she not splinted Jem Beamis's broken leg last fall when he was injured during the harvest and they were not able to locate Adam? Did Adam think the stranger a dangerous marauder who could not be trusted in the same room with a lady, even though he was laid by the heels with a whack on the head?

Considering the aspect of the man who now lay in her best

spare bedchamber, however, Catherine suspected that Adam's assessment might be correct. Despite his present debility, and though he was docile enough while flat on his back, there was a definite aura of a temporarily inconvenienced predator about him. Laughing at her own fancy, she strode off to attend to her household duties.

The man in the bed opened one eye to observe a gentleman of professional mien bending over him. His muscles tensed in an unthinking urge to leap at the man's throat, but, surprised at this savage reaction, he suppressed the instinct and lay quiet. No one was holding him prisoner, after all. Were they?

"Well, then," grunted the gentleman, "let's have a look at you."

A doctor then, and one who seemed to know his business. His fingers were cool and sure as he prodded bone and sinew. The foot, he pronounced, was not broken, but merely sprained. He applied a cool compress and bound it efficiently, which action brought considerable relief.

"I am Dr. Beech, by the way—Adam Beech. Catherine—that is, Miss Meade, tells me you have lost your memory," he said as he assisted his patient in replacing his disarranged bedclothes.

"Apparently," murmured the patient. "At least, I do not seem to know who I am."

As he spoke, the doctor's brows lifted momentarily. "Extraordinary," said Dr. Beech, the skepticism on his face unmistakable. "Well, perhaps we can determine in just what areas your memory has failed you. Do you know where you are?"

The patient smiled briefly. "In England, I assume, though I have no idea where."

"Can you tell me the name of the reigning monarch?"

"George, the third, but his son is Regent."

"What year is it?"

The man frowned. "Eighteen twelve—but I'm not sure of the precise date."

The doctor grunted. "It's August fourteenth. Where is your home?"

"I have been trying to remember, but that knowledge, too, is gone; nor can I remember the names of any family that I might have."

"I see. Are you aware that England is at war?"

"Oh, yes. With France, under the leadership of Napoleon." The man chuckled. "Or, rather, the Corsican Monster, as I believe he is called."

The catechism went on at some length, until at last, the doctor leaned back in chair, apparently satisfied.

"As far as I can tell," he said somewhat portentously, "your amnesia seems to fit the parameters of the affliction, at least in as far as I am familiar with it."

"Can you tell me how long it will be before I regain my memory?" The question was asked with an almost painful intensity, but the reply—as the man had expected—was not encouraging.

"Nn-no, I'm afraid not. Little is known about the condition, neither what causes it—for it can come on with mental trauma as well as from a blow to the head—or what causes it to go away— for, there is no real cure. We must rely on Mother Nature to heal your unfortunate condition, as I'm sure she will sooner or later."

"Let us hope it is the former rather than the latter," said his patient dryly.

There was a moment's hesitation before Dr. Beech continued. "I noticed a horse in the stable, a stallion. Apparently, he is yours."

There was another long pause as the patient once more searched within his mind. A horse? A stallion? A great black shadow flickered in his mind, and the sound of a soft whinny and huge teeth pulling at his pockets for sugar. Desperately, he fastened on the fragmentary image, but in the next instant it was gone. Damn! The little piece of his memory had been so close, it was as though he could have grasped it with his fingers. Now, his mind was just a bottomless blank again. Damn!

"I suppose he might be," he murmured cautiously. "I don't know."

"It seems strange," said the doctor meditatively, "that you carried no identification on you. No cards, no letters addressed to you, nothing of that sort."

"Unfortunate," said the man.

"Well, then." Adam Beech rose and picked up his bag. "Let us hope that a few days' rest will heal your mind as well as that foot." He moved to the door, only to find Catherine waiting in the corridor. With her were Lady Jane and Mariah.

"Good God," said Adam. "I was not expecting a reception committee."

Catherine smiled with a hint of apology. "Grandmama is anxious to meet our guest."

She ushered the old lady into the chamber, and allowed Mariah to precede her, but when she would have followed, Adam laid a hand on her arm.

"It is not necessary for you to wait on him any further," he pronounced. "Mariah can do all that is necessary for him."

"Do you not trust me in the same room with an unattached male?" she asked, her irritation warring with amusement.

"Trust has nothing to do with it," Adam relied stiffly. "Except that in this case it is the male I do not quite trust. He seems a pleasant fellow, but I find that he speaks with the accents of a gentleman, while his clothing seems to place him several ranks lower. There are so many rogues about that I would not wish to see you exposed to trickery."

"Now, see here, Adam," said Catherine, "the man is a guest in my house, and I shall decide how much attention he needs and from whom."

Adam was still protesting when she pushed past him into the room.

From his bed, the injured man listened to the altercation taking place at the doorway. With some interest, he sat up and, patting himself into a semblance of respectability and drawing the comforter about him, awaited events.

As he had surmised, the doctor proved no match against his determined hostess. In a few moments, Miss Meade hove into view behind the other women, Mariah Something?—and a very old woman, small and spare and leaning heavily on a cane. Dr. Beech brought up the rear, disapproval writ large on his face.

At that moment, the man caught Miss Meade's eyes on him. For an instant his gaze locked with hers. His breath caught in his throat, for it seemed to him that he was being drawn into an emerald whirlpool. The moment was gone so quickly, however, that he thought he must have imagined that silent little eternity of communion.

Miss Meade smiled, and the man was surprised at the vivacity thus lent to her countenance. Her remarkable eyes glinted like jewels in the afternoon sunlight that slanted through the windows.

"We meet again, mister, er." She stopped, an expression of perplexity spreading across her well-shaped features. "We must think of a name for you," she said awkwardly. "We cannot keep addressing you as, 'Um.' "

"Completely unacceptable," he replied promptly and with great earnestness.

"What do you think of Smith?"

The man grinned. "Somewhat pedestrian, but suitably generic." He put out his hand and smiled invitingly. "Do call me John."

Pointedly ignoring this pleasantry, she assisted the old woman to a chair.

"Grandmama, allow me to present Mr. John Smith. Mr. Smith, my grandmother, Lady Jane Winter."

Were there no men in this household, wondered the newly christened John Smith? If not, his situation had just improved noticeably. If he couldn't charm three lone women, his name wasn't—he grinned sourly—John Smith.

"Forgive me for receiving you in such a ramshackle fashion, my lady," he said, lifting his hand with a flourish. "You find me temporarily discommoded."

Lady Jane did not return the disarming smile he bent on her, but he was encouraged by the twinkle he discerned behind her wire-rimmed spectacles.

"You find your situation amusing, Mr. Smith?" The old lady's voice was cool.

"Hardly, my lady. I am merely pleased to have been—apparently—of some service to Miss Meade, even if it resulted in my, ah, present difficulty."

He ignored the faint snort from the doctor's direction and settled back into his pillows. There, he thought with some satisfaction. Nothing like creating a sense of obligation in one's benefactors. He shot a glance at Miss Meade from under his lashes, and was surprised to see her quirk an eyebrow in amusement. No fool, then, this green-eyed beauty. It behooved him to proceed with care. It also behooved him to discover precisely who was in charge of the household. Mariah, he discounted. Barring the existence of a male lurking somewhere in the woodwork, it was either the old lady or the young beauty who ran things.

"Yes," Lady Jane was saying, "I heard about your rescue of our resident damsel in distress." Her chuckle was unexpectedly rich and robust in such a fragile body.

"I am happy I was able to be of assistance," said John with aplomb. "I appreciate your taking me into your home, my lady."

"This is my granddaughter's house," replied the old lady, her tone noncommittal and discouraging further questions.

John knew a stirring of surprise. If this room were any indication, the house was an elegant residence. It would be very strange if it were owned by an unmarried female. The probability loomed larger of a man on the premises. On the other hand, the good doctor behaved as though Miss Meade was his private property, to be guarded assiduously against dangerous marauders. Perhaps she truly was unmarried.

He supposed it didn't make a great deal of difference. Whether or not he regained his memory in the near future, he must make it his first priority to leave this place without delay. Why he had this sense of urgency to be away from here, to find a hiding place into which he could plunge, he did not know, but he felt it would be unwise in the extreme to ignore his instinct.

Meanwhile, he would enjoy the company of the lady with the emerald eyes, and take advantage of the hospitality of these nice people. He waited for some sense of shame to creep into his reflections, but he was possessed instead with the feeling that he had done worse things than take advantage of people who trusted him. He shrugged. Apparently, he was conditioned to the philosophy that one did what one must. He searched within himself, but all he felt was a certain sense of soiled resignation. He closed his eyes briefly.

Watching him, Catherine felt a stirring of pity. It must be frightening to lose one's memory. She allowed her gaze to rest on him for a moment, absorbing that sense of coiled tension she had noticed before. Even beneath the comforter, it was apparent that he was accustomed to athletic pursuits. The forearms exposed beneath a shirt of inexpensive cotton were muscular, ending in strong, well-shaped hands.

Her gaze drifted back to his face, and she recalled the moment, a few minutes earlier, when she'd inadvertently caught his gaze. What a strange sensation it had been, as though part of her had been locked into his being with an almost audible click.

She drew in a quick breath. "Mr. Smith, can you think of no one whom we could contact? Your family will be worried when you do not arrive home. Your—your wife will be most concerned."

His wife? John Smith stiffened and stared at her in consternation.

Chapter Three

His wife! Good God, he hadn't thought about that. Did he have a woman waiting for him somewhere? Somehow, the idea filled him with a certain panic. A vision loomed over him of a trim little female, busying herself with her embroidery, humming to herself as she breathlessly awaited his arrival.

It felt all wrong. He could not picture himself as married, although he could not have said why. The whole idea seemed ludicrous. Marriage meant commitment—responsibility—and tedious explanations as to one's whereabouts and activities.

He frowned. What was there, he wondered uneasily, about his whereabouts and activities that would not bear explaining. He lifted his eyes once more to Miss Meade.

"I'm sorry, but I can think of no one. If I am married, I have forgotten that, too."

"Of course, Catherine," grumbled Dr. Beech. "If he truly has amnesia, he can't remember anything at all about himself or anyone close to him."

John did not care for the note of skepticism in the good doctor's tone. Was he suspected of prevarication? Something told him it would not be for the first time.

Dr. Beech stepped forward. "And now, I think it would be a good idea to let the patient rest. Perhaps after he has slept, his mind will be in better working order."

So saying, he began to shepherd the ladies from the room. Shooting a keen glance at John, he promised to look in on him the next morning.

Catherine turned to John as she moved toward the door. "I shall send some dinner up to you in a little while, and if there is anything else we can do, please don't hesitate to ask. Oh, yes." She halted, and smiled suddenly. He wished she wouldn't do that; it had the most peculiar effect on him. "We must do something about your clothes. I'm afraid your efforts on my behalf have rather ruined them. I shall try to procure a nightshirt for you from

Timkins, our butler, so that we may do something toward refurbishing them. Or no." She surveyed him briefly. "It would never fit. One of the footmen perhaps."

John nodded bemusedly, and the little party passed from the chamber.

As soon as the door closed again, he tossed aside the bedcovers and cautiously rose from the bed. He still could not put any weight on his foot, but by using the back of a straight chair as a crutch and pushing it across the floor, he was able to move to the window. It overlooked a fairly vast park area, and in the distance, a sheet of ornamental water glittered in the sun. The requisite number of trees and neatly trimmed shrubs dotted the landscape, and some sort of yew alley slanted off to the left.

Well, well. It looked as though he had fallen into a honey pot. The perfect place to regain his strength and his memory. If only it didn't take too long. Again, he was swept by a nagging sense of urgency.

Slowly, he sat down on the chair and gave himself up to thought. He still had no idea where he was, except, of course, that he was in the country. In the south of England, by the looks of it, but he could be mistaken. Cursorily, he examined his clothing, hanging on the back of the chair. Even the pockets of his coat proved unproductive. He had money, but not much. Except, no—what as this? A rustling sound drew him to the coat collar, which, when turned over revealed a narrow, hidden pocket. It contained—my God, over five hundred pounds! Where had he got that kind of gelt?

But there was nothing else. Not a scrap of paper with a name on it. Not a bill, not a letter, not even a handkerchief with an initial. Lord, what kind of man sets out from home with nothing in his possession except enough money to choke a mule?

A man who is heading off for parts unknown and wants to keep his identity a secret, that's who. Well, he'd done a damn good job, hadn't he? Thoughtfully, he tucked the roll of soft back into its hiding place, and returned the coat to its place on the back of the chair. His efforts had tired him, and he hobbled back to bed, where he explored the blank void that was his mind. Search as he might, however, no clue glimmered in the fog. At the end of a half hour's fruitless concentration, he still had no idea what kind of man it was who had inhabited his body for what he guessed was some thirty years.

But he *had* to remember. Somehow, he knew that his very survival depended on his return to sanity.

He jerked his head at a tap on the door, which opened immediately to admit a housemaid bearing a nightshirt. He affixed an engaging smile to his lips.

"Well, now," he said, "here's a sight to bring a man back to good health."

The maid giggled shyly. She laid the nightshirt on the bed and made as though to leave the room, but John spoke quickly.

"Surely, you don't have to go so soon? And me fretting myself to flinders with loneliness."

"Oh, no, sir. I mustn't stay," she replied with a smile, but she advanced to the bed.

"Ah. Will your mistress beat you if you spend a few minutes with a poor, wounded fellow?"

The maid giggled again. "Oh, no, sir, but I have my duties."

"One of which, I'm sure, is to see to the needs of a guest in the house."

"Oh, now, sir, and what is it you're needing?" she asked archly.

"Why, just a bit of company." He patted the bed suggestively and, after a moment's hesitation, the girl hopped up to seat herself on the edge.

"And how are you feeling, sir?" she asked, a little breathless at her own temerity. "They say belowstairs that you don't know your—that you can't remember—"

"That I've somehow lost myself," John said with another smile. "They're perfectly right; I can't remember so much as my own name, but I'm told it will all come back to me with a little time. Tell me something about you. What's your name, pretty miss? Have you worked here long? Is it a good place?"

The girl giggled once again. She seemed much given to giggling. "I'm called Doris, sir. I've been here about two years, sir, and yes, it's a good place to work. Lady Catherine is all that's kind. Mrs. Mariah can be a bit of a tartar sometimes, but she's a nice lady."

"How is it Miss Meade owns this big place all on her own?"

"As to that, I couldn't say. It used t'belong to the old one—that is, Lady Jane."

"I see," said John thoughtfully. "And the three ladies live here alone? I shouldn't think that would suit them—at least the two younger ones."

"Well, I've wondered about that meself," said Doris confidentially. "But, I think something happened a long time ago to Miss Meade. Something real bad that made her hide away like a scairt child. I think some of the older servants know what it was, but they don't say much."

The girl seemed to recollect herself suddenly. "I don't know what got int' me t'be chattering away like this." She slid off the bed. "I really do have t'go, now, sir, but I'll be bringin' yer dinner up in a while, so maybe we can talk more then."

John flashed a practiced smile. "I'll look forward to it, Doris."

The little maid whisked herself out of the room with a flip of her skirts, and John donned the nightshirt. This accomplished, he lay back once more.

So, there was a mystery surrounding his lovely hostess. Too bad, he could not stay around to unwrap it. Even more, he would like to unwrap Miss Meade. He had a notion that one might find something under her cool, patrician exterior well worth investigating. A fleeting memory shot through him of an emerald gaze connecting with his in a sudden, unexpected moment of intimacy.

He waggled his foot experimentally. And winced. He would be going nowhere for a day or two at least. Well, a lot could happen in a day or two, if one put one's mind to it. If her ladyship had been shut away by herself without masculine attention for years, she ought to be ripe for a spot of dalliance.

Unless, the good doctor was attending to her needs. Somehow neither conveyed the impression of an amorous relationship with each other, but impressions could be deceiving. Mmm. One would see what one would see.

In the meantime, it would be a good idea to make one's way down to the stable to examine the stallion that supposedly belonged to him. He could not manage this on his own as yet, but perhaps if he were, oh, so charming, a crutch might be forthcoming, or a stalwart footman or two to tote him about.

His hopes in this direction, however, were doomed to failure. To his pleased surprise, it was not Doris who brought his dinner tray, but Miss Meade herself.

"Absolutely not" was her response to his request for conveyance to the stable. "Tomorrow or the next day, perhaps, but for today, you must rest, Mr. Smith."

He put out a hand as she prepared to leave the room.

"Can you not stay for a few moments?" he asked plaintively.

She hesitated. "I'm afraid not. Mariah and Grandmama are waiting for me downstairs to go in to dinner."

He assumed an expression of humble resignation. "Of course, ma'am, I realize I have no claim on your attentions. Perhaps if you could have someone bring up a book or a journal after a while, I could while away the rest of the evening in a relatively pleasant occupation."

She burst into laughter, and John found that he very much relished the sound of it.

"You are the most complete hand, Mr. Smith. I wonder if you are ever at a loss—or if you ever exit a conversation without obtaining what you want."

He bent a stare of wounded innocence on her, but found he could not maintain it. Instead, he found himself chuckling guiltily. "Was I successful this time?" he asked.

Still smiling, she replied, "No, I'm afraid not. I do not wish to keep Mariah and Grandmama waiting. However, I shall send up some books, and after dinner, we will come up to keep you company."

He would rather have had Miss Meade all to himself, but he murmured a suitable expression of gratitude.

"Now, is there anything else we can do for you, Mr. Smith? I'm afraid we are unused to gentlemen visitors."

"You are far from a city here?" he asked carefully, and she dropped her gaze.

"Actually, no. We live in Hertfordshire—near Buntingford, and we are a scant thirty miles north of London."

John drew in an involuntary breath. Somehow he felt this information was important.

"Ah." He hesitated for a moment. "Earlier, you asked if I had come to visit you? Was I indeed on your land when we first, er, encountered each other?"

"Yes, I had been out for a ride, and Silk accompanied me. She had run into the shed in pursuit of some small creature. You were evidently riding along the track that runs by it. It's just a path, really, and it's quite a way into my estate from the main road— and not a great distance from the house, which is why I thought you must have made your way there purposely."

"But, if I am unknown to you, why would I be visiting you?"

"Indeed, Mr. Smith."

Neither referred to the fact that, in view of his humble raiment, the possibility loomed large that he might have been a trespasser on Miss Meade's land.

"I shall see you later, then." Miss Meade bestowed another of her charming smiles on him and left the room.

Shrugging philosophically, John addressed himself to his dinner, which proved to be a simple meal, but well prepared. He had finished his broiled chicken with vegetables in an Italian sauce and had just tucked into a *pupton* of fruit, when a footman entered, bearing several books and an armful of newspapers.

Setting the books aside, he casually perused the *Times*. The front page bore today's date. Evidently, living so close to London, the family was able to receive the current journals in a timely fashion. The stories dealt mainly with the progress of the war in the Spanish peninsula. There was also a piece on the king's health, which appeared to be unimproved. Last was a report that the authorities were still looking into the matter of the escape of the French General Rivenchy, captured after the Battle of Salamanca. It appeared, that the initial suspicion that he had been assisted in his flight by a British officer, one Major Lord Justin Belforte, was now confirmed by the discovery of a body, identified as that of the major, just beyond English lines. The traitor had apparently died in the escape, and any coconspirators in the operation were still at large.

John yawned. There was little else of interest in the paper, and a quick glance at the books revealed them to be two volumes of poetry and an alarmingly thick history of Rome. Lord, had they been Miss Meade's choice for his entertainment, or merely a random selection on the part of the footman?

Pushing back the tray, he settled back for a further contemplation of his predicament.

Downstairs, Catherine and the other two ladies were also just finishing their meal.

"So you still do not trust him?" Catherine asked Mariah.

"It's not that I don't trust him—precisely. I just think it would be wise to keep an eye on the silver while he's here."

"But what is there about him to arouse suspicion?" Catherine asked the question, well knowing that she hoped for a reply that would answer her own uneasy reflections on the stranger with the polished-metal eyes.

"I don't know. He speaks and acts like a gentleman but he dresses like a peddler. And then there's that devil with four feet in the stable. The grooms tell me he's wild as bedamned and won't let anyone near him. They had a time of it just getting him into a stall. I just think we ought to watch the fellow," she concluded, more or less coinciding with Catherine's own assessment.

"Well, we can do that starting this evening. I promised him we would visit him after dinner."

"Excellent," interposed Lady Jane. "I do love a mystery, and dredging up that young man's past may prove vastly entertaining."

Catherine's face shadowed momentarily. "Perhaps that would

be unfair. I mean, sometimes one's past is better left uninvestigated. I would not want to cause the man needless discomfort if there is something in his history he'd rather forget."

"Catherine, really." Lady Jane spoke with asperity. "If you are going to bring up all that tedious nonsense—"

Catherine smiled warmly at her grandmother. "No, of course, I'm not. How could I repine over a dismal little episode that occurred so long ago, when I have so much happiness in my life now." She reached to grasp the hands of the other two ladies.

"You'd be a lot happier," said Mariah dryly, "if you'd let a man in, as well. Adam Beech has been very patient, Catherine, but he deserves—"

"We've been over this ground before—many times, my dears. Adam deserves a woman who will love him unreservedly, which I cannot. He is my friend, and for that I am grateful, but I do not wish more from him."

"Bah," Lady Jane uttered a barely stifled snort. "You can't let one unhappy experience with love discourage you from dipping into the pool again. Lord, if I'd let that sort of thing stop me, I never would have married Carstairs. He wasn't much of a husband, but he was malleable, and I did enjoy being a countess— and he did give me four beautiful children."

Catherine and Mariah exchanged grins. "And how about Mister Winter?"

Lady Jane's expression softened. "Ah, dear Charlie. My only regret is that I never had any children with him—although—" She glanced about her with satisfaction. "I was left with Winter's Keep." She chuckled. "Lord, what a rumpus there was when I told my family I was going to marry a cit! But there wasn't a thing they could do about it. If you want to talk of love matches— well, the real thing came to me late in life, as it may do for you, Catherine. But you're not getting any younger."

"And, as I have told you, Grandmama," retorted Catherine, "if I die an old maid, I will not count it a tragedy. I am pleased that matrimony brought you happiness, but, as you can see, I have achieved that state by remaining single."

"Well," interposed Mariah judiciously, "I like being single— but, I liked being married, too; and if I were to stumble across the right man, I could be persuaded to try it a second time."

Lady Jane shot a glance at Catherine before replying to Mariah. "Spoken like a sensible woman. Now, if you could just persuade your friend to set foot in London again, the odds of your finding the right man to stumble across would increase considerably."

"Grandmama, we have been all over that, and—"

"Yes, and I realize I'd be wasting my breath to point out—again, that your precious scandal has long been forgotten, and you still have friends there who—well, never mind," she concluded at the signs of real anger that were rising in Catherine's eyes. "I shan't say anymore."

"Good," said Catherine firmly. "And now, if we're finished, shall we rejoin our patient?"

When they entered Mr. Smith's room a few minutes later, they discovered that a servant had just come into the gentleman's room to light the candles in the wall sconces and to set a taper alight on his bedside table. Smith had just taken the draft left for him by Dr. Beech, and they found him dozing over the history of Rome. His delight at their appearance was patent. The visitors grouped themselves in chairs around his bed, and Catherine and Mariah addressed themselves to the needlework they had brought with them. After a desultory exchange of conversation, John said lightly, "I do apologize for not being able to tell you more about myself, but won't you ladies tell me something of your histories?"

The three women exchanged wary glances, and Lady Jane spoke first.

"I am a widow, Mr. Smith. I was married at eighteen to George, the fifth Earl of Carstairs. After twenty-seven years of marriage, he died—took a tumble in the hunting field—and I re-married two years later, this time to Charles Winter. He passed away three years ago, after thirty-two years of happy marriage. I had four children with the earl—my oldest daughter married Catherine's father, and my son is now the sixth earl."

"And now," said John gravely. "You have retired to the country?"

"Yes," replied Lady Jane tightly. "Although—well, that is neither here nor there. I am happy here and surrounded by people whom I love and who love me. What more could I ask?"

"What more, indeed, my lady. And you have a lovely home—or, no, you said this is Miss Meade's house, did you not?" He turned a carefully casual glance on Catherine, who flushed slightly.

"Yes," replied Lady Jane. "Winter's Keep was getting too much for an old lady to maintain, and, since I had been planning to will it to her, I simply signed it over in advance, a year or so ago."

"Perhaps, I might be allowed to see more of—what is it?—Winter's Keep—tomorrow. I should need a crutch, of course, but—"

"We shall see how you go on tomorrow, Mr. Smith," interposed Catherine, "before we speak of crutches and tours of the house—or visits to the stable."

The patient smiled graciously. "Of course, dear lady. It shall be as you wish."

"Yes, it will," she replied, a martial light in her eye. Why was it, she wondered somewhat dizzily, that she felt constantly obliged to spar with this man? He was helpless, for heaven's sake. Flat on his back in bed. Yet she persisted in seeing him as some sort of threat to her well-being. He had already seriously impaired her peace of mind, for no good reason that she could discern. Now she gasped a little as the laughter in his eyes flowed into hers with a gentle assault. His gaze shifted almost immediately to Mariah.

"And you are Miss, er, Bredelove—although we have not been properly introduced."

"That's Mrs. Bredelove. I, too, am a widow, Mr. Smith, and—"

"Mrs. Bredelove is my cousin, Mr. Smith—my third cousin," Catherine interposed, "as well as my very dear friend. She agreed to come to live at the Keep after the death of her husband in the Peninsula. It is she who manages things here, and I do not know what I should do without her."

Mariah laughed. "Actually, we divide the labor. I take care of the house, and Catherine looks after the estate."

"Looks after the estate?" echoed John in some surprise.

"Yes," replied Catherine, her amusement apparent. "As in overseeing the Home Farm, keeping the accounts, seeing to the maintenance of the tenants' cottages, and all the rest."

"But do you not retain the services of a bailiff?"

"Oh, yes." Catherine laughed. "For Grandmama has put her foot down when it comes to supervising the planting and harvesting. She thinks it improper for a lady to ride atop a hay wain, although there is nothing I like so well."

An image flashed before John of the graceful Miss Meade, tendrils of hair curling about tanned cheeks as she strode along the furrows, pitchfork in hand, like a goddess of the grain. Something in him leaped in response, and he found his fingers itching to plunge them into the glorious mass of her hair, to breathe in the glowing energy that radiated from her. Shaken, he turned back to Mrs. Bredelove.

"Your husband lost his life in Spain?" he asked quietly. "Where?"

"He died in a skirmish outside a small village near Abrantes." Mariah's voice was soft, and her eyes very bright. "And I don't know what I would have done but for Lady Jane and Catherine." She reached to clasp the hands of her two friends.

John, watching, felt his throat tighten, and with an instinct he barely recognized as defensive, he derided the scene inwardly. Unfortunate, he thought, that females so tended toward the mawkish. These three believed themselves to be the most devoted of friends, but just let the self-interest of one of them conflict with that of one of the others, and see how fast their affection for each other would disintegrate.

He did not pause to ask himself what, in the life that was so stubbornly hidden from him, had caused this cynicism. He only knew that to trust one's welfare to another was to court disaster.

The ladies stayed but a few moments longer before Catherine rose.

"I think we must take our leave," she said, noting John's pallor and the dark smudges under his eyes. "I fear we have tired our guest with our chattering."

He protested, but was forced to admit the truth of her statement. His day's adventure had taken its toll on his body, and he was aware that his eyelids were drooping. With a promise to visit him first thing in the morning, they trooped out of the room.

Catherine, who exited last, turned at the doorway. "Sleep well, Mr. Smith."

"Thank you, Miss Meade." He smiled sleepily. "I hope, you, too, will sleep well. I look forward to seeing you in the morning."

To his surprise, he realized that he meant the words sincerely. Miss Meade, her spectacular assets aside, was a most unusual woman, and he was glad to have made her acquaintance.

He picked up the history book and began to delve further into the glory that was Rome. After just a few moments, however, his eyelids drooped beyond his ability to keep propping them open, and he set the book on his beside table with a thump.

Blowing out the candle, he lay staring into the darkness. If he were forced into a layover on wherever he'd been going, he reflected, he could not have asked for a better bivouac. Feeling a laudanum-induced drowsiness creep over him, he nestled into his pillows and muzzily contemplated his course of action for the next few days.

Tomorrow, he'd see about getting that crutch, then he'd take a look at the rest of Winter's Keep. Perhaps he could turn his stay here to some advantage. Then he'd make his way to the stables and see how Caliban was getting on. After that—

He sat up in bed, sleep forgotten, as the significance of his last sentence sank in.

Chapter Four

Caliban! That was the name of his horse. He had remembered! And his own name? Why, it was Justin Belforte, of course. How could he have forgotten? Lord Justin Belforte, and he was a major in His Majesty's army, and—

And he was in the devil of a lot of trouble. Along with the sorry details of his life, the circumstances of his arrival at Winter's Keep rushed in on him, and for a good quarter of an hour, he simply sat in the midst of his rumpled bedclothes, contemplating his situation in growing horror.

Lord, he thought, with renewed panic, he had to get out of here. He was supposed to be miles away by now, tucked safely in the fastness of Longbarrow. He was supposed to be hot on the trail of whoever had tried to implicate him in Rivenchy's escape and had subsequently tried to have him snuffed. He was supposed—but wait a minute.

He almost fell to the floor in his haste to reach the newspaper that still lay on the bedside table. Yes! There it was, the story of his supposed demise in Spain. What a stroke of luck! He had been granted the opportunity of moving about London at will, as long as he maintained some sort of disguise. Nobody would be looking for a dead man.

Except, of course, for the person or persons who had arranged to have him attacked on his return to London. That man knew he was still among the living, and was taking great pains to remedy that situation.

Carefully, he tore the article from the paper. Looking about the room, he finally slid the article between his mattress and the lacings beneath.

He continued his ruminations. In disguise, and with a bolt-hole to which he could return after his investigative forays, he should be able to manage to stay alive. Lord, he had to get to Robbie. Except, of course, that he had been forbidden to contact Robbie.

Well, he would have to go against Charles's orders, just this once. He had, after all, nothing to fear from Robbie, who had been his best friend—almost his only friend—since the two had been at Eton together. Their relationship had begun one spring day when Justin had come upon a group of older boys tormenting a puppy. Justin, with a lamentable lack of foresight had attempted to interfere, and the boys had immediately turned their attention from the puppy to his own underfed self. If it had not been for the advent on the scene of one Robert McPherson, things would have gone very badly for the Duke of Sheffield's little boy, Justin. Robbie, or the McPherson, as he had liked to be called, was a year older than Justin, and large and powerful for his age. Between the two of them, they had dispatched the bullies. An odd but tenacious bond was formed between the small, slightly bookish Justin and the big, rawboned Scottish lad, and they remained friends throughout all their school years and into the army. They had covered each other's tracks and pulled each other out of more scrapes than Justin could remember, and he was prepared to trust Robbie with his life—as Robbie would trust him.

Justin's thoughts returned to the subject of the bolt-hole. Who would have thought that an ill-advised and wholly unpremeditated good deed on his part would land him in this snug little paradise? His good angel, whom he thought had turned away in despair years ago, must obviously have been sitting on his shoulder on this occasion.

All he had to do was keep this amnesia thing going. Miss Meade would surely not boot him out into the cold, cruel world while he had no place to go. Particularly, with an injured foot. He must take care not to appear to heal too quickly.

He supposed it was an unpalatable trick to serve on his hostess. Miss Meade and her little household had been all that was kind to him. But then, unpalatable tricks were his specialty, were they not? A thoroughly bad man, his father had called him, and he'd done his best to live up to that dubious encomium. On the other hand, he was not actually doing her any harm. When it came time to leave, he would explain all, and he'd make sure no notoriety befell her as a result. He had a feeling that coming under public scrutiny would be devastating to her.

What was it, he wondered, that had happened to her, causing her to retire so completely from society? With her looks and her breeding and what was apparently a comfortable fortune, she should be a married woman with a pack of little ones at her heels.

He shrugged. Not that it was his affair. No, his affair was looking out after Number One, for if he did not, he might likely find himself either hanged for treason or dead in a ditch someplace, neither of which concepts greatly appealed to him. Hopefully, he would have the business completed within a week or two—a month at the latest, and then he would be on his way with a tip of his hat to Miss Catherine Meade.

He tasted her name on his tongue, and with it came a sudden, vague sensation of familiarity. Surely, they had met before, perhaps in that long-ago time when Justin had still been an acknowledged member of his family, gracing balls and routs with his presence.

He became aware that sleep was once again closing in, and he burrowed into his pillow. He smiled as he thought of Caliban, no doubt stomping and champing among the alien straw of his stable stall. Tomorrow would bring a joyful reunion. His last coherent thoughts, however, were of Catherine Meade. He was uncomfortably aware that duping her for an extended period of time would be no easy task, and it would take every ounce of skill and charm at his fingertips to stay ahead of her.

The next morning, as it happened, did not bring Miss Meade, but her henchwoman, Mrs. Bredelove, with a tray full of breakfast. He greeted her with a carefully crafted expression of woe on his features.

"Oh, my," said Mariah, settling the tray on his lap. "I was going to ask how you're feeling this morning, but I can see by your face that you're not yet, ah, in the pink."

He sighed. "No, indeed, ma'am. I am much better, but I had hoped to awaken this morning with a full complement of memory, and that has not happened. My mind is still a blank," he concluded lugubriously.

"Well, now, that is too bad," replied Mariah briskly. "Catherine will be sorry to hear of it. She said to wish you good morning, by the way, and she will be up to see you when the doctor arrives."

"And when might that be, do you think?" asked Justin. "I am most anxious to view that horse in your stable. He must be, as you seem to think, mine, and I am hoping that the sight of him might jar my memory."

"Well, now," said Mariah, seating herself on the edge of his bed, "I hadn't thought about that. I'm sure Catherine will get you a crutch or something—if Dr. Beech thinks it's all right."

"The, ah, the doctor and Miss Meade seem to be good friends," said Justin casually.

"Oh, yes. Ann, his wife, and Catherine knew each other since they were children. Adam and Ann came here to live when Adam went into practice, just in time to . . . That is," she finished hastily. "Since his wife died five years ago, he's been rather lonely and spends a lot of time here."

"Ah, I see." Justin nodded sagely.

"Yes, I thought you might. The doctor is a very good man," she added inconsequentially.

"Mm, so he seemed to me—and an excellent physician, as well."

Mariah rose. "Well, I'll leave you, then. You asked when the doctor might arrive. I don't know, really, but I should think you wouldn't have to wait long."

Justin thanked her, and after she had whisked herself from the room, addressed his meal. He was pleased to note that whoever had ordered its preparation had done so with a masculine appetite in mind. He made short work of the eggs, York ham, and beefsteak, washing it down with the tankard of ale that accompanied the little feast.

Replete, he availed himself once more of the chair he had used the day before as a crutch and made his way to the pitcher and basin that rested on a commode near the window.

Before he had finished his ablutions, Doris, the maid, appeared with the clothing that had been removed from him yesterday. Shirt, waistcoat, coat, and breeches had been cleaned, pressed, and mended, so that, while he was no more sartorially acceptable than he had been when he arrived, he was a least presentable.

Doris also provided him with an ancient, but gleamingly sharpened razor, so that, a half an hour or so later when Catherine entered the room, he felt ready to face whatever the day might bring. He was already grateful the day had brought him Catherine Meade, he thought jauntily.

Then he saw that Dr. Beech had entered the room behind her, bearing his medical bag and a crutch.

"Morning," he grunted. "I see you're up and about. Mariah reports you still have no memory."

"I'm afraid not." Justin hobbled weakly from the commode to the bed, easing himself into it with a spurious wince of pain.

"Oh, dear," said Catherine solicitously. "The foot is still bothering you."

"A little," replied Justin, phasing the wince into a brave smile.

"Well, let's have a look." Adam Beech took Justin's stockinged foot into his hands. "Mm. Swelling seems to have gone down. You still have some edema, but I see no reason why you should not try getting around with a crutch. Are these yours?" He indicated the boots that still lay near the foot of the bed, where they had been tossed yesterday.

Adam picked them up and assisted Justin in pulling them on. He held one in his hands for a moment, staring at it with narrowed eyes.

Damn! thought Justin. Those boots were by Hoby, and, though they were worn and scuffed after a hard year in Spain, their quality was apparent. They were the only part of his apparel he had not been willing to exchange for something shoddy and nondescript. Frankly, he hadn't thought anyone would notice, but he'd apparently been mistaken. Beech was a good doctor, and good doctors didn't miss much.

He said nothing, however, merely handing the boot to his patient, and a few minutes later Justin stood up, fully clothed and shod. With the aid of the crutch, he moved slowly about the room.

Well, now, this wasn't going too badly. His foot was apparently not seriously sprained. He could even put a little weight on it, he discovered. Better and better. Now, if they'd just let him out of his room, he'd nip down to the stable to see how Caliban was getting on. The poor old fellow was no doubt missing him, and without proper exercise, he'd soon be up to no good.

Catherine watched him as he navigated the distance between the bed, the window, and then the writing desk at the far end of the room. He moved awkwardly, but with a silent intensity. Even hampered as he was by the crutch, the power of his stride was apparent, and Catherine was reminded of a caged lion she had seen once at the Tower. Suffering from a sore paw and confined by the bars of his cage, the big cat was still the king of the beasts—still menacing in his sheathed power. It was obvious from the way Mr. Smith clamped his lips together that he was in pain, but he persevered until he had made his way around the perimeter of the room.

"I'll be leaving now, my dear."

She turned with a start to observe that Adam had picked up his bag and was ready to depart. Catherine put her hand out to him. "Thank you for coming, Adam."

He took her hand and sent her a speaking look. "You know I'll come any time you ask, Catherine."

Catherine could feel a blush creep over her cheek at the warmth of his words, spoken in front of a stranger. Was he sending Mr. Smith a message? she wondered. She experienced a spurt of irri-

tation. She shot a glance at Mr. Smith, who was studiously sur-
veying the scene outside the window.

An awkward silence fell, and at last the doctor cleared his
throat.

"Good day, then," he said gruffly, and Catherine produced a
stiff nod. She followed him from the room and was surprised to
find, upon reaching the corridor, that Mr. Smith had remained on
their heels.

"But I can't just stay in bed all day," he said, his eyes wide. "I
thought I might visit the stables. To take a look at my horse," he
finished hastily as he was treated to two blank stares. "If you
would be so kind as to point me in the right direction . . . ?"

"Of course." Catherine's voice was still tinged with embarrass-
ment. "I shall take you myself if you will wait a moment while I
see Adam to the door."

She placed a hand on Adam's arm and swept away, not sure if
she was hurrying to escape those too perceptive gray eyes, or to
get Adam out of the house before he committed any further faux
pas.

"It's all right, Catherine."

Adam's brown eyes suddenly sparked with mischief. "I could
find my way around your house blindfolded by now. I'll see myself out."

Turning to Justin, he added, "Miss Meade and I are such good
friends—I am sure you will understand, we do not stand on ceremony."

With a wave, he set off down the corridor, leaving Catherine to
fume impotently. Justin, availing himself of the arm Catherine
held out for his support, was forced to grin to himself in appreciation. Rather a master stroke that. The doctor had managed to convey several messages in that brief statement, none of which was
meant to offer encouragement to an importunate stranger taking
up residence—even temporarily—in the house of Miss Meade.

Winter's Keep was a very large house, Justin discovered.
Catherine led him through several corridors, passing rooms of
various functions, all elegantly furnished. Leaning heavily on her
arm, he managed without incident the great staircase that led from
the upper story of the house to the ground floor. The entry hall
was impressive, to say the least. From the stairs, an ocean of polished marble flowed to a massive front door, lapping along the
way at doors leading to small salons, elegant as jewel boxes, lying
along the hall's perimeter.

They did not cross to the entry, however, but turned toward the back of the house, which involved more passages that became darker and narrower as they approached the service wing.

"Whew!" breathed Justin at last. "Perhaps we should have packed a lunch."

Catherine grinned. "Yes. Charlie Winter had a healthy respect for the concept of high living."

"And all this is yours?"

"Yes. I really did not wish for anything so—so ostentatious, but I spent a good deal of time here as a child. In addition, Grandmama said it was the only home she had to her name, so I would have to make do."

"But are there not other relatives . . ."

Catherine's face hardened. "Indeed there are. My uncle and his sons all considered, and with good reason, I suppose, that Winter's Keep should have gone to them, but Grandmama was adamant."

Recalling her family's howls of rage and anguish and the frantic machinations at Grandmama's decision to give Winter's Keep to their niece and cousin, Catherine smiled sourly.

"And do you feel at all overpowered to be the mistress of so much grandeur?"

"Oh, no. Since it is familiar to me, I rather enjoy it. It's a little like living in a museum, surrounded by beautiful things. And I like being involved in the lives of so many people—the staff and the tenants, to say nothing of—"

She bit the words off sharply. Really, she thought, the man had a knack for asking the most outrageous questions in such a matter-of-fact tone that one was prompted to answer as though he had asked for the time of day.

Catching her kindling glance, Justin laughed.

"You're quite right, your Grandmama's decision about where you should live is none of my business. It's just that I cannot help being interested in how you live your life. Perhaps it's because I seem to have none of my own at the moment."

She shot another look at him. As he had no doubt intended, she felt a pang of compunction for his situation.

"You're quite right, Mr. Smith," she said coolly. "It is none of your business, but I somehow feel you rarely let that fact interfere with your actions."

"You may be right," Justin returned unrepentantly. "But, you must admit, I gain more information that way than I would by being polite."

"As well, I should think, as the occasional punch in the nose."

By now, however, Catherine was laughing, robbing her words of much of their sting.

They had reached the rear of the house, and Catherine led Justin through a back door. Crunching along a neat gravel path that took them past the kitchen garden, he soon found himself facing the stable block, a well-kept series of brick buildings trimmed with white. From one of these the sound of agitated voices could be heard. Inside, they were met with the sight of three stable men gathered about one of the stalls that lined the interior. Within, the largest horse Catherine had ever seen reared repeatedly, pawing the air and heaving against the restraining ropes that had been tied to its bridle. He was black as night, and his eyes rolled wildly. He was startlingly unattractive, thought Catherine, for his head seemed too large for the rest of him and his front hocks seemed to bulge out in all the wrong places. Lord, what a monster!

To her surprise, Mr. Smith did not hesitate, but approached the horse without fear. Moving past the grooms, he grasped the animal's bridle and began speaking to it. She could not hear what he said, but his words had a marked effect. Almost immediately, the stallion stopped his mad bucking, and within a few seconds he had dropped his massive head into Mr. Smith's bosom.

One of the grooms approached Catherine.

"We wasn't doing anything to 'im, Miss Catherine. One of the lads came to 'im with a curry brush, and you'd 'a thought he'd brought up a whip 'n chain. We only wanted to spruce 'im up a bit. The contrary beast wouldn't even take any grain nor water from us. Just tried t'murder us where we stood."

"It's all right now," said John Smith over his shoulder. "He didn't know where I'd got to and thought you all must be up to no good." He hesitated. "Sometimes he just needs things explained to him."

Indeed, the horse now seemed perfectly amenable to being handled. He whickered encouragingly at the groom nearest him, pushing at the lad's cap with his nose as though to make amends.

"How very extraordinary!" exclaimed Catherine. "Do—do you recognize him? That is, has he made you remember—"

"I'm afraid not," replied Mr. Smith, his face falling. "I have the feeling that I'm very familiar with him, but . . . It's hard to explain. When I look at him, I can see myself on his back, and it's as though I've been there many times. Oh!" He halted abruptly, his fingers busy with the horse's bridle. "Look here! There is a name scratched on the leather." He peered at it closely. "It's very faint—the bridle looks old—but, I think it says—" He spelled out the letters. "C—A—L—I—and, I think a B. Why, it spells Caliban. That must be his name."

He stroked the horse's nose. "Is that it, old fellow? Is your name Caliban? Seems a little harsh, but I must say it rather fits."

Caliban did not reply, but nibbled contentedly at his master's hair.

Marveling at the sudden change in the animal's mood, Catherine murmured, "Well, judging from his temperament—and his looks, too, to be honest, I'd say it's the perfect name."

Odd, thought Catherine. Mariah had said the horse looked expensive, and Mariah was an excellent judge of horseflesh, however, it looked to her as though three pounds might be too much to pay for such a misshapen animal, let alone three hundred guineas. Why, even his tail was crooked, she observed, as Caliban flicked the appendage in question, sparsely endowed and almost comically ill formed.

"Well," said Smith, "I must have had some reason for purchasing him. He looks strong, at least."

"Mm," responded Catherine, eyeing Caliban's deep chest and muscled withers.

"D'ye want him saddled, then?" asked one of the grooms. "He ain't been exercised yet this morning, and I have t'say, sir, that none o'us is p'tick'ly anxious t'get on 'is back."

Smith laughed. "You have nothing to fear now, lad. But, yes, I'd like a good gallop above anything right now." He turned to Catherine. "Could I persuade you to join me, Miss Meade?"

"Oh, no!"

Catherine was surprised at the spurt of nervousness she experienced at his invitation. She had no reason to shy away from his company, after all. Why should she feel so uneasy at the thought of spending a pleasant hour in the saddle at his side? "That is, I'm not dressed for riding," she concluded a little breathlessly.

"Ah," said Mr. Smith regretfully. "Another time, perhaps."

They chatted for another few minutes while Caliban was led out of his stall and made ready for his outing. Then, with the aid of one of the grooms, he swung rather awkwardly into the saddle. Once in place, however, it was, thought Catherine, as though he had somehow become part of the great stallion. Man and animal moved with a fluid grace that made her breath catch in her throat.

With a wave, Smith galloped from the stable yard and out onto the gravel path, and in a few moments he was a blur against the parkland that swept away from the house. Slowly, Catherine dropped her hand from its returning wave and made her way back to the house.

Astride Caliban's broad back, Justin reveled in the feel of the wind in his face. God, it had been a long time since he and the great horse had enjoyed an all-out gallop. What a good thing he'd embellished Caliban's bridle with his name those many months ago in—where was it?—somewhere in the Estremadura, he rather thought. He himself might be able to get along without his name, but Caliban would be another matter. He doubted the horse would respond well to, "Oy—you!"

He recalled the day he'd cut the name in the leather. He'd been out all day, perched on a stony mountain side, waiting for the appearance of Soult's troops. At that time, Justin had been one of the corps of "runners," men with superbly bred horses who scouted out troop movements, then sped to Wellington's headquarters with such details as number, speed, and direction of movement, contents of the baggage train, quantity of foodstuffs carried. Being an agent had still been a glorious adventure then.

When had it all begun to go sour? he wondered. Could he pinpoint an hour or a moment? Certainly, the day he had betrayed Paulo Albendondez, a man who had called him friend, must rank as one of the first black moments of his career. Since then, of course, there had been many men—and women—into whose good graces he had wormed himself only to use them to his own ends.

And now, with the end of the war in sight, he had thought he was done with all that. But no, now it was all beginning again, with the very nice Catherine Meade and her little family. Only now, he was fighting for his very survival, and he could not afford the twinge of conscience that snaked through him at the thought of the ill he was about to do them all. No, he would do what he had to do, just as he had done all his life.

Turning, he urged Caliban back to Winter's Keep.

Chapter Five

Dinner that evening was a convivial affair. Justin had established his ability to maneuver at will about the house, with the aid of his crutch and the ostensible assistance of a footman. Thus, he declared himself available to join the ladies, and lost no time in making himself the life of the party.

"But, do tell me something of your other neighbors," he said to Lady Jane over his portion of veal fricandeau. "Squire Wadleigh sounds an excellent landholder, but if he's the homebody you describe, he cannot be much company. Is there a family with whom you enjoy regular visits?"

"Oh, yes," interposed Mariah. "There are many. The vicar and his wife appear here as regularly as the postman, it seems. And then there are Mr. and Mrs. Woodcombe. They are lovely people, and they have a daughter and son near Catherine's age."

"Ah," said Justin with an air of interest that was not altogether spurious. Might the son have a romantic interest in Catherine? So far, he had been unable to unearth the slightest hint of a man in her life, with the possible exception of Adam Beech, a fact he found difficult to understand. His hostess was not conventionally beautiful, but many men must find her attractive. More than attractive. Her eyes, green and deep as a jungle pool were by themselves enough to win masculine admiration.

As though reading his thoughts, Catherine spoke up. "Indeed, the Woodcombes' attention is very much taken up these days with wedding plans, for both Jonathan and Melisande recently became betrothed. Jonathan is to wed Miss Morival from Shinglehead, a village some twenty miles from here, and Melisande will marry Squire Wadleigh's son. Both ceremonies will take place this fall."

"And Dr. Beech?" Justin spoke the name smoothly, edging it into the conversation like a spoonful of sugar into a teacup. He was not pleased when Catherine smiled widely.

"Goodness, Adam is a mainstay in our lives. His wife was one of my best friends. She passed away while I was still living in London with my parents, before I—left to return here."

"You were raised in Winter's Keep, then?"

Lady Jane waved a hand. "Catherine spent a good part of every year here with me until—what was it, '97 or '98—when my daughter, Matilda, and her husband decided she must spend more time with them. He is a barrister." Her voice sharpened. " 'It was for Catherine's sake,' they said. 'What kind of prospective husband would she meet in this backwater?' they said." She clicked her tongue. "It was unfortunate that it was of such importance to Josiah Meade that his daughter make a good match. Matilda had no social ambition—although she did prefer the bright lights of society to rural solitude."

Across from him, Justin observed the flush that spread across Miss Meade's cheeks at her grandmother's forthright speech. He smiled. "Such is the case with many ladies, I understand." He turned back to Catherine. "But you were saying about Dr. Beech?"

"Only that he is my dearest friend. He showed me a great deal of kindness when—when I needed it the most. I owe him a great deal," Catherine concluded in a rush.

Mmm, thought Justin. So much so that if he urges you to dislodge your unwanted guest, you would follow his suggestions unquestioningly? For there was little doubt in his mind that the doctor was not in favor of a prolonged convalescence on the part of his latest patient in the home of his dearest friend.

Again, Justin was intrigued by the mystery of Miss Catherine Meade. Where, he wondered again, had he heard her name?

Ah, well. He shrugged philosophically. If he stayed at Winter's Keep long enough, all might be revealed to him. Otherwise, the lady would remain in his memory as a pleasant enigma.

"By the by," Catherine was saying, "I sent a message to our local constable about you."

Justin turned to her, a startled question in his eyes.

"I asked him if he knew of anyone reported as missing in the area. If not, I asked him to pursue the matter further—to send to London for information."

Justin shook his head a little at this unwelcome piece of news. Certainly, Lord Justin Belforte would not have been reported missing, since he was believed to have been killed in Spain. However, the man or men who knew him to be still alive might well be interested should they come across the information that an unknown person had turned up in a small village outside London, a man, further, who seemed to have no knowledge of his identity.

One could only hope that should Miss Meade's inquiry proceed farther afield than the office of the local constabulary, it would be received with indifference at Bow Street and therewith die a natural death with no further ado. Since this seemed like the most likely outcome of a request for investigation instituted by a reclusive spinster living in the hinterlands beyond the metropolis, Justin allowed himself to relax.

It was rather pleasant, relaxing—something he had not managed for longer than he cared to consider. He should have been bored, for the range of conversation that might have been expected from three single ladies living on the edge of oblivion was certainly not what he was used to. He was surprised to discover, however, that they kept abreast of current events and their observations were in turn keen and acerbic.

"Really," commented Lady Jane. "It appears that the behavior of our troops after their long-postponed victory at Badajoz was disgraceful. One might expect raping and pillaging from the French, but it has always been my understanding that Wellington will not put up with that sort of thing."

Justin flushed. He had not been a part of the madness that had descended on the troops after Badajoz, but the bestial shouts of the men and the screams of terrified women still rang in his ears. He opened his mouth, but Mariah was before him.

"I understand that the fortress of Badajoz was taken only after days of unimaginable hardships to the men," she said quietly. "The reports said that many died in unspeakable torture from the methods used by the French in defense of the stronghold. Men— even the best of them—can sometimes give way under such stress and behave in a way they would not normally."

"Did you follow the drum, Mrs. Bredelove?" he asked curiously.

"Yes." Her eyes were moist and her look faraway. "William and I were married when he first purchased his commission. I went to Oporto as a bride."

"Lord," Justin said, startled. "What an introduction into the state of matrimony. That is," he added hastily, "I have heard that conditions for the women in Oporto were dreadful."

"They were." Mariah grinned. "It had been raining for a month before our arrival, and I spent my first week there trying to keep the water out of our tent. Despite my best efforts, it was rather like living at the bottom of a river. I don't know what I would have done if it were not for Mrs. Canfield, our colonel's wife. She was an old hand at army life and took me under her wing."

Justin smiled sleepily. The next moment, he was obliged to stifle a yawn. Lord, the fresh country air hereabouts must be having more of an effect on him than he realized. In a few moments, he made his excuses to the ladies and retired for the evening.

Silence fell among the women after Justin's departure. Mariah spoke at last.

"He's a likable chap, isn't he?"

"Mm," replied Catherine.

"You don't like him, dearest?" asked Lady Jane, her brows lifting in surprise.

"I don't know him well enough to like or dislike him."

"But, you don't precisely trust him." This from Mariah. "I must own, I feel the same way. He's charming as he can hold together, but I get the feeling he's not being completely honest with us. For example, for all his claims of memory loss, he remembers that he served in the Peninsula?"

"What?" exclaimed both of the others.

"Did you not observe the expression in his eyes when Lady Jane mentioned Badajoz. There was a lingering horror in them that I think would only be felt by someone who had been there. And, when I spoke of Oporto, he knew right away what a hellhole it had been. I'd be willing to wager a great deal he was there."

"But if he says he cannot remember . . ." said Catherine slowly.

"It may be," put in Lady Jane, "that he is only aware that the battles took place, without any personal recollection."

"I suppose so," admitted Catherine. "Still . . ." She shifted in her chair. "Do you know, he reminds me of Francis."

A shocked silence greeted her remark, and she hastened on.

"Please don't take my words amiss. It does not bother me to speak of him, you know. That would be the height of foolishness. Just because I made a complete fool of myself over a conscienceless rascal like Francis Summervale, doesn't mean that I cannot bear to hear his name. I don't intend to spend the rest of my life repining."

"I'm glad to hear that," said Mariah briskly. "But," she added tentatively, "in what way does Mr. Smith make you think of him?"

"Oh, the charm you mentioned. And the fact that I feel there's something he's hiding. Of course, he did put himself in jeopardy to save Silk and me in that shed—something Francis never would have done. It's just that I can't escape the feeling that it would be a mistake to put out one's hand in wholehearted friendship with Mr. John Smith—or whatever his name is."

The three ladies nodded in accord, and conversation became general. It was not long before they dispersed to seek their beds. In her chambers, Catherine gave herself up to her maid and grew reflective as she gazed in the mirror while the woman brushed her hair.

She had changed in the years since she'd returned to Winter's Keep. Not only was she older, but she had matured in a hundred subtle ways. She had said that she did not repine over the matter of Francis Summervale, and that was true. She would never entirely dispel the regret she felt, however, at her blind stupidity at the time.

At the ripe age of three and twenty, she should have known better. She had become accustomed to masculine attention from the time she had left the schoolroom. Her birth and breeding were unexceptionable, and she was not unattractive. Also her fortune was generous. Thus, she had garnered her share of proposals for her hand. She had refused them all, for none of the gentlemen who buzzed about her like bees to a honey pot had touched her heart.

Until Francis.

The Honorable Francis Summervale appeared on the London scene during Catherine's third Season, after a sojourn on his family's estate in the West Indies. Though tall and well formed and with hair the color of the sun, he was not precisely a handsome man. However, his eyes were of a piercing azure-blue, and to gaze into them was to lose oneself in a realm of tropic skies and the promise of unimagined delights. The ladies of the ton sighed over him and jealously detailed his amatory successes over the teacups.

The scion of an ancient and honorable family, he carried the weight of his name gracefully. Little was known of his material worth, but it was thought the family had, of late years, seen a diminishing of their fortune. Thus, while the maidens of the *beau monde* vied for his attention, their fathers looked on him with suspicion and concern.

From the moment he and Catherine were introduced to each other at Lady Clifford's ball, he had eyes for no other damsel. And Catherine, who had come to believe her heart was inviolable, fell headlong in love. When he proposed marriage, she was ecstatic, and she urged Francis to address her father without delay. As might have been expected by anyone less used to getting her own way, Catherine's parents did not smile on the proposed union. Josiah Meade, a perspicacious, socially ambitious barrister, having seen which way the wind was blowing, had investigated Mr. Summervale thoroughly and discovered that not only was the gentleman poor as a church mouse, but had managed to land himself heavily in debt. To Catherine's outraged astonishment, her father not only refused his permission for them to wed, but banned Francis from his home and forbade Catherine to have any more to do with him.

Nothing, of course, could have been more guaranteed to propel Catherine even further into the sanctuary of her beloved's arms. She and Francis began a series of clandestine meetings that culminated, perhaps inevitably, in plans for an elopement.

Recalling the night she and Francis had fled to Gretna, Catherine uttered an involuntary cry.

"I'm sorry, miss," gasped Winthrop, her maid, bringing Catherine back to the present with a jolt. "Did I pull your hair, then?"

"No, no, Winthrop. Please go on."

Catherine closed her eyes once more under the soothing strokes of the hairbrush, and the night when her world crashed about her came rushing into her mind.

She could even remember the smells of the dark, silent house as she had tiptoed from her bedchamber. How strange, she had thought, that she was leaving the familiar cocoon of her home, never to return. For she knew she would not be forgiven for this night's work.

Francis was waiting at the appointed spot and had gathered her in his arms, kissing her until she was a mass of quivering sensation. Then he had bundled her into his carriage, and they had plunged headlong into the night. They made good time, reaching Leicester by morning. They traveled hard all the next day and stopped at a charming little inn just outside York. After a cozy dinner spent in making plans for their future, Francis had escorted her upstairs. He had, of course, reserved two bedchambers, but as they reached the door of the one selected for her, it became clear that he did not intend to go on to his own.

His lips were warm, and his hands slow and soft as they caressed her. It had taken everything she possessed to draw back from him. He had first laughed, but then became angry at her insistence that they wait until they had said their vows before engaging in the pleasures of marriage. Eventually, at the risk of raising the house, he had given way. Swallowing his impatience, he bade his bride-to-be a stiff good night and retired to his chamber.

Full of excitement and unappeased desires she barely understood, Catherine did not sleep well in her chaste bed. When she finally fell into an uneasy doze an hour or so before daybreak, she was aroused by a commotion belowstairs.

"Father!" she breathed through bloodless lips, recognizing the voice raised the loudest in the altercation.

When she and Francis and Josiah Meade gathered in the inn's tiny parlor, however, her father had scarcely glanced at Catherine.

"You have been with my daughter for the better part of two night," he bellowed.

Francis made no denial, and Catherine was surprised to observe a small smile curve the corners of his mouth. "Yes, sir," he replied in a low voice. "I tried to abide by your refusal of my suit, but I love Catherine and I could not stay away."

"Bah!" was her father's only reply. "If I had my way, I would tie you to a manure cart and horsewhip you to within an inch of your miserable life." He drew a deep, shaking breath. "However, Catherine's reputation is already hanging by a thread. Come, Catherine."

"Papa! No!" Catherine had cried. Francis had moved to her side, flinging a protective arm about her.

"You—you cannot separate us, my lord. We must marry!"

"On the contrary, you vile young snake. Catherine's mother and I have put it about that she has been laid in her bed by a putrid sore throat. No one knows of her departure. If we move quickly, all will be well. You will leave the country, sirrah, and count yourself lucky you still have all your body parts."

By now, Francis was pale and perspiring. He, too, seemed to have forgotten Catherine's presence in the room.

"If you think to fob me off in such a manner," he all but shouted, the desperation in his voice plain, "you are much mistaken, my good sir. Do you think I will skulk away without my due? Whether Catherine and I marry or not, you will pay well to be rid of me. What will the world think when they know your daughter is no longer a maiden?"

Catherine gaped at him unbelievingly. What was he saying? Of course, she was still a maid. How could he lead her father to think . . . ? To threaten to expose her to—

"Your due!" echoed the earl. "You haven't tuppence to rub together, and you sniffed out *my* daughter to recoup your fortune. Well, you chose unwisely, puppy. I am not without power, and if

you think I will wed my only child to the likes of you, you have
badly miscalculated. Come, Catherine!"

Unresisting, nearly blind with grief, Catherine allowed herself
to be drawn from the inn.

And then disaster struck.

Sir Geoffrey Witbolde and his lady chose that precise moment
to break their journey from their home in Durham to London. The
couple were known as the most voracious gossips in the *ton*, and
their mouths dropped open as they disembarked from their carriage to behold Josiah Meade, one of His Majesty's most promi-
nent barristers and husband to the daughter of the Earl of
Carstairs, hauling his daughter from the inn, with a protesting
Francis Summervale in his wake.

"Well!" breathed Lady Witbolde.

"As I live and breathe," echoed her husband.

With a supreme effort, Josiah affixed a smile to his face. Greeting the baronet and his wife courteously, he declared himself
pleased at their happenstance meeting. However, he explained
through teeth gritted together so hard they hurt, he could not stop
to chat. As they must have surmised, they had surprised his
daughter and her affianced husband in a domestic spat, and he
had been forced to take a hand.

Their little eyes glittering like those of wild dogs falling on a
doe, Sir George and Lady Witbolde protested that they had no intention of keeping Mr. Meade from family matters. He could, of
course, rely on their discretion, and they cordially wished the
young couple their heartiest congratulations.

Catherine watched a triumphant smile spread across Francis's
features, and thought she would be sick. Numbly, she allowed
herself to be bundled into her father's carriage, but when Francis
reached for her hand, she jerked it away as though she had
touched something slimy. Glancing at his betrothed in sharp surmise, Francis said nothing, but addressed himself to making himself agreeable to his future father-in-law.

"Never mind that," Josiah had snarled. "What's done is done.
You have your wish, Summervale, and may you rot in hell. Now,
we must begin making plans. You must be married by special li-
cense, of course. No telling if Catherine is with child. The wedding will take place in St. George's in Hanover Square with as
much pomp as we can manage. No matter—"

"No," said Catherine in a small, firm voice.

"No matter what the expense," continued her father as though
she had not spoken. "We must—what?"

"I said, no," repeated Catherine, this time in a louder voice. "I will not marry Francis."

Francis shot her a look of pained bewilderment. "But, beloved, I don't understand—"

"I thought you loved me," Catherine said in a choked wail. "I didn't believe Papa when he said you were nothing but a fortune hunter, but now I perceive that he was right."

"There, there, dearest, you are distraught," murmured Francis.

"Yes, I am," she replied, pulling away from him. "But, that does not alter the fact that I am not going to marry you. You have broken my heart, Francis, and I shall never forgive you."

She knew she sounded like the persecuted heroine from a Gothic novel, but the words might have been written for her sole utterance. How could she have been such a fool? She looked at Francis, and it was as though she had never seen him before. How could she never have noticed that those magical blue eyes were close set and hard as marbles? That his golden hair owed its gleam to the artifice of pomade and curling iron? Miserably, she huddled in a corner of the carriage.

"Catherine," said Josiah reasonably. "I don't like the situation, either, but you have made your bed, and you must lie in it. You may be sure that the Witboldes will have the story of your elopement spread through every drawing room in London by week's end. If your betrothal announcement does not appear within a few days, you will be ruined."

Her voice trembling so that she could hardly speak, Catherine replied, "I am sorry for that, Papa, but I will not marry Francis."

To all of Francis's pleadings and cajolery over the next several days, and to all of her father's blustering threats, as well as her mother's tearful exhortations, she stonily repeated herself until at last she was left alone in her misery. All alone. Her father virtually disowned her, and her mother, though she mouthed words of sympathy, eventually acquiesced in her husband's abandonment of their daughter. Her friends, while commiserating with her to her face, gradually withdrew, and their sly murmurings when they thought she could not hear, cut her to the soul.

Only Grandmama Winter remained at her side. Her comfort was astringently phrased, but sincerely offered, and she steadfastly faced down the whispers and the cuts direct.

At last the day came when her father declared that he washed his hands of her. She was to be packed off forthwith to a cottage in Yorkshire, to remain there for the remainder of her days. Not only would the rest of the family have no more to do with her, but she was forbidden to remain in contact with those few of her friends in London who had sided with her.

It was at this point that Grandmama had taken a hand. Her granddaughter would not, by God, be made a pariah for holding to her principals. She was not to be punished for spurning a man who had taken advantage of her youth and innocence in such a despicable manner.

In the face of her family's vituperative opposition, Grandmama whisked Catherine away from London to the sanctuary of Winter's Keep, and there allowed her to heal in her own time. She saw to it that Catherine renewed her friendships among the local gentry, and, although those worthies at first looked askance at Catherine's presence in the neighborhood, such was Lady Jane's influence—and the fact that they had all known Catherine since she'd been in short skirts—that they gradually accepted her among them as one of their own.

When Cousin Mariah had returned from the Peninsula, dazed and in shock, much like a young doe shot by hunters and left for dead in the forest, the household at the Keep had expanded to enfold her, as well. She became a fixture there, and had made herself an indispensable part of their family.

As for Catherine, she was happy. She almost repeated the words aloud like a talisman as Winthrop at last braided her mistress's hair for sleep. When she climbed into bed a few minutes later and blew out the candle, she wondered why she suddenly found it necessary to reflect on her good fortune. She had a lovely home, good friends, and family who loved her. What more could she want?

As she turned into her pillow, her thoughts returned unwillingly to the stranger who lay in her guest bedchamber. A stranger whose gun-metal gaze seemed to bore within her to an uncomfortable depth, raising disturbing and unwanted questions in her mind.

Chapter Six

The following morning, having intercepted Catherine in the breakfast room, Justin repeated his invitation to her for an early ride. Since she had come downstairs dressed in riding garb, planning a brisk, early gallop, she was obliged to accept with a show of good grace.

"Do you always rise so early?" she asked, pulling on her gloves of York tan.

Justin was about to answer in the affirmative, when he caught himself. He smiled cautiously.

"I think I must, for it feels natural to be doing so. I should imagine, however, that I rarely venture forth in such charming company."

He watched in some satisfaction as a delicate flush swept over her cheeks. Was the lady so unused to even the mildest of compliments?

Once mounted, they cantered sedately past the environs of the house. During his solitary excursion the day before, Justin had been struck by the beauty of Winter's Keep. Palladian in style, it lay in a fold of hills, an exercise in symmetry, its two main wings spread on either side of a graceful portico.

"The house was built early in the seventeen hundreds," explained Catherine, "by the Earl of Stanchin, and it was owned by the family until about fifty years ago, when it was purchased by the Duke of Berkshire for a younger son. Charles Winter acquired it in 1792."

"It's very handsome," remarked Justin. He glanced around. "The parkland is quite extensive."

"Yes, the whole estate covers about two thousand acres."

He whistled silently to himself. What was Charles Winter's chosen field of endeavor that he had attained such an impressive success?

Catherine grinned. "Charlie had his fingers in a number of pies. He started out in mining, and he moved on to manufacturing. Toward the end, he had some interest in the East India Company and liked to call himself a nabob—although he did not actually spend much time in that country."

Justin shook his head abruptly. He wished she'd stop doing that. Reading his mind, that is. For years he had prided himself on the ability to keep his own counsel, but he was apparently an open book to this chit.

As they progressed past the Home Farm and onto fields ready for harvest, he continued to probe gently for information on the estate. Why he found it necessary to avail himself of this information, he could not have said, for surely he could see no benefit to himself in it. He was simply interested, he discovered with surprise. He wanted to know more about Miss Catherine Meade and her little family. He could not think why this should be, except that she was an unusual woman. She had chosen to live apart from society, without benefit of masculine support, and she seemed completely happy in her decision.

He wondered again why she had never married. He grinned to himself. If he were in the market for a wife, he might consider laying siege to the lady. Not that any female in her right mind would consider him as husband material. On the other hand, females so seldom were. In their right minds, that is. They were almost universally susceptible to skillful blandishment, as he had discovered much to his profit, early in his checkered career.

Once again, the familiarity of Catherine's name niggled at the back of his brain. Miss Catherine Meade. He rolled it around in his mind. Daughter of a barrister. Had he met the gentleman somewhere? In White's perhaps? Certainly not at Horse Guards. He'd surely remember if the fellow were with the Foreign Office.

"You are fortunate that Winter's Keep lies so close to London," he remarked idly.

"Why is that, Mr. Smith?" Her tone was not precisely sharp, but it held little encouragement.

"You have all the benefits of living in the country, yet you can avail yourself of all the delights provided by the city."

Catherine stiffened. "I'm afraid that the delights of the city hold little temptation for me."

Justin lifted his brows. "Surely, you jest! A lady who does not enjoy shopping in town? Or the theater? Or the museums?"

She was silent for a moment. "Yes," she replied at last. "I suppose I do miss some of those things. It is simply that—that I do not care enough for them to risk—that is, I—I do not like all the noise and dirt and—and encountering persons one would rather not talk to."

She bit her lip, obviously vexed at having said so much. Justin proceeded smoothly.

"Of course. Actually, I cannot say that I am anything but pleased that it is your habit to stay close to home. Otherwise, I would not have enjoyed the good fortune of meeting you."

She sent him a sardonic glance. "Do you call it good fortune to have sprained your ankle and sustained a serious head injury all on my account?"

Oops. Justin backpedaled. "I count the cost light at becoming acquainted with a lady of such breeding and charm as yourself."

As soon as the words were out of his mouth, he regretted them. Lord, what was the matter with him, spouting such shopworn, not to say smarmy phrases? He could feel himself coloring as Catherine sent him a derisive glance.

She smiled coolly. "Really, Mr. Smith, it is not necessary to turn me up sweet. You are welcome to stay at Winter's Keep as long as necessary until you regain your memory—and the use of your foot. It is not my custom to turn beleaguered strangers away from my door, particularly those to whom I am in debt."

My God, she was doing it again. Seeing into his thoughts as though his head were made of glass. He was usually a little subtler in his methods. He flushed.

"I suppose I deserved that," he said, affixing what he hoped was an engaging smile to his lips. "But you are, in truth, a lady of breeding and charm. And," he continued in a more serious vein, "I do most sincerely appreciate your allowing me to stay here. I'm sure I must have a home somewhere, but until I can remember where it is, behold me greatly in your debt. There," he concluded, once more having recourse to the grin, "is that better?"

"Minimally," she retorted.

Justin sighed in mock despair. "Really, I never encountered a female so averse to compliments. I find it hard to believe that you are unused to receiving them."

"I appreciate a sincere compliment as much as the next woman, I should imagine. It is pretty, empty phrases to which I object."

"But—"

"Oh, please, Mr. Smith, may we talk of something else? I have nothing but disgust for men who mouth polished little nothings. In any event, I think it is time we returned home."

With a jerk on her reins, she wheeled her little mare about and cantered off in the direction of the house.

Justin followed slowly, his eyes on her rigid back. Phew! It appeared he had been right. The cause of Lady Catherine's withdrawal from the polite world had been a man. A man, he'd wager his best curly-brimmed beaver, who had gained her trust with his empty, polished little nothings and then had broken her heart.

The question remained why was her heart still in such a state of disrepair that she had shut herself away for the past seven years or so? Interesting.

Interesting, but of no concern to him, he reminded himself firmly. He had enough to worry about without meddling in the affairs of a spinster of uncertain years, even an attractive spinster with jeweled eyes. He galloped after her, and, while making no overt apology for his unwelcome flattery, he maintained an inconsequential flow of chatter during the remainder of the ride home. By the time they clattered into the stable yard, a reasonable degree of amity had been reestablished between them.

He spent the rest of the day making himself agreeable to Lady Jane and Mariah. When Adam Beech arrived that afternoon to check on his patient, Justin made himself agreeable to him, too. This proved not to be an onerous task, since the doctor was an eminently likable fellow. He was not, however, very forthcoming on the subject of Lady Catherine.

"Yes," he replied in answer to a carefully phrased question from Justin, "I suppose some might consider it odd that Catherine has chosen to abandon the city. However, urban life does not appeal to all of us."

"Yourself, for example?"

"Yes. I could be making a good deal more money practicing in London, but, like Catherine, I prefer rural life, and I don't mind being paid with the occasional chicken or pig."

"And did your wife enjoy the solitude of the country, as well?"

Adam smiled. "Oh, yes, Ann loved it here, although she was raised in London. We met there shortly after I returned from Edinburgh, and once we had settled here, she vowed that nothing would pry her away from her garden and her animals again."

"Animals?"

Adam's smile widened. "Yes, Ann collected them the way some people acquire objets d'art. I think her name was put on some sort of animal telegraph, for our doorway was always cluttered with stray cats and dogs or wounded birds, rabbits and even hedgehogs."

"Miss Meade says that she and your Ann were good friends."

The doctor's face shadowed. "When Catherine returned from London, she was greatly at a loss without Ann."

"Was she so unhappy, then?"

"Unhappy! She was devastated. She—" Adam broke off. "I have said too much. Catherine's secrets are hers to tell, not mine."

"Of course," said Justin hastily. "I did not mean to pry." Which was an out-and-out lie, of course, but the wise man knew when to abandon the chase—at least, temporarily. "Mrs. Bredelove appears to be a good friend to Lady Catherine, as well."

Adam broke into a wide grin. "Lord, yes, Mariah is the salt of the earth."

"And very attractive, too."

Adam stared at him blankly. "Well, yes—I guess she is, isn't she? She's been a great support to Catherine—as has Lady Jane."

"A formidable old lady."

"To say the least. I think if she could have laid her hands on a dueling pistol, she would have shot Francis Summervale right through the eyes."

"Francis Summervale?"

Adam looked up suddenly. "It seems I have misspoken again," he said shortly. He sighed. "Or, perhaps that fellow's name still sticks in my craw. The gentleman was the cause of much grief for Catherine. I do not intend to say more—except," he added meaningfully, "that if any other such as he were to cross Catherine's path again, I'd shoot him myself."

"Ah," said Justin.

Upon Adam Beech's departure, Justin contemplated the name the doctor had inadvertently dropped. Well, perhaps semi-inadvertently. Francis Summervale. Again, he was struck by a certain familiarity. No—more than that. He was sure he had known someone by that name.

Yes, of course! He had known a Francis Summervale in the Peninsula. Big, beefy fellow with yellow hair. Served with the Rifles, if he weren't mistaken. He and Summervale hadn't been well acquainted, but had encountered each other more than once. Hadn't liked him much, as he recalled. The captain seemed rather too full of his own consequence for Justin's liking. He'd purchased his commission only recently and, though he hadn't seen any action, swaggered among the ladies like a seasoned warrior.

He managed to enjoy a notable success in this arena, in spite of—or perhaps because of—the whisper of scandal that accompanied his arrival in Spain. It seemed as though he had thoroughly compromised a young woman, bringing her to the point of ruin.

He had, he told his cronies, proposed marriage, but the chit proclaimed that she had no wish for husband or family. If the truth were told, said Summervale, he was relieved to be out of the situation, for the lady was not altogether to his taste. At least he had done his duty.

The young woman's name was, of course, Justin now remembered clearly, Miss Catherine Meade.

So, Justin mused, Miss Meade's cool composure was a facade. Behind that cool green gaze, lay a passion willing to be stirred. He thought it unlikely that she was a wanton, but she had allowed herself to be seduced by a pair of blue eyes and a head full of pretty yellow curls. Moreover, in refusing to marry Summervale, once having flung her fling, she had shown herself willing to flout the conventions of society.

Hmm, perhaps his little pastoral interlude would prove a little spicier than he had expected. The picture flashed in his mind of a thick mane of honey-colored hair spread out on a pillow beneath him and a pair of green eyes grown cloudy with desire.

Lord, he thought, perspiring, it had been too long since he'd been with a woman. It was apparent that he would have to exert a greater degree of charm than he had managed so far. Catherine had been speaking to him after their ride this morning, but just barely. And at luncheon, her conversation had been only borderline civil.

Well, he'd just have to hone up those empty blandishments. He was not used to failure with the fair sex, and he saw no reason to expect anything less than his usual achievement this time. He hummed in anticipation as he made his way downstairs.

His first opportunity to put his campaign into effect came later that evening. After dinner, Justin once again joined the ladies in the Keep's gold salon. However, they had barely begun a game of piquet when Lady Jane rose from the table.

"I do apologize, my dears," she said in a rather thready voice, "but I believe I shall be obliged to retire early this evening."

Justin stood to assist her. "Does your head hurt very badly, then?" he asked softly.

She glanced at him in surprise. "I'm afraid it does. I get these pesky headaches only rarely, but they are indeed extremely painful. I shall be right as rain, however, tomorrow."

With Justin's hand under her arm, she moved toward the doorway, and Catherine jumped from her chair to join her.

"I shall see you to your room, Grandmama, and instruct Hannah to make you a posset. She always knows just what to do for you."

"No, Catherine, never mind." Mariah, too, left the table. "Let me go up with her. I think I shall retire, too, for I have an early day planned for tomorrow. I am promised to Mrs. Sylvester directly after breakfast for a linen inventory."

"Yes, dear," put in Lady Jane. "Do stay here and entertain Mr. Smith. I shall do very well with Mariah, and"—she waved to them with a hand that shook visibly—"I shall see you both in the morning."

After seeing her grandmother from the room, Catherine sank once more into her chair at the table.

"Poor Grandmama. She has been plagued with those headaches for years. They are wretchedly severe, but fortunately, as she says, they do not last long." She glanced curiously at Justin. "How did you know she was in pain? She hates anyone fussing over her, and always takes great care that no one know when one of her migraines comes on. Even I did not realize there was anything amiss with her tonight."

"I had an—" He stopped short. He had almost mentioned his Aunt Mowbry, who had suffered from the same malady. "I had a notion," he said instead. "The way she held herself—a certain tension around her eyes."

"I see."

Catherine knew a moment of surprise. She would not have thought the charming Mr. Smith observant enough of the cares of others to have noticed those of an old woman who meant nothing to him. She had, however, noticed the hesitation in his speech.

"Tell me, Mr. Smith," she asked, fixing her gaze on him, "have you noticed any improvement in your memory?"

He shook his head ruefully. "Not a glimmer. Well, no, that's not quite true. Every now and then some recollection tickles at the back of my mind, but I cannot seem to grasp it."

"It must be extremely uncomfortable to lose one's identity," said Catherine meditatively.

"Indeed it is," responded Justin earnestly. "I know not what responsibilities I may be leaving untended, or what loved ones I may have left to fend for themselves. Have you received any word on the request you left with the magistrate?"

He certainly seemed the picture of a man who could not remember his own name, Catherine thought dispassionately. His gray eyes stared unseeingly, apparently into a past that was closed to him. She felt a twinge of compunction. Why did she persist in attributing such unworthy motives to him? What reason could he have to lie about such a thing?

On the other hand, what had he been doing at Winter's Keep in the first place? He was obviously a gentleman. Why had he arrived dressed in clothes one of their footmen would have scorned? And then there was that mesmerizing charm that he oozed like honey from a comb. Even as she told herself it was as false as tinker's gilt, she had to fight the urge to purr under his compliments. It had reached the point, she admitted to herself, where she must take pains to avoid his gaze, e'er she fall into the quicksilver pools that were his eyes.

Oh, the devil take it! She was not the susceptible ninny she'd been when she'd fallen victim to Francis's wiles. She had never been one to blush at a honeyed phrase from a good-looking man—even Francis's fulsome praises had made her uncomfortable, and she was not going to start acting the simpering maiden now.

She took a deep breath and answered his question. "No, we have received no word from the magistrate, but it was only yesterday that I sent to him. It is highly unlikely that we would have heard anything from him so soon. In any event, I think we must assume that you do not live anywhere in the immediate vicinity. We are well acquainted with everyone who lives within ten or twenty miles."

"And you are sure you do not number me among your acquaintances?" he asked with a smile.

"Quite sure." Her returning smile was thin. "And now," said Catherine, rising once more, "you must excuse me. I, too, wish to retire and I want to look in on Grandmama before I go to my room."

"Of course," he murmured.

He followed her into the great hall. Most of the other candelabra in the great chamber had been extinguished, so that when Justin lit two of the candles placed on a small table by the stairs and handed one to her, they were immediately enclosed in an intimate pool of light. He moved with her, step for step up the staircase and she was intensely aware of the latent strength in his thigh and shoulder as he brushed against her. When they reached the top, Catherine turned to her own bedchamber and was unpleasantly startled as Justin moved to accompany her.

"I know my way, Mr. Smith," she said sharply, but she may as well have remained silent.

"It would be remiss of me not to perform this mundane courtesy," he replied smoothly. Upon reaching her bedchamber, he opened the door with a small flourish. She stepped inside quickly, and, though he made no move to follow her, he prevented her from closing the door behind her by the simple expedient of placing his foot against it.

"Sleep well, Catherine," he said, his voice flowing over her like warm silk. "And let me thank you again for your hospitality. Despite the inconvenience to myself that you mentioned earlier, I would not have missed this encounter with you for the world."

For a moment, she simply gaped at him. Then, before she knew what he was about, he had bent his head over hers and brushed her lips with his. So light was the contact, it could hardly be called a kiss, but she felt his touch as though he had penetrated to the core of her being.

She started convulsively, and without thinking, raised her hand to deliver a stinging slap across the mouth that smiled at her so invitingly. The sound seemed to reverberate through the corridor and, with a strength she did not know she possessed, she shoved at him so violently that, caught off guard, he caromed into the opposite wall. Without waiting to measure his response to her action, she whirled into her bedchamber and slammed the door behind her.

Chapter Seven

The sun was high in the sky when Justin opened his eyes the next morning. Hastily, he threw back the covers. Lord, he hadn't slept this late in donkey's years. Perhaps, he reflected ruefully, it was due to the fact that he had not closed his eyes until nearly dawn.

He still could not believe what had transpired last night. The image of Catherine's fiery green glare had stayed with him far into the night. Who would have thought, for God's sake, that a woman of her years and experience would take such snuff at a moment's harmless dalliance? All he'd intended was a chaste little salute there in the intimate darkness of the corridor, but one would think he'd attempted rapine and murder. Lord, it was a wonder she hadn't brought the household down on them.

His rambling meditations during the night had consisted of these and other, similarly virtuous protestations, but it was not long before he admitted to himself that, had she responded to the light, perfectly harmless kiss he had bestowed on her, he would probably have essayed a further, perhaps slightly less harmless attempt on her virtue.

All right, if she had given him the slightest encouragement, he would have seduced her on the spot. It was not his habit to seduce gently bred maidens, for it seemed a tad thoughtless to ruin a young girl's life for a few moments of pleasure—particularly when the world was so full of another sort of female, the kind who, for a consideration of some sort, was more than willing to give a few moments of pleasure, perhaps taking a few for herself as well. However, this particular maiden was already ruined, apparently willingly so. Thus, it might have been expected that after a judicious amount of blandishment, Miss Catherine Meade would be ripe for a spot of seduction. After walking up that darkened stairway in such close proximity with her, inhaling the delicate scent she wore, he was more than ready to pursue this pleasant course of action.

However, though he was not usually so maladroit in estimating a woman's sexual appetites, it seemed he had sadly misread the situation with Catherine Meade. He seemed to have misread nearly everything about her, so perhaps he shouldn't be too surprised. Still, she had definitely overreacted. To his mind there was nothing in his behavior to warrant the haymaker she'd delivered to his jaw. A simple "Unhand me, you varlet!" would have sufficed.

Justin might have been surprised to know that, in her own bed-chamber, Catherine was reflecting in a similar vein. Really, she thought for at least the hundredth time, she had behaved like the veriest peagoose last night. To be sure, the man had sullied her hospitality by kissing her, but it was not as though he'd assaulted her. A dignified, "Sir, you forget yourself!" would have sent him on his way.

With a blush of mortification, she contemplated the image that was fairly burned into her consciousness of Mr. Smith, his eyes wide with astonishment, his cheek white with the outline of her fingers. For an instant, she thought she must have harmed him as she sent him hurtling across the corridor, but she hadn't waited to find out. No, she'd slammed the door and cowered behind it as though the man had been attempting to ravish her. What must he think of her?

Not that it made any difference. No matter her—her startled reaction, it was he who was in the wrong. John Smith had been trying to beguile her with his disingenuous prattle ever since he'd arrived. Earlier last evening, she had been lulled by the sensitivity he had shown toward Grandmama's headache. Now, however, her first impression had been confirmed. He was just like Francis! And it was this instant response to his caress that had caused her to fly into such a rage with him. How dare he try to use her! She had already told him she would allow him to stay at the Keep, but that was not enough! Oh, no, she was expected to warm his bed as well.

Her thoughts continued for some time in what she at last admitted was an effort to fan the flames of her anger. For, if she were to be honest, she would have to acknowledge the fact that she had been tempted. Just for a moment. His lips were warm and firm, his body lean and muscular. She had been shocked at the unfamiliar maleness of him, so very close. Adam had certainly never presumed to attempt such an intimacy with her, and she suspected that even if he had, her response would not have been so immediate or so frightening.

She turned her face into her pillow. She simply did not want to think about this anymore. Lord, how was she to face John in the morning? Of course, she had no intention of apologizing to him. No, she would continue to treat him with courtesy, of course, but she would *not* apologize. She would remain aloof and dignified— and hope to God he would regain his senses soon. The sooner John Smith left Winter's Keep, the better off they'd all be.

Again, the thoughts of Miss Catherine Meade and the ersatz John Smith were, unbeknownst to them, running in similar channels. As Justin left his bed betimes the next morning for a gallop on Caliban, he mused that his stay in the little haven that was Winter's Keep had already begun to pall. The pursuit of a lady who appeared to view him as a combination of the worst features of Casanova and Attila the Hun had lost its luster. It was a very good thing that within a day or two his ankle should be healed enough for him to proceed to London, where he would take up the threads of the mystery that threatened him.

As it turned out, Justin's estimate was a trifle optimistic. It was not until one night almost a week later that he made his way stealthily down the front stairs at Winter's Keep. The house was dark and silent, for he had waited until everyone was asleep before he ventured out. Quietly, he saddled Caliban and led him away from the manor. Once clear, he mounted the stallion and let him have his head, for there was a full moon this night.

Arriving in the city, he made his way to the lodgings of the accommodating whore who had provided him with shelter on his return to England a scarce week ago. This soiled dove, who went by the salubrious name of Highlife Kate, was no longer in the trade, having decided to abandon her reasonably lucrative career after the birth of her fifth child. However, she was as soft of heart as she was fertile (however inadvertently), and her door was always open to those favored few who had treated her with kindness in the days she plied her trade in the unsavory streets of Limehouse.

"Ooh, Luv," she squealed with delight when he appeared in her doorway. "I thought mebbe you was off and away again t'Spain or one o' them other heathen places."

On being assured of his continued presence in England, and on being apprised of his most pressing need at the moment, she supplied him with a grimy coat, breeches, and a shabby waistcoat. Adding a pair of torn hose and cheap, scuffed boots, she plied him with a savory stew before he set out on his appointed rounds.

His first stop was a tavern not far from Kate's digs. Here, he took a seat in one of the darkest corners of an already stygian taproom. He was halfway through his second pint of bitters when a gentleman sauntered into the room. Although, "gentleman" was perhaps not the sobriquet one would choose in describing what was, for all intents and purposes, a walking bundle of dirty laundry.

He was very large and had obviously not come nigh or near a bar of soap for some months. His hair, greasy and black as tar, hung down over a threadbare coat collar. A crust of beard spread over a misshapen jaw.

Justin lifted his tankard in a barely perceptible gesture as this apparition made his way into the room. It was enough. In a few moments the man had settled himself in the chair opposite, and Justin raised his hand once more, this time to order a second measure of ale.

"Good to see you, Jack," he murmured.

"Yer a sight for sore peepers yerself, sojer," responded his guest. "Hear you've had some interestin' adwentures of late."

"You could say that."

"In fact, heard you was dead."

"As you can see, that somewhat overstates the case. It was a near thing, though, and as you can imagine, I'm more than a little interested in discovering who has taken such an interest in snuffing me."

Jack squinted at him over the top of his tankard. "I'll tell ye somethin' else, sojer. Word is ye've been givin' aid and comfort to a certain French general."

Justin stiffened slightly. "You shouldn't pay so much attention to rumor, Jack. For example, that one's a flat-out lie."

Jack stared at him unblinking for several seconds before nodding. "Glad t'hear it. I has me standards, after all, and treason is somethin' I don't hold with."

"Nor I, Jack. Nor I. And now that you mention it, I'd very much like to know who helped Rivenchy escape and then blamed it on me."

"Orright, then. What d'ye want me t'do?"

John leaned forward and issued a short but precise list of instructions, following which he placed a small roll of soft on the table.

"I think this should cover your expenses, plus a little something for yourself."

Jack swept the roll into a capacious pocket without examining it, and finishing the remainder of his tankard in one gulp, he stood.

"Thank 'ee, sojer," he said, wiping his mouth on the back of one hirsute paw. "You can count on ol' Jack Nail."

"I know that, Jack," replied Justin, his mouth curving in a brief smile. "And I know I can count on your discretion as well."

Jack did not answer, but nodded abruptly in a gesture of affirmation. The next moment, moving extraordinarily swiftly for one so bulky, he had exited the taproom.

Justin left a few moments later, setting out in a westerly direction. Some forty minutes later, he arrived in Ryder Street, in a sedate area between St. James's Street and the square of the same name. After pacing the street in front of a certain elegant town house for some minutes, he disappeared into a tidy alley just to its left. From there, via a few barrels and a drain pipe, he scaled the outside wall and eased himself through an upstairs window. He did not light a candle but, sinking into a nearby chair, waited in the dark.

He waited for a very long time. His eyes had begun to droop in a light doze, when the click of the door latch alerted him. Muscles tensed, he watched a figure enter the room, illuminated by the candle he carried in from the corridor outside.

"Hullo, Robbie," said Justin.

The man in the door showed no sign of surprise, but peered into the darkness.

" 'Lo, Justin," he drawled. Moving about the room, he lit other candles from the one he held in his hand. "I was wondering where you'd got to, but I didn't think it would be long before you'd show up here."

Having finished his task, he turned to Justin, who had risen to move toward him. "Good God." Robbie surveyed his friend. "Changed tailors, have you? You look like last week's dirty dishes."

Justin grinned. "This from a man who once spent a month in the hills of Beira without once changing his underwear?"

"Ugh. Don't remind me." Robbie shuddered delicately, a gesture at odds with his shambling, muscular frame and features that could most kindly be described as craggy. Robbie McPherson was wholly a product of the Scottish Highlands. His hair, an untamed thatch of brick-red, seemed to possess a life of its own and was matched by a flourishing set of mustachios. His hands, as one of his fellow officers had once described them, "Could choke an ox while he was balancing a caber." His eyes were the color of a glenful of heather—a bottomless gray-green, and at the moment they were narrowed in scrutiny.

"So what have you been up to, laddie?" he asked, pouring a generous measure of brandy for himself and his guest.

It took some minutes for Justin to outline his recent adventures, but he held Robbie's undivided attention.

"And she believes you've lost your memory?" he asked, when Justin at last paused for breath.

Justin nodded. "To her, I'm a poor, wayfaring stranger who came to grief in the performance of a heroic deed on her behalf. As such, I am entitled to consideration, commiseration, and her unlimited hospitality."

Robbie shook his head. "Honest to God, me lord. You could fall into a manure pit and come up with diamonds in your mouth."

"Mm, yes. I suppose you could say I have a certain element of luck in my favor, but I prefer to think that my present circumstances are the result of sheer cunning."

"I suppose I don't need to ask if the lady is attractive."

"Well, she's not what you'd call a raving beauty, and she appears to be coming up on thirty, but she's exceedingly well preserved."

"And already smitten with her mysterious guest, I suppose."

Justin's smile faded. "If she is, she's hiding it remarkably well." He rubbed his jaw reminiscently, and Robbie's brows lifted in mock astonishment.

"What? Don't tell me you suffered a rebuff? From a spinster?"

"A sp—? Mmm, yes, I suppose she is." It was difficult, Justin realized in some surprise, to think of Catherine Meade, she of the glorious golden hair and the jeweled eyes as an ape-leader. "At any rate," he continued briskly. "I did not slither into London at considerable personal risk and climb rickety drain pipes to discuss my amatory failures. Tell me, what did you discover before leaving Spain?"

Robbie leaned forward in his chair, his face serious. "Not nearly as much as we'd hoped. Everyone is very closemouthed about your supposed defection. Even Wellington has been unwontedly silent on the subject." He shifted uncomfortably. "I think that, having so often expressed his confidence in your ability and your dedication, he now feels foolish and—no doubt—betrayed."

Justin's expression hardened. "I expect you're right. What about Scovell?"

"He seems to have accepted without question the story of your death at the hands of the French after you delivered Rivenchy to them."

Justin swore long and fluently. "My God, Robbie. George Scovell and I go back to Corunna. I was one of the first men he recruited for the Guides." He rose to pace the floor. "Do you have any idea whose body was substituted for mine in that ditch?"

"Not really. However, a private in the Rifles went missing just before Rivenchy escaped. It was assumed he took himself some unauthorized leave, and no connection has been made between the two events. However, his description almost exactly matches yours. His uniform was discovered in his barracks by one of his mates, so it was assumed he changed into mufti for his little holiday. Nobody but me, it appears, thought it odd that, though you'd been seen leaving camp for the bridge at Huerta wearing full uniform, when your body was found, it was clad only in breeches and a shirt, with nothing in the pockets except a handkerchief with your initials in one corner."

"How convenient," said Justin thoughtfully. "Well, hell, anyone could have crept into my tent and stolen those."

"Mmm, yes, but it would almost have to have been someone from the Light Bobs. A stranger skulking around the camp would surely have been noticed. Remember, the reason for your mission was the concern over French soldiers fleeing the battle field after Salamanca. Wellington had ordered extra guards posted. There were a few outsiders, of course, as there always are around a military camp—peddlers, beggars etc. In fact, I thought I saw—" He shook his head and grinned. "Well, no, it couldn't have been. I guess I'm getting of an age where everyone I see reminds me of someone I already know."

"Did anyone leave camp at about the same time I did?"

Robbie rubbed his chin. "No one that I noticed. As you may remember, most of us had gathered in Bertie Freeman's tent the night before. You were there, too."

"Lord, yes. I dropped more than I should have at cards that night. Must have been that liberated sherry of Bertie's. Morning came at an ungodly early hour, and I barely made it out of camp at my appointed time."

"I do remember that I didn't see anything of Roger Maltby all that day or the next. When he finally did show up, he said he'd been holed up with that senorita he'd been keeping in the village."

"Maltby," said Justin slowly. "Now, there's a fellow who would send his bowl up twice for soup."

"Yes," replied Robbie shortly. "Do you remember the time he

won almost a thousand pounds from young Breckenridge? I always suspected he cheated."

"As did I—but that doesn't make him a traitor."

"No, but if I had to suspect anyone in the Light Bobs of dirty work, he'd be right up at the top of my list."

"Agreed." Justin paused. "But there's something else. I did not mention this to you in Spain, because—well, I could not bring myself to believe . . ." He took several turns about the room before continuing. "Robbie, after I was captured—while I was being interrogated by the French Officer—Captain Bassinet, his name was—Paul Bassinet—he seemed to know a great deal about me. In fact—"

"Yes, you told me. Knew where you'd been raised and how long you'd been in the Peninsula and that you were under Scovell's command, and—"

"What I didn't tell you was that I was able to catch a glimpse of the papers spread out on his desk, to which he referred frequently during the course of our little chat." Justin drew a deep breath. "One of those papers was covered with St. John's handwriting."

Robbie's mouth dropped open.

"Your brother, St. John?"

"The very same. I suppose there could be a perfectly innocent explanation. Whoever, for example, had supplied the good *capitán* with such an exhaustive portfolio on my humble self could have done so by simply scooping up a handful of my own papers from my study at Longbarrow, among which might very well be a letter or some other piece of business from St. John. God knows we never corresponded on a regular basis, but he did send to me now and then concerning matters that required my attention."

"Yes, I suppose it could be coincidence, but there's never been any love lost between you and St. John. On the other hand, St. John doesn't seem like the type to carry a grudge that far. Would he be sorry to see you sent to your grave?"

Justin pressed his lips together. "You're forgetting Susan Fairhaven. Don't you remember? St. John was betrothed to her."

"Mmm yes. Pretty little thing. You and Sinjie had some sort of a dustup over her, didn't you?"

"It all happened while you were still at Oxford. It was more than a dustup. Susan was in London when I was sent down. As you may recall, I went to earth in the metropolis for a few months before I purchased my commission. I stayed with Charles for a while and then, with his largesse, I took lodgings in St. James's.

"I was still smarting from Father's treatment of me, and it was only because Charles kept his hand on my neck that I didn't get into the same sort of trouble that had got me exiled from Oxford. As it was, I played the tulip and decorated all the ton functions with my presence. Naturally, I saw quite a bit of Susan. She was a born coquette, you know, and Sinjie did not have the sense to guard his interests. He was spending most of his time at Sheffield Court, learning the business of the estate, or some such. Seeing an opportunity to ruffle his feathers, I began a mild flirtation with her. I meant no real harm, but as so often happened, my little prank caught up with me. She cooperated enthusiastically with my endeavors, even going so far as to creep from her window several times for midnight assignations."

"Oh, my God," muttered Robbie.

"I swear to you, Robbie, we never went beyond a few kisses and a little heated fumbling. However, not long thereafter, and several months before the wedding was to take place, it was discovered that Susan was pregnant. She pointed her pink little finger at me, tearfully insisting that I had seduced her cruelly—although she made it sound more like a rape.

"St. John came to see me, and it was only by the most dexterous of footwork that I avoided being shot on the spot. I protested my innocence, to no avail. He seemed to think I had arranged the whole scenario with the express purpose of humiliating him, and he raged at me for hours. When I left him, he was vowing vengeance and swearing that he'd make me pay, if it was the last thing he ever accomplished on this earth."

"Good God," said Robbie again. "I suppose St. John refused to marry her?"

"Well, of course he did. He would not dream of soiling the Belforte line so grievously, but he seemed to think—as did Father—that it was necessary for yours truly to escort her down the middle aisle instead, thus salvaging the family honor.

"Fortunately, I was due to sail away with my regiment at just about that time, and before Father could marshal his forces, I was safely away to the Peninsula. Thus, I was spared the consequences of my supposed crime against maidendom. She's dead now, you know," Justin added almost as an afterthought. "She caught the French pox."

"Good God!"

There was a long silence as each of the gentlemen sipped thoughtfully at their brandies.

"I suppose," said Robbie at last, "it's not surprising that he'd enjoy seeing you dead in a ditch, but do you really think he would contrive a plot of treason and a subsequent ambuscade simply to even the score between you?"

"That's the part I can't reconcile," responded Justin slowly. "I can't see him as a traitor. Plus the fact, of course, that arranging to have me accused of such a heinous crime would well and truly out-stain all the other clots of mud I've tossed onto the family escutcheon. But I've seen men perform irrational acts in the name of vengeance. At any rate, I've set a watch on Sheffield House here in town. I want to know who visits him and when—and why."

"Who's going to do that?"

"Jack Nail."

Robbie grunted. "Good choice. What do you want me to do?"

"You'll be going back to Spain soon. It sounds as though Roger Maltby could stand some watching. It would be interesting to discover if he's come into any money recently. In addition, you might nose out any friends of the mysteriously disappeared private in the 95th. It appears to me that someone went to a great deal of trouble to find a body with a marked resemblance to yours truly."

"And if any of said friends recently underwent an improvement in their finances, that, too, would be of some interest."

"Precisely. That's all I can think of for the moment. You may come across something on your return to the Peninsula that will lead you to further investigation. In the meantime, I believe I'll pay a visit to Jerry Church."

"Church? I don't believe I—wait a minute. Doesn't he work at the Horse Guards? Lord, Justin!" he exclaimed at Justin's affirming nod. "Are you *trying* to put your head in the noose? You aren't all that well acquainted with him, are you? What makes you think he won't turn you over to his superior? You've already got a connection there in Charles. Hasn't he already promised to do what he can?"

"Yes, but he's so highly placed I don't think he has access to the really informational rumor mill that grinds so exceedingly fine in the lower echelons in any department. Also I need someone there who will follow *my* orders. And I do know him fairly well. He had lodgings near mine when I lived in town. I was in a position to do him a spot of good when he got into trouble over in

Procurement. In fact, I was responsible for getting him a position on the Top Floor under Wilkerson. I don't think he'll turn me in. At any rate, I need someone in his position, and I think he'll do as well as anyone."

Robbie shrugged. "Well, it's your neck, I suppose, but I think you're making a mistake."

"Objection noted." Justin smiled, then hesitated. "I must thank you for your efforts, old friend."

Robbie shuffled uncomfortably. "Good God, don't be daft."

Justin laughed softly, but he noted with satisfaction the affectionate gleam that warmed Robbie's gaze. "By the by, what is that sickly growth you've sprouted under your nose since the last time we met?"

Robbie stroked his mustache complacently. "You like it? Drives the ladies wild, of course."

"No doubt. Nothing like tickling a female into submission." This time Justin's laughter sounded aloud.

Their business concluded, Justin found himself reluctant to leave Robbie's company. It was a relief to relax into the security of his friend's company, for truth to tell, the lie that was his constant companion in Catherine Meade's house was beginning to take its toll. He glanced round Robbie's sitting room and eyed the fashionable cut of that gentleman's coat.

"Come up a bit in the world, haven't you, old horse? The last time I visited you in your digs, they were on the upper floor of The Three Tuns, over in Shoreditch. And your coat—Weston, is it not? How did you make the leap into what one perceives is almost the lap of luxury?"

"Ah," murmured Robbie, flushing. "Do you remember my Aunt Ilverhampton? She passed on to her reward last year and left me a few shekels. I found life above The Three Tuns a bit more adventurous than I desired, so the first thing I did was to hie me to more nobbish quarters."

"Hmpf, you never mentioned any of this to me."

"Did I not? Ah, well, who knows how many dark secrets I have clasped to my breast?"

Justin chuckled and settled more comfortably into his chair. It was good to be with Robbie again, he reflected. It was a relief simply to be able to speak his mind—and his fears.

The two spent another hour talking of a number of things. Thus, the night was far advanced when Justin at last took his leave. When he arrived back at Winter's Keep, a faint lightening of the eastern sky presaged the imminent arrival of dawn.

Entering the gate, he bent forward in his saddle to whisper to Caliban. A remarkable transformation swept over the great horse. He drew to an immediate halt. At a slight pressure from Justin's thighs, he resumed his forward progress, but in a most peculiar manner. He walked slowly, and if it could be said that an animal tiptoed, such was Caliban's demeanor. His movements became fluid, and not a creak of leather or jingle of harness could be heard in the night air. Staying to the grass verge rather than the gravel paths, Justin reached the stable yard with no more sound than a cloud's shadow passing beneath the moon.

Justin dismounted and removed the stallion's tack before easing open the stable door and leading Caliban inside. The horse did not whinny or whicker or blow, but stepped docilely into his stall, and with a nudge from his velvet muzzle, bade his master good night.

"Good night, old fellow," whispered Justin. "You have done well."

Slipping from the stable, Justin made his way into the house without incident, and a few minutes later reached his bedchamber, where he divested himself of his rather gamy ensemble. Hesitating a moment, he lifted his mattress and carefully laid the clothing next to the newspaper article he'd placed there earlier. Donning his nightshirt, he climbed wearily into bed and lay for some time with his arms folded behind his head, staring sightlessly at the ceiling.

He was not sure how much, if anything, he had accomplished this evening, but at least he had set something in motion. Perhaps Roger Maltby really was the traitor. He hoped so. In fact, it would give him great pleasure to wrap his fingers very slowly around Roger's thick neck and squeeze the breath from his body.

But what if it wasn't Roger? Or perhaps Maltby was merely a tool in the scheme? Here Justin's thoughts skittered to the paper whose image had burned itself into his brain the night of his interrogation by Captain Bassinet.

Did St. John really hate him so virulently?

No, he would not think of that now. There must be some other explanation for the presence of the paper in the officer's little packet of information on Lord Justin Belforte. He wondered idly what St. John was doing at this moment. Probably sleeping the sleep of the just and pure either in London or at the family seat near Barkway.

And his father. How was the duke faring? The newspapers hinted that he was desperately ill, felled by reports of his younger son's treachery. Justin's stomach tightened for a moment before he shrugged. The old man should have been inured by now to the failings he had so often bewailed to the skies.

Lord, how often had he stood before his father's desk, first as a small boy, bracing himself for a caning, and later as a young man, slouched sullenly under a withering hail of sarcasm and imprecation? Afterward, St. John would compound Justin's resentment with a comprehensive lecture on his shortcomings. At least he did until the day Justin, having grown to manhood, retaliated in a forceful and somewhat bloody confrontation. Since that time, the two brothers had scarcely spoken.

Justin sighed heavily. He had always known St. John disliked him—his brother had made that fact known in a hundred small and not-so-small episodes of boyhood humiliation and ill-usage. And then there had been that final confrontation between them. St. John had, admittedly with good reason, given his belief that his brother had ruined his fiancée, sworn an undying enmity toward Justin; but was his hatred enough to plot a treason for which his brother would be blamed? To say nothing of seeing him murdered into the bargain. For certainly the man who had planned Rivenchy's escape had arranged for that ambush in Spain.

Justin's features hardened. Well, if that were the case, so be it. He had long ago lost any familial affection for either his father or his brother, and if he were obliged to ruin St. John—or worse, for the crime he had committed, he would feel no remorse.

He turned his face into his pillow and prepared to slip into a sleep that he knew was neither just nor pure.

Chapter Eight

It seemed to Catherine that August had never passed so quickly. There was the harvest, of course, which was always a hectic time for her. Most of her days were spent in the fields, where, though she did not actually wield a scythe or a rake, she closely followed the activities of her workers who did.

On the first morning, as she rode her little mare behind her troop of laborers armed with their implements, she looked about her with some satisfaction. The scent of the hops, past which she now rode, hung as heavy in the air as did the fruit from their long poles. Further afield, acres of wheat waved tall and golden in the sun, and past them, oats and rye lay ripening for harvest in a few weeks' time. In the distance, the fruit orchards lay serene and full, their branches bending with apples, cherries, and plums. The Lord had been good to her in His bounty, and all who depended on her could be grateful that their well-being was thus secured for the coming year.

Her reverie was interrupted by the sound of hoofbeats, and she was startled to behold John Smith riding hard behind her.

"You want to what?" she asked in astonishment at his reply to her query.

"I wish to help with the harvest," he answered with a grin, gesturing to the little parade ahead of them. "Your agent, Mr. Crestwick, was telling me the other day that with the opening of the factory at Carringford, you're finding yourself a little shorthanded this year."

Catherine simply gaped at him. His breeches and homespun shirt, obviously borrowed from someone a little shorter and more rotund than he, did little to disguise the feral grace with which he sat astride Caliban.

"But you cannot mean you plan to work in the fields."

"That is precisely what I mean. I need the exercise to help me maintain my fine figger, me girl." He flexed his arm pridefully.

Catherine refrained from availing herself of John's mute invitation to examine his forearm, and sank into an embarrassed silence.

Really, she chided herself, she had allowed herself to fall into the oddest state of mind since Smith's arrival. She had maintained her fury over what she persisted in calling his attack on her for a good two days. It was at this point she realized the futility of remaining in a quarrel with someone who refused to acknowledge that he was being quarreled with. It was as though the incident outside her room had never occurred. Smith treated her with the same courtesy and laughing deference he accorded Grandmama and Mariah. He was a charming companion at mealtimes, and helped while away the long evening hours with games of whist, songs at the pianoforte (he was possessed, not to her surprise, of a fine baritone voice) or readings from the works of currently fashionable poets and writers. He did not apologize for his scandalous behavior, nor was there any repetition of what had occurred in that shadowy corridor.

Eventually, she had been forced to fall back on a dignified silence regarding the episode. She smiled disbelievingly at the compliments he paid her and took care to avoid being alone with him. Withal, she had the uncomfortable feeling that he was laughing at her—not unkindly, but with a certain errant mischief.

She wished she could tell herself that she was immune to his charm, but no woman with breath in her body could remain entirely indifferent to him. Riding beside him now, she chided herself for her unbecoming fascination with the beauty of his hands as they controlled the restive Caliban without effort, or the way the homespun clothing clung to his muscular shoulders and lean hips. Most of all, she resented the feeling of connection that sprang up between them every time he was near. Did he feel it, too? That sense of unspoken communion—of laughter silently shared and thoughts communicated without words.

She shook herself. How ridiculous she was being. She sounded like a smitten schoolgirl with a crush on her music master. He was only a man, after all, and she had resolved long ago that she would never again succumb to masculine importunities.

She frowned. She knew that in her resolve, she would receive no support from Grandmama and Mariah, for the rogue had insinuated himself in their good graces and they all but preened under his carefully designed attentions.

There were moments when it seemed to her that he reveled in the display of his wickedness. It was almost as though he were saying to her, "Yes, I am a perfect rotter at heart, and I am manipulating you and your household. But see how cleverly I am going about it. You will come to no real harm—probably, and we all are having such a lovely time."

And they were. Catherine had to admit that he was good for Grandmama, for Lady Jane was in better spirits than anyone had seen her in years. John had the knack of making her laugh, and he was adept at anticipating her every desire. Her spectacles appeared in his fingers just as she turned to look for them on the lamp table beside her chair. Wine and biscuits were conjured, seemingly out of thin air, the moment she suggested that "a little something" would taste good right now. John was the first on his feet when she asked in a querulous tone for her shawl.

Oh, yes, it was all nicely calculated. And Mariah! Goodness, they spent hours talking about the war with Napoleon and the difficulties of life as a soldier's wife. For someone who claimed not to know so much as his own name, he was certainly familiar with the most minute details of the war in the Peninsula.

There, he was doing it again—prancing about in his ridiculous getup and grinning as though he were playing at being a harvester for her sole amusement. She pursed her lips, and wheeling her mare about, resumed her journey to her fields.

The question uppermost in her mind was—why? Why was this stranger in their midst going to such trouble to ingratiate himself? She had told him he need not fear being sent out into the cold, cruel world without a penny to his name, nor a clue as to his identity. What more could he want from them? Or was his entire predicament a pretense? Had he really lost his memory? But why create such a charade for their benefit?

Pretense or not, she thought some hours later, none of her workers had labored harder at his task than John. From the moment they had set scythes to the hay in the morning until now, near sunset, when they were bundling up their tools to begin the trek home, he had toiled unflaggingly. When the laborers had paused for their noon meal, John had settled into the grass with them, swilling great drafts of ale. He regaled the men with ribald stories and sent the women into storms of giggles as he flirted with young and old alike.

Catherine realized that he genuinely enjoyed the camaraderie. Had he really been a soldier? she wondered. It scarcely seemed a profitable career for a self-aggrandizing rogue. Later that night, she found herself again pondering his motives. There was no doubt he had tired himself today. Yet, after dinner, he spent a good two hours reading to Grandmama from a book of rather mawkish poetry by Thomas Chatterton, simply because her rheumatism was fretting her. She was sure, though she did not understand how she knew, that his solicitude was not feigned.

She leaned back in her chair, closing her eyes. She was tired as well, pleasantly so after her day in the sun-warmed fields. Mariah, too, looked as though she would like to make an early night of it. Her cousin did not take an active part in the harvest activities, but usually took the opportunity to give the house a good turnout. She had spent the day supervising a thorough cleaning of all the chandeliers in the place—a formidable task.

Catherine was not surprised when, shortly after ten o'clock, Grandmama declared herself ready for bed. John rose with what seemed to Catherine a suspicious alacrity to help the old lady to her feet. Mariah yawned and announced that she, too, would retire. Catherine, nothing loathe, followed the two women from the room, observing as she did so that John was also moving toward the stairs. He laughed at her questioning glance.

"Yes, I am going to seek my rest as well. I'm sure that if I were a few years younger, I could keep up with the laborers in the field all day and still while away the better part of the night in a tavern, but being stricken in years, I can feel every stroke of the scythe. Tomorrow, I shall be stiff as a pike."

Catherine nodded sedately, and bidding him a polite good night, began to ascend the stairs. On an impulse, however, she stopped abruptly, causing John, who was behind her to bump into her. She laughed self-consciously.

"I—I just wanted to say thank you." At the questioning lift of his brows, she continued hastily, "For your work in the fields and—and for spending your evening reading to Grandmama. I know you cannot have enjoyed such an interminable length of time with Thomas Chatterton, for I recall your saying he is among your least favorite poets. It—it was kind of you to give Grandmama such pleasure when she is so uncomfortable."

John's brows flew into his hairline. "Kind? My dear Catherine, you have not known me for very long, but surely our acquaintanceship is of long enough duration for you to know that I rarely do anything out of kindness. As it happened, Chatterton fit precisely into my mood tonight. I wished nothing more than to lull myself into a stupor with soporific verse prior to falling into bed for a hard-earned slumber."

She smiled tentatively. "Mmm, I somehow find that hard to believe—that you do nothing out of kindness." The smile dropped from her lips at his next words.

"Believe it," he said in the sharpest voice she had yet heard him use. His expression phased quickly into one of light mockery. "Kindness is simply too fatiguing, I've found, and so utterly profitless. There, I've shocked you," he added. "I shall amend my statement. I try to repay a kindness, of course, for a gentleman always pays his debts, but . . ."

"But the word 'altruism' is unknown to you," she finished.

"Completely foreign."

"Mmm," she replied skeptically, thinking of his blind rush into that little shack to rescue her and Silk. What an odd gentleman, to be sure. Most people tended to claim benign natures undeservedly. Here was someone who denied having one. Heretofore, she had suspected him of using his charm for his own ends, and she still believed this to be true. However, perhaps he was deliberately painting himself worse than he was. Why he should wish to do so was beyond her, unless—Unless, he did not realize he was doing so.

The thought startled her, and she fell silent for a moment. At the top of the stairs, she turned to bid John good night once again, only to find that he had availed himself of her hand. She knew an urge to wrench it from his grasp, but realizing that this would make her look singularly foolish, she contented herself with a frigid stare.

To her surprise, he shifted awkwardly. "I—I believe I misspoke myself just now. I did not mean that I do not appreciate the kindness you have shown me. It is my good fortune to find myself in your household, Catherine, and I shall try not to abuse your trust."

As though aware of the peculiarity of what he had just said, John bent over her hand and brushed her fingers with his lips. With a small, almost shy smile, he turned on his heel and moved away down the corridor, leaving Catherine to stare after him.

Upon reaching his bedchamber, Justin closed the door behind him and leaned against it, breathing as heavily as though he'd just escaped the furies of hell. Lord, how had he come to make such a complete ass of himself? Perhaps, he reflected as he wiped his forehead, because never before had he undergone such a complete upheaval of emotion as he had climbing that single flight of stairs.

He had been taken aback at Catherine's expression of gratitude, for he knew it was completely undeserved. He did not understand the instinct that had surged within him to give her such a disgust of him that she would be under no further illusions as to his character. This, after he had spent the better part of his stay so far ingratiating himself with her. He had thought himself undone after

his blatant attempt on her virtue only a few night before. He
counted himself lucky he hadn't been driven from the portals of
Winter's Keep with a fiery sword.

However, he had apparently redeemed himself with his attentions to Lady Jane. And the cream of the jest was that his ministrations to the old lady had been performed without a thought to
the main chance. He simply liked her. He supposed it was because she reminded him of his Aunt Mowbry, one of only a few
of his relatives who did not agree with his father and brother that
he was a disgrace to the family name.

He moved across the room and, drawing forth the disreputable
ensemble he had placed under his mattress, began to change his
clothes. He stretched his aching muscles. Lord, he didn't feel like
a ride into London tonight, but he'd made an appointment with
Jack Nail and he'd better keep it. He was eager to discover if his
associate had come up with any information of value, and it was
time to initiate contact with Jerry Church. In addition, it was time
to pay another visit to Charles, who would by now think he had
dropped off the edge of the world.

In her own chamber, having prepared for bed, Catherine dis-
missed her maid. She did not immediately seek her rest, but remained standing by her window for some moments. It was a
lovely night. The scent of the shocked hay drifted across the park,
blending with that of the ripening oats and rye from farther afield.
The stars hung, huge and liquid in the sky, while a crescent moon
sailed delicately across the tops of the trees. For a moment, she
felt part of the night, as though she might take wing and soar into
the filigree of clouds that cast lacy patterns on the grass below.
Leaning against the window's velvet hangings, she inhaled
deeply, absorbing the sounds of crickets chirping and the hoot of
a distant owl. Suddenly, a wave of yearning swept over her, a
wanting for she knew not what.

She knew she was being ridiculous. She had everything she
needed. She had family and friends to love and who loved her in
return. What more could anyone want? The embrace of a man?
How absurd. She'd had that and found it sorely wanting. She
turned away from the window abruptly. Climbing into bed, she
thumped her pillow, but before she could sink into it, a sound
from the corridor caught her attention.

She frowned. It was merely a creaking—probably the house
settling in for the night—however, thoughts of her grandmother
and the restless nights she sometimes endured pulled her from the
bed. Opening the door cautiously, she peered into the corridor,

but saw nothing. Another soft creak, this one from farther away, drew her toward the stairs, and she reached them just in time to observe a dark figure move swiftly from the hall below to the back of the house.

She darted back to her room and ran back to the window. Yes, there—just below her, emerging from the kitchen exit, was a man. He was dressed in dark clothes and moved so silently that she might almost have thought she imagined his shadowy progress. A few minutes later, she observed a horse and rider gliding across the landscape, disappearing at last into the path that led away from the house to the outside world.

What the devil? Only one explanation for this extremely odd situation occurred to her, and without thought she hurried to John Smith's bedchamber. When there was no response to her soft knock, she entered the room. It was empty. Moonlight slanted across bedcovers that had not been disturbed.

"I'm tellin' ye, sojer, 'e ain't 'ere." Jack Nail inhaled a lengthy draft from the tankard in front of him. "It's a ruddy shame, but there it is. 'E left town t'be with the old gaffer—the duke that is, when the old man took sick. I can't watch a cove 'oo ain't around t'be watched."

"Damn!" exclaimed Justin explosively, causing some of the other patrons of the Pig and Whistle to eye him curiously. "I suppose I should have known my father would hole up at the Court when he became ill, and, of course, St. John would see it as his duty to minister to him. Little Sinjie would never fail in his duty," he added bitterly. "What the devil am I to do now?"

"Well," said Jack cautiously. "I did put out some feelers, as ye might say. It don't appear 'e's been 'avin' any queer dealings with anybody of me acquaintance. And I do have a pretty wide circle of acquaintants," he added with satisfaction.

"That you do," replied Justin appreciatively. "Still, you can't accomplish much here in town. Tell me," he continued speculatively, "how would you like to spend some time in the country?"

"Eh?" Jack thunked his tankard on the table.

"Yes, I do believe a week or so of fresh air and sunshine, with a touch of birdsong, would do you no end of good, Jack."

"Birdsong!" exclaimed Jack in accents of extreme disgust. "I think your attic's gone to let, sojer."

It took another fifteen minutes of cajolery and judicious bribery to convince Jack of the benefits of a rural sojourn, but at last he agreed to take up lodgings in the inn in Barkway, close to the Duke of Sheffield's seat.

"It will be better, of course, if you can obtain a position at the Court. Perhaps a slight indisposition will befall one of the stable grooms, leaving a temporary position open for his cousin from London. Or some such."

"Oh, orright," said Jack grudgingly. "I'll see what I kin do."

The next stop on the evening's itinerary was the lodgings of Jerry Church in Gardiners Lane, not far from Whitehall. Jerry lived above a baker's shop, and a swift scrutiny of the upstairs windows indicated that his quarry was not at home. With a sigh, Justin settled into the doorway of the shop, now closed for the evening, to wait. Less than twenty minutes later, he was rewarded by the sight of a rotund figure ambling toward him. The gentleman, whom the streetlights revealed to be in his mid-twenties, stopped at a doorway just to the left of the shop and, fumbling for a moment in his waistcoat pocket, produced a key.

Before he could unlock the door, however, Justin approached him.

" 'Evening, Jerry," he murmured as the young man turned a startled face to him.

"What d'you want?" Jerry Church attempted to jerk away from the hand Justin had laid on his arm. "Leave me alone, or I'll call the Watch." He drew in a quick breath as Justin turned his face to the light. "Good God! Do—do I know you?"

"Of course you do, Jerry," replied Justin, maintaining his hold on the younger man's arm. "Yes, it is I, but let us not make a present of my name to the street. Shall we go up?"

"No!" Jerry's face shone a sickly white under the glow of the lamp. "My God, you're dead—aren't you?"

"Actually, no," replied Justin in some amusement. "However, as it happens, my continued existence is the very subject I wish to discuss with you." His grip tightened. "Now, let us repair to your domicile before the Watch does indeed come to investigate."

Jerry opened his mouth to protest, but, grimacing a little as Justin twisted his arm ever so slightly, unlocked the door and led the way up to his rooms on the top floor of the building.

His first act on entering his sitting room was to hasten to a cupboard, where he withdrew a bottle and a glass. Pouring from the one into the other, he imbibed it in a single gulp. He poured another, then, with a glance at Justin, grudgingly filled a second glass. Bringing both to a small table set before a worn settee, he gestured to Justin to be seated.

"What the devil are you doing here?" was his first question, followed by a rain of others. "Why aren't you—that is, what happened? Do you know how much trouble you're in? How did you get back to England? My God—everyone believes you to be a traitor! What—?"

"Slowly, Jerry. I am here because I need your help. I will explain all."

And, with frequent interruptions from Jerry, he did so, omitting certain pertinent facts.

"Well, if that don't beat the Dutch!" exclaimed Jerry, at the conclusion of the monologue. "What d'you mean, you need my help?" he asked, grasping at what to him was the salient point of Justin's monologue.

"First of all, I want your promise that you will not tell anyone you've seen me."

Jerry was silent for a moment.

"Well, I won't, then," he said at last. "I never really believed you'd help a French general escape, and if someone's trying to frame you—I know well enough how that can ruin a man. But, Justin, there's nothing I can do for you. Those bastards in the front offices will sit on their fat arses and see you hang. You know they will, and I can't—"

"That's precisely my point, Jerry. If I show my face in public, it's going to end up with a bullet in it, or a noose 'round the bottom end. All this is limiting my scope of activity pretty severely. I need some eyes and ears in the Horse Guards."

"But, I can't—" repeated Jerry weakly.

"I'm not asking you to risk anything—much. And, frankly, my boy, you owe me." Justin spoke softly, but there was an edge of meaning in his tone that obviously did not escape his host. Jerry bristled.

"I know that. I know that after that—that hatchet job somebody arranged for me over in Procurement, I very nearly paid the price for someone else's dirty work. If it hadn't been for you—well, believe me, I know what I owe you."

"Very well. Now, here's what I want. First of all, someone had to provide a uniform and false identification for Rivenchy so he could cross our lines. You know the people we generally use for expert forgery. See if you can find out if any of them were hired for this particular job. Second, I want all the information you can dig out on a Captain Roger Maltby of the Light Bobs. His associates in civilian life, his debts if any—you know the sort of thing. And finally, just keep your eyes and ears open for any stray scraps of rumor you think might be helpful. Please, Jerry," he added after a moment, forcing an expression of candid appeal to his gaze. "I know I'm asking a lot of you, but—I've always considered you a friend, and, frankly, I have nowhere else to turn."

Jerry stared speculatively at him for a long moment before he finally erupted into a harsh chuckle. "By God, it would give me a good laugh to see those bastards made fools of. I'll tell you what," he added easily, "I've always liked you, Justin. You're not like the others, ready to grind a heel in somebody's face for his own ends. On the other hand," he asked curiously, "what made you think I wouldn't run straight for the nearest constable?"

"Ah." Justin smiled genially. "As it happens, I think better of you, Jerry. In addition, I do have one or two good friends left who know I have come to you and would take it sorely amiss if I were to come to harm at your hands."

Jerry gulped convulsively. "I'll see what I can do for you. Um, where can I reach you?"

"You needn't concern yourself, my friend. I'll be in touch."

With that, Justin swallowed the last of his drink and rose to his feet. With a bow and a wave of his hand, he made his farewell and swiftly exited the room.

His final stop of the evening was at the home of Charles Rutledge. Charles's greeting to Justin was explosive.

"Where the devil have you been, you unconscionable whelp? I'd just about given you up for dead."

"Why, I've been adventuring, good sir. You will be surprised to know that I am suffering from amnesia."

"Justin—" began Charles warningly.

Justin treated him to an expurgated version of his recent activities.

"And she thinks you don't know your own name?" asked Charles, unconsciously mimicking Robbie's reaction a few nights earlier. "Who is she?"

"I don't think I shall tell you that, Charles, nor where she lives—at least, not yet. Whoever is so interested in helping me shuffle off this mortal coil, no doubt, knows I've likely been in touch with you. I don't want that person leaning on you for information."

Charles grunted. "Fine. But what's your next step?"

Justin hesitated. He had told Charles of his suspicions of St. John, but found himself loath to discuss this particular aspect of his situation.

"I am thinking of going to see my brother," he said at last.

Charles's mouth pulled down. "I think that's not one of your brighter ideas."

"Why? Do you think he'll shoot me down in the drawing room at Sheffield Court?"

"Not if he's got any sense, but that isn't to say he couldn't make things difficult for you."

"As in turning me over to the authorities?"

"Well, yes."

Justin laughed shortly. "He could certainly try. But I can't see him doing that. What would people say? You must know that propriety is the god of St. John's idolatry and for the heir to the Duke of Sheffield to turn in his own brother to the tipstaffs—well, it simply isn't done, you know."

Charles did not smile. "Justin, listen to me. If St. John is truly responsible for your, er, predicament, you're right. Turning you in is the most unlikely course of action for him. But that isn't to say he might make a try—possibly not the first—to have you eliminated. And then there's your father. He is already laid down in his bed over this business. He thinks you are dead, and he's trying to deal with that. Have you considered that resurrecting yourself only to plunge into a trial for treason may very well do him in?"

Justin's only reaction to this speech was a hardening of his expression. "You don't seriously think the subject of my father's health is of the slightest consequence to me?"

"But he is your father!"

"A fact for which he never ceased to express his regret—and one I've tried to forget. However," he continued, a smile curving his lips at Charles's concern. "I'll agree to wait until I have more information to go on." He stood. "And now I must return to my little haven before the cock crows and I turn into a pumpkin."

Charles, took, rose from his chair. "Justin, you must tell me how I can reach you. If Scovell—"

"I'll be in touch, old friend."

With that, Justin departed through the French doors of Charles's study, leaving his friend to stare after him in angry frustration.

Chapter Nine

"Dear God in heaven," groaned Justin. He limped toward Caliban, tethered in the shade of an ash tree near the edge of the road. He waved wearily at the rest of the workers laying down scythes and rakes and the short badging hooks used to gather the stalks into sheaves. Calling their farewells, they began to make their way home from the fields.

Catherine, preparing to mount her own little mare, turned a questioning stare on him.

Justin patted Caliban's misshapen nose. "I've been at this for a week now. Why do I still feel at the end of every day as though I've been trampled on by a water buffalo?"

"Ee, Muster Smith," called a laughing voice, and they turned to behold a dark-haired young man bearing down on them. "That'll teach ye to try t'out-reap them that's been doin' this all our lives."

"I expect you're right, Will," replied Justin ruefully. "Besides, I fear old age is taking its toll. Will someone please fetch me my cane?" He bent over in an exaggerated crouch, one hand on his knee, the other on his back.

Catherine chuckled and lifted a small pouch tied to her saddle. "And here's your reward, Will. You've captured it every day this week, just as you've done each year since you began coming out for harvest."

The young man grinned proudly. "Ay, Miss Catherine, and me and me mum are grateful. Ye're the only landowner here abouts who gives a prize every day for the most hay scythed."

"And it gives me great pleasure to do so." She handed the pouch to Will, who hefted it appreciatively, listening happily to the resulting clink of coin. To Catherine's surprise, he reached inside his shirt for a second, heavier pouch, and added the contents of the first one to it.

"Have you been carrying all that money around with you?"

"Just today, miss. I've promised Mum one o'them new fangled washing machines with this year's winnings, and now I have enough. I'm goin' into Buntingford this very night to collect it from Ben Foley, the ironmonger."

"Washing machine?" interposed Justin.

"Aye, sir. I'm not sure just how it works, but you attach it t'the washtub and turn a crank, and it paddles the clothes about, better nor a person could scrub 'em herself. It's got rollers on it, too, to wring 'em out. It'll sure save Mum's old back." He laughed aloud. "Now, mebee she'll stop raggin' at me t'bring home a wife t'help 'er with the housework."

"I wouldn't bet on it, my boy," said Justin. "It's been my experience that once a woman gets started nagging on a subject, it's like a toper with strong drink. She pretty much becomes addicted to the taste of it."

Will snickered, and with a wave of his hand, started off in the opposite direction as most of his fellows. John swung Catherine into her saddle, and she watched as he mounted Caliban. For some moments they rode in companionable silence.

"Still," said John at last, "I must say I think the exercise agrees with me. I can feel muscles strengthening that I didn't even know I possessed. And, if I do say so as shouldn't, I manage to keep up with those young giants back there."

"Indeed you do," replied Catherine, smiling. "Perhaps you will win the prize yourself one of these days."

"I think not." John sighed gustily. "I fear me old mum will have to look elsewhere for a new washing machine."

Catherine laughed. "Will's mother is a bit of a tartar. And he's such a good lad. He brings every penny of his wages home to her and helps her with her little garden."

"He sounds a dull dog," remarked John.

Nettled, Catherine looked sharply up at him. "Oh? Does doing one's duty by his family make a man dull?"

"No, of course not. That's merely a symptom. If Will—What is it?" he asked, as Catherine suddenly glanced over her shoulder, frowning.

"It's that man." She indicated a burly individual who was moving along the road taken by Will. "I wonder why he's walking in that direction."

"Is he your tenant?"

"No, he's a stranger. I hired him temporarily, with two others. I did not like their looks at the time, but I was in need of workers."

"Perhaps he lives down that way."

"I don't think so." She continued hesitantly. "Will is carrying a good deal of money with him."

John's brows lifted. "Surely, you don't think—"

"I think perhaps we should follow."

She began to turn her horse about, but to her uneasy dismay, John merely shrugged.

"It's not my habit to become involved in other men's concerns," he said easily. "I'm sure you are wrong in your suspicions, but in any event, Will is a stalwart young brute and well able to take care of himself."

"You mean, you would simply turn your back on someone in trouble?" she asked, her voice brittle. Disappointment in his response settled in the pit of her stomach, as though she had swallowed something cold and heavy.

"I'm simply saying," he said in a tone of great reason, "I see no need to meddle in an affair that is none of my business. I have a strict policy of noninterference, you see and—hmm."

John halted abruptly, his gaze on two other men, who were now scurrying after the man following Will. By now Will could no longer be seen, concealed by a bend in the road that led through a small spinney, and in a few moments, the three men had also vanished.

With a muttered curse of exasperation, John pulled about, and, to Catherine's astonishment, he spurred Caliban along the road after Will.

Catherine followed at a gallop.

In a few moments they had rounded the bend to be met with the sight of Will, in the center of a vigorous struggle with the three men. The young man, though giving a good account of himself, was clearly losing the battle. Such was their preoccupation with their task, that the three assailants did not notice the newcomers until John, dismounting in haste, had reached the group. Grasping the shoulder of the largest of the bullies, he wrenched the man away from his prey.

" 'Ere—watcher think yer—oh." He burst into a loud guffaw. "Well, if it ain't the gentleman farmer."

At his words, the other two looked up from the task at hand. Their eyes widened when they saw Justin. They dropped their hands from Will as they caught sight of Catherine, but the large man, evidently their leader, seemed unworried.

"Eh, lads, looks like we've got company, but no matter. I b'lieve we'd had enough o' sweatin' in the fields, anyway. We ain't bloody hayseeds, then. Let's just finish the job 'ere and be on our way. Nobody knows us hereabouts, so we kin be off clean as soon as we relieves this young fella of his burden. Ere, Caleb, take care o' 'is lordship."

So saying, he pushed Justin into the arms of another of the assailants and began to work again on Will, twisting the young man's arm behind his back.

Caleb, who was some inches taller and a great deal broader than Justin swaggered forward, apparently foreseeing no difficulty in dispatching " 'is lordship." Catherine cried out in alarm, but Justin merely crouched in a waiting attitude. He flicked a glance toward Will, then sent a low whistle in Caliban's direction.

To Catherine's astonishment, the stallion ambled to where Will manfully defended himself against the remaining two attackers. Caliban butted one of the men with his great head, sending him tumbling across the turf, leaving the other to Will's capable ministrations.

When John's opponent reached him and pulled back a meaty fist, John sprang from his crouch in a blur of motion. Pivoting on one foot, he spun around, delivering a high kick that landed on the point of Caleb's chin. Hurtling backward, the thug landed on his backside with an astonished thump. Undeterred, he repeated his attack, only to be felled again by the same method. This time, Justin followed up his attack by grasping the man by the shirt, hauling him to his feet, and planting a fist in the middle of his face. The man sank to the ground, more or less a spent force.

Justin then went to Will's assistance. In a few moments, the remaining two attackers joined Caleb on the ground, gasping and holding their hands to various portions of their anatomies.

Justin mounted Caliban, and held out a hand for Will to climb aboard as well.

"Perhaps," he said a little breathlessly, "you could postpone the washing machine purchase for another day, and I think," he added with a questioning look at Catherine, "that we can leave those lads for the constabulary to scoop in later."

"Oh. Yes," agreed Catherine, who stared at him in some bemusement.

Later, after they had deposited Will at his mother's doorstep, still voluble in his admiration for the part Justin had taken in subduing the three ruffians, Justin and Catherine rode home in the lengthening twilight.

"You handled yourself very well, Mr. Smith," Catherine remarked with a smile.

"John," said Justin automatically. "I—I appear to have had some experience in that sort of thing."

"So it would appear. Tell me, what happened to your policy?"

"My policy?"

"The one about noninterference."

"Ah. Um, I thought Will capable of handling one bully, but three seemed to shorten the odds in what I could only consider an unacceptable manner."

"I see." Catherine's lips curled in a small smile. "You know," she continued meditatively, "I have never seen anyone fight in just that manner."

"I shouldn't think you have seen many men fight in any manner at all, have you?"

"Well, no, although I have seen some of the local lads go at it from time to time. I don't think," said Catherine carefully, "that they ever used their feet. Wherever did you learn to do that?"

Justin smiled, recalling the Oriental gentleman who had served as his batman for several weeks in the Peninsula. Chang had bestowed upon him a great many pieces of inscrutable wisdom, not the least of which were some useful street-fighting tactics. "Just something I picked up somewhere, I daresay."

"Mm," returned Catherine noncommittally, and Justin shot her a sharp glance.

"It appears Caliban picked up a little something as well."

At the sound of his name, the stallion tossed his head with an unmistakably self-satisfied nicker.

"Er, yes, what a good thing he chose that particular moment to blunder into the melee."

Catherine, who had heard John's low whistle to his horse, merely nodded, her brows lifted skeptically.

Justin discovered that his own brow was heavily bedewed with perspiration that owed nothing to his recent skirmish. He reflected, not for the first time since his arrival at Winter's Keep, that Catherine Meade was a shade too perspicacious for his comfort. Shifting in his saddle, he searched for a change of subject.

"Who would have thought to find such adventure so far removed from London? Do you often get these little crime sprees here?"

Catherine laughed. "No, of course not. Oh, we hear of the occasional highwayman out on the Cambridge Road, but we seldom get so much as a farthing stolen from the poor box in church. We all know each other around here, you see."

"Except for vagrants who come up from London looking for work at Harvest," finished Justin.

"Precisely."

"Tell me," he asked casually. "Do you never regret your decision to leave the city?"

Catherine stiffened. "I told you, Mr. Smith—"

"I know—you don't care for the bustle and scurry of the metropolis. Still, I find it hard to believe that you never avail yourself of its many undeniable charms. You and your grandmother and Mariah keep up with the news. Do you not ever go in to partake of the theater? Or the museums? The art exhibits?"

Catherine remained silent for some moments. "Well, yes," she replied carefully at length. "Every once in a great while, Mariah and I go in to attend the theater. We spend the night at a hotel and return early the next day."

During this speech, she became increasingly agitated, clenching her reins spasmodically. Lord, she wished she could get over this irrational feeling of panic every time she so much as mentioned leaving Winter's Keep. Her rare forays into London were always the result of an unremitting bout of nagging on the part of Grandmama and Mariah, and were spent in a constant panic lest she should meet someone she had known previously. She was at a loss to explain to herself why she so feared a repetition of the malicious slurs and cuts she had endured following the abortive elopement. She supposed it was because she had previously thought of her tormentors as her friends.

Now, when she returned from the city, she fairly catapulted herself from the carriage into the house, almost slamming the door behind her in her relief to be home again.

Evidently her distress was apparent, for John slowed his mount and peered into her face.

"What is it, Catherine?" he asked in a low voice. "What happened in London to cause such an upheaval in your life—to cause you to hide away from family and friends?"

"Nothing!" she said sharply. "That is—I really do not wish to discuss my personal life, Mr. Smith—not that I can see what possible interest it would be to you."

"Can you not?" John's voice was like warm honey flowing over her in sensuous waves. "For such a perceptive young woman, I should think it would be perfectly obvious by now that there is very little about you that is not of interest to me."

Catherine gasped, and she could feel her cheeks go hot. "I am not a young woman, Mr. Smith," she snapped, regretting immediately the inanity of her remark. "This conversation is growing ridiculous," she concluded pettishly. She raised her reins preparatory to slapping them against her mare's neck, but John reached to lay his hand on her arm.

"I'm sorry," he said in a tone more serious than any she had heard him use so far. "But you must know that you're a damnably attractive woman. It seems a crime against nature that you should immure yourself here in the fastness of the Keep—how aptly named it is, by the by—waiting to wither away into spinsterhood—with nothing to occupy yourself with but your grandmother's needs and those of a home four sizes too big for you."

By the time he had finished this speech, a flush of anger had tinged the sharply chiseled plains of his cheeks. A moment later, an expression almost of surprise leaped into his eyes, and he dropped his hand away from hers. He spurred Caliban and moved ahead of her, his eyes fixed on the road ahead.

Wordless, Catherine stared at her arm, almost expecting to see the outline of his fingers, still warm against the cloth of her habit. She lifted her eyes to gaze at John's back, feeling as though she might choke from the suddenly frantic beating of her heart.

Chapter Ten

"It is rare, as I understand it, for amnesia induced by a blow to the head to continue for so long." Adam Beech spoke noncommittally, crumbling a piece of bread onto his plate.

"Is that so?" responded Justin courteously, his voice equally colorless. "I must say, then, that, while making medical history confers a sort of distinction, I think I would rather pass on this one."

Catherine drew in a sharp breath and glanced around at the other guests at her table. The vicar and his wife smiled sympathetically, while Squire Wadleigh harrumphed in agreement. Lord, John held them all in the palm of his shapely hand. (And when, she wondered in some irritation, had she taken to thinking of him by his first name?—or at least his pseudo-first name.) This was not the first time he had met those gathered in her home on a warm evening in late August. Since he had been a guest in her home, he had gone visiting with her and Grandmama more than once, and had been on hand to help receive callers on several occasions. The whole neighborhood, of course, had made it their business to come see the oddity currently being entertained by Miss Meade and her grandmother.

Only fancy! Report had it that he was ever so handsome and spoke like a gentleman, but he could not even remember his own name! He had snatched the reclusive Miss Meade from a burning building, or was it a collapsing building? Catherine smiled mirthlessly to herself.

She wasn't sure why she had arranged this dinner party. She was, after all, not in the habit of entertaining, and tonight's group was small. Most of her guests had known her since her childhood, and they had all been generous with their support when she had come back to the Keep in disgrace.

Perhaps she hoped to lull John Smith into lowering his guard. For, the longer he was a guest in her home, the more certain she was that he was not being completely honest with her. In the week since his nocturnal venturings from the Keep, she had probed relentlessly with seemingly innocent questions and innocuous remarks, all to no avail. If he was lying about his amnesia, he was maintaining his hoax brilliantly.

But why?

The question still nagged at her. If he were pretending, did it have anything to do with his stealthy departure that night a few weeks ago? Where had he gone? She had lain awake, listening, for several hours, but she had not heard his return. In the morning, he appeared at breakfast, a trifle heavy-eyed, but declaring himself ready for another day in the fields.

She had meant to tax him with his disappearance, but she hesitated. His explanation might be perfectly innocent. Perhaps he was restless and had succumbed to the lure of the night. She might easily have done so herself, she thought, recalling the moment of longing she had experienced at the window. She had in the past gone for late-night walks, especially during those first few months after her return to the Keep when she had lain awake night after night, sobbing her heartache into her solitary pillow.

Never, however, had she saddled a horse and gone for a midnight gallop. Of course, she was not a man, and thus, perhaps, not in need of such a physical outlet for her emotions.

Emotions. Is that what had driven John Smith to leave bed and pillow in the middle of the night? She was sure he had made two or three nocturnal excursions since then. Mmp. If he were troubled by emotions, she rather thought he had them well in check. He did not strike her as a man given to frenetic ramblings.

She felt oddly reluctant to ask him where he went. It was as though by letting him know she was aware of his peregrinations she would lose an advantage over him. No, she would watch and wait. She would display the same distant courtesy she had maintained so far toward him, and, in the meantime she would—in Mariah's words—keep an eye on the silver.

This program, however, was not so easy to maintain as she might have expected. It was impossible not to join in the conversations that sparkled and fizzed in the drawing room after dinner since his arrival, nor was it any easier to remain silent on the way to and from the fields when John conversed easily and knowledgeably on a number of subjects, from the progress of the war in the Peninsula to the likelihood of the king's regaining his health. He drove with her into the village now and then, and escorted her and Grandmama and Mariah to church on Sundays. She took him on an inspection of her tenants' cottages, and he surprised her with his sensible comments regarding the improvements she planned.

She glanced down the table now to where John sat, at Grandmama's left hand. He was perfectly at his ease among this sprinkling of county gentry, just as he would have been, she surmised, at the Prince Regent's table or sprawled on a settle in a country inn. Over his faint protests, she had purchased two suits of clothing for him in the village. They fell far short of what could remotely be called fashionable, but they were a considerable improvement over what he had been wearing when he arrived. He was garbed now in an ensemble suitable for evening wear, and he looked every inch the gentleman.

Across the table, Archie Glasham, the squire's visiting nephew, eyed John uncertainly. Strongly bent toward dandyism, the young man favored florid waistcoats and high-pointed shirt collars. A veritable cascade of fobs dangled at his waist, and he sported an ornate quizzing glass that he brought to his eye with a flourish at every opportunity. Earlier in the evening, when the two had met, Archie had glanced contemptuously over John's ensemble and attempted to put John firmly in his place as a nonentity scarcely entitled to sit at table with such a top of the trees as himself.

As the evening progressed, however, it became apparent that his opinion of Miss Meade's mysterious guest had undergone a marked reversal. No one, even a budding tulip concerned solely with the cut of his clothes, could mistake John Smith for a nonentity. Catherine smiled. John was being unexpectedly kind to the boy. Archie had given him the opportunity on several occasions during dinner to skewer his ridiculous pretensions, but John had refrained. With an understanding twinkle in his eye, he had turned aside, softly and courteously, Archie's fatuous platitudes and uninformed opinions on world matters.

"Yes," he said sometime later, after the guests had departed, "I imagine he is somewhat of a trial to his family, but a nice young man for all of that."

"I thought you were quite forebearing," said Mariah with a laugh. "Did you see that waistcoat? It would have made a good signal flag."

"It was a bit on the gaudy side," replied John. "But it would be cruel to make sport of him, poor lad. Actually, he reminds me—" He stopped suddenly, and his eyes widened.

"What is it?" asked Catherine quickly. For the merest instant she could have sworn a look of chagrin flashed over his features, but the next moment it was replaced by one of disappointment.

"It—it's nothing," he responded quickly. "Only—" He sighed. "I get these—these lightning images. Something will trigger a picture in my mind, only to be gone the next moment. How can memory seen so close at some times, but so elusive at others?"

Lady Jane patted his hand. "There, there, my dear boy. I know it must be most frustrating for you, but you will come about eventually."

"I cannot help wondering," said John in a troubled tone, "what my family must be going through, with my being gone without explanation for so long. Or"—he smiled painfully—"perhaps I have none. At least, no one seems to be looking for me with any degree of diligence." He lifted his gray gaze to Catherine. "You have had no response to your inquiries?"

It was more of a hopeless statement than a question, and Catherine's heart stirred. She thought of herself as an outcast, yet she knew were she to disappear without a trace, those she thought of as family would comb the kingdom for word of her. How awful it would be to think that no one cared. No one at all.

In another few minutes, Lady Jane bade the others good night and made her way upstairs. Mariah followed a few moments later, and John, too, ascended the stairs. Catherine, informing Lady Jane that she would be up in a few minutes to say good night, remained behind. Snuffing the candles in the drawing room, she moved along the corridor to the library, where she browsed restlessly among the shelves.

Lord knew she was tired enough to fall asleep instantly without the aid of a book. She had been in the fields all day, for although the hay was done for the year, harvest had just begun on the corn for winnowing. She had been out among her laborers, as had John, as soon as the dew was off the grass, and had worked until sunset. Still, she was not yet ready for sleep.

She had experienced difficulty getting to sleep for some nights now, and she knew her wakefulness had nothing to do with the state of her body, and everything to do with her confused state of mind. She was sure she had taken John Smith's measure just minutes after she had locked gazes with him in his bedchamber the afternoon she had brought him to the Keep. She had thought him a charming rogue, a species with which she was all too familiar. Yet he kept confounding her original assessment. His kindness to Grandmama and Mariah, his willingness to work in the fields was certainly unlike the self-serving charm displayed by Francis. And then there was his rescue of young Will from those three ruffians a couple of days ago. True, he had at first refused to become involved, but Catherine had the definite impression that his initial reluctance to go to Will's assistance had gone against his grain—as though he were forcing himself to take the coward's way. It was only when it became obvious that the boy was facing insurmountable odds that John had allowed himself to follow his own inclination.

But why would a man deliberately choose to portray himself as a scoundrel? And was it a conscious effort on his part, or one that he had been practicing for so long that it had become second nature? Sighing, she turned again to the bookshelf. Really, she must get some sleep tonight. Perhaps something soporific from the pen of the poet, Chatterton, would help. Unthinking, Catherine's lips curved upward as she recalled John's patient reading from the tome for Grandmama's benefit.

As she moved to pluck the book from its place on the shelf, the door opened behind her. Catherine realized without turning who had entered.

Swinging slowly about, she affixed a bright smile to her lips. "You could not sleep, Mister Smith?"

"I am John in the fields, Catherine. Can you not call me by my first name, such as it is, here in the house, as well—at least when we are alone?"

Uneasy at this pointed intimation of just how alone they were at the moment, Catherine's laugh sounded brittle in her own ears.

"I suppose it does not make a great deal of difference what I call you, does it, since the only name I have for you is not yours?"

For an instant, a look of pain flashed in his eyes, and Catherine was shamed.

"I'm sorry," she said. "I should not have—"

"But it is quite true. For all you know my name could be—well, not John Smith, but—oh, John Bellingham."

"John—Oh, Percival's assassin." She smiled uncertainly. "But he was hanged weeks ago."

"Yes, but I might be someone else of his ilk. Or a smuggler's apprentice, or a Luddite, or—"

"Or a perfectly ordinary gentleman who suffered a misfortune while trying to help someone."

John clapped a hand to his forehead. "Good God, an ordinary gentleman? That would be worst of all! No, I insist I must be someone with a little dash—a convict escaped from the hulks, perhaps."

Catherine laughed dutifully, noticing with some dismay that

during the course of this conversation, he had moved farther into the room and now stood at her side.

"Ah, Chatterton and his monk again. Well, that should send you off to dreamland in nothing flat. My question is, why this need for a literary sleeping draft after the day you put in?"

Casually, he leaned across her shoulder to riffle the pages of the book, and Catherine was intensely and irritably aware of his nearness and its effect on her. She turned her head and nearly gasped on discovering that his eyes were mere inches from hers and that the candlelight had turned them to a glittering silver.

She laughed shakily. "Perhaps, I am overtired. Have you never been positively numb with fatigue but found yourself unable to go to sleep?"

He leaned closer, and when he spoke, his voice was a silken whisper. "Now, how would I know that? Particularly, when fatigue is the farthest thing from my mind right now."

A maelstrom of emotions churned within her. She was by now sure that, while he possessed Francis's easy charm, he was far different from her erstwhile lover in character. Yet she suspected him of being dishonest with her. And of using his undeniable charm for his own purposes. On the other hand, she thought she discerned something of value beneath the casual courtesy and behind those laughing gray eyes. Why it had become important to her to get to the truth of the man, she was unwilling to contemplate. She knew she should step away from him, but she was suddenly consumed with an urge to throw caution to the winds, to allow herself to be drawn into the magic of that molten gaze.

He was very close to her now, so close that she could feel the soft caress of his breath on her cheek. His hands came up to grasp her shoulders, and she was intensely aware of the warmth of his hands through the flimsy muslin of her gown. He was going to kiss her. The knowledge was a fire, building inside her, but she remained motionless under his touch. When he bent to cover her mouth with his, his lips were cool and firm, and oddly tentative.

When she made no demur, however, the kiss deepened. Instantly, a wave of pure sensation swept over her. She was terrified at the sense of violation that engulfed her—not from John's gentle offensive, but from the tumult of her own emotions. Distantly, she heard a faint, mewling sound, and realized to her horror that it came from her own throat. His mouth moved over hers more searchingly now, more urgently—almost demanding.

And she responded. Lord, it was as though her very bones had turned to flame, and she was consumed with wanting. Even in

Francis's embrace, she had never experienced this need to press herself into him, to somehow absorb him. His hands moved on her back, caressing a spot at the nape of her neck that she had not known was exquisitely sensitive, then moving down her spine, creating a trail of fire that left her gasping. He abandoned her mouth momentarily to spread the heat over her cheeks and down her throat until she thought she would burst from the throbbing deep within her.

Dear God, Catherine cried inwardly. She was losing control! Blindly, she pulled away, and it was as though she were peeling part of her skin from her body. John released her immediately, but his breathing was harsh and his hands trembled. His eyes were the color of a storm at sea, and she fancied she could discern flashes of lightning in their depths.

In a moment, however, his demeanor had returned to its normal air of benign mockery.

"I suppose I should apologize for that, but I cannot bring myself to do so."

Her pulse was still beating wildly, but with a supreme effort she forced her voice to calm. "There is no need," she replied with creditable coolness. "It is I who am at fault. I made no effort to rebuff your advances."

"No." His laughter was smooth, albeit a trifle shaky. He rubbed his jaw reminiscently. "At least I came away relatively undamaged this time."

John stiffened slightly, but the gleam of his smile remained undiminished. "A wise decision on your part, my dear," he said, after a moment's hesitation. "A lady cannot be too careful of her virtue, and to entrust it to, 'an importunate stranger,' is certainly the height of folly."

Catherine made no reply, but turned away swiftly. On legs that would scarcely carry her, she walked from the room.

Reaching her bedchamber, she found her maid awaiting her, but after dismissing her, she flung herself across her bed.

What in God's name had come over her in that darkened, book-lined chamber? She had been curious, that was all. She wanted to know what John Smith was all about, and she had wanted to settle the nagging question of her attraction to him. Well, she certainly had done that, but she could not have foretold that the answer would overwhelm her in such an avalanche of emotion. Why had she responded in such a manner? She had expected that she would enjoy his kiss—nothing more.

But this—this ravishing of her very soul, was as astonishing as it was unwelcome. She placed her fingers on her lips. They were swollen, and probably bruised as well, she thought. Dear Lord, whoever John Smith was, he was an expert in rendering a female helpless with desire. Particularly a female as inexperienced as herself, she realized sourly. Surely, if she were more sophisticated, she would not have reacted like a bedazzled schoolgirl to his embrace.

And, she realized irritably, she did not know any more about her infuriating guest than she had before. She knew only that she was dangerously attracted to him, as the proverbial moth to a flame, and if she did not want her wings thoroughly singed, she had best make it her first priority to get Mr. Smith out of her house.

She had promised him that he could stay as long as his identity was in question, but she was beginning to wonder seriously if he were making a May game of her and that he knew perfectly well who he was. Well, there was no way right now of deciding this issue, so she would simply have to redouble her efforts to discover his real name. It was possible that John Smith resided far from London, and that his family was searching for him to no avail in Yorkshire or Lincolnshire or some other remote location, not realizing that he had traveled to the south of England.

She would send to London for a Bow Street Runner. Yes, that sounded like the most sensible course of action. Those men were adept at finding missing persons; surely they would manage just as well at turning up missing identities.

She realized with an unpleasant start that she would miss John Smith when he returned to wherever he had sprung from. Not, of course, that she was in any real danger of losing her heart to him—she had learned her lesson too well to be lured into that trap again—but, she must guard against lapsing into a serious indiscretion. She had always thought of herself as a virtuous woman, but she was not at all sure that her rectitude was strong enough to withstand John Smith's beguiling assaults. And she certainly had no desire to be added to his no doubt long string of conquests.

There were times, she had admitted to herself long ago, when she almost wished she had allowed Francis to seduce her on the night of their elopement. She had undergone all the penalties of ruination with none of its pleasures. If she had allowed Francis to bed her, she would at least have sampled the delights of a carnal embrace once in her life. Perhaps there might even have been a child. A familiar stab of longing surged through her.

Now, she was forced to another admission. The desire she had felt for Francis to continue his fevered caresses was a frail thing compared to the almost uncontrollable spiral of wanting into which she had been drawn at the first touch of John's mouth on hers. Francis's embrace had resulted in a pallid imitation of passion—an apprenticeship into the wickedly delicious precincts of sin to which she had been so persuasively invited by John Smith.

She turned her face into her pillow, but her last thought before drifting into a restless sleep was that oddly, she had experienced no sense of sin in her response to his kiss. In fact, the one aspect of the episode that she remembered clearly was the shattering sense of rightness she felt in his arms, as though she had been enfolded in a welcoming haven.

Which was absurd, of course. John Smith was dangerous, she reminded herself muzzily, and she had better not forget it. She must not be lulled into losing the peace of mind she had struggled so long to acquire.

Her eyes closed, and her breathing deepened; and she slept, only to dream of polished-pewter eyes and a dark, lean visage hovering above her own.

Chapter Eleven

It seemed as though she had been running for a very long time. Her breath came in short, deep gasps, and behind her she could hear the hoofbeats of her pursuer. He was getting closer! Her feet, tiny and fur-covered were bloody from the rocky terrain over which she traveled. Behind her, she could feel the full brush of her tail, catching occasionally in the brambles covering her path.

She stumbled and fell. Instantly, the hunter was upon her. Dismounting, he ran to her and bending, he cradled her in his arms. She raised her head and gazed into the gun-metal eyes of John Smith.

Oddly, now that she was caught, she felt no fear as he stroked her luxuriant red pelt. Her whole body tingled as he ran strong, gentle fingers over her pointed ears.

She strained against him, and now she stood on two feet. She was human once more, and her hands as they reached to touch him were again white and slender and smooth. She lifted her face, and John bent his to meet her.

For a moment, she waited in breathless acquiescence for his kiss, but as he moved closer, and closer still, his features began to blur. Before her terrified gaze he changed! He was no longer John Smith. He was a stranger—or—no, he wore the face of—of Francis Summervale.

She shrank away from him, aware as she did so that she had resumed the shape of a fox. Frozen in her fear, unable to move, she watched Francis draw a dagger from his belt. He held it high over his head, and when he brought it down, it flashed in a glittering silver arc, plunging straight toward her heart. Her mouth opened in a long, silent scream, and—

Catherine jerked upright in her bed. Wildly, she glanced about the room, absorbing with difficulty the familiar surroundings of her bedchamber. With a conscious effort, she calmed her breathing and listened to the thunder of her heart.

It took several minutes for her to regain her composure, but at last she sank back into her pillows. Lord, what an odd, frightening nightmare! She had barely begun to drift into another, uneasy sleep, when a creaking noise from the corridor seemed to ring like a gunshot in the room and brought her bolt upright again.

She sprang from her bed and hurried to her window. In a few moments, as before, a now familiar figure exited the house and glided over the graveled path that led to the stable.

Catherine waited until the man, mounted on the equally familiar figure of Caliban, disappeared into the distance. Then, lighting a candle from the embers that still glowed in the hearth, she slipped from the room and moved along the dark, silent corridor to John's bedchamber.

Without pausing to knock, she opened the door and whisked herself inside. She lit a few candles and stood for a long moment of indecision in the center of the room. At last she moved hesitantly, first to the desk that lay near the window, then to a large commode positioned against one wall. She ran her fingers lightly over their surfaces, finding, as she expected, nothing of note.

She was beginning to feel a little foolish. What on earth did she think to find in here? Surely, a man of John's intelligence—assuming he had something to hide—was not likely to leave a conveniently crumpled letter with a scrawled signature, or a monogrammed kerchief.

Finding nothing in her first, cursory search, Catherine drew a deep breath and began on the wardrobe and bureau. The paltry contents of each—the suits she had purchased and the one he had worn on his arrival at the Keep, plus a few items of underclothing—were all that met her inspection. She reached for one of the suits, but halted, her fingers poised midair.

No, she simply could not make herself rifle the man's pockets. With a sigh, she turned toward the wall sconce. Pursing her lips to blow out the candles, she halted suddenly, struck by a thought. The three ensembles that hung in the wardrobe comprised, to Catherine's count, John Smith's entire complement of clothing. If they were all present and accounted for, what the devil was he wearing tonight? His nightshirt? No, that lay neatly folded in a bureau drawer.

She looked around the room again, and this time she paused at the bed. The coverlet had been turned down, but the bed obviously had not been slept in. Yet the foot of the bed was oddly disarranged.

Moving to it, she lifted the bedclothes.

Nothing.

The mattress lay crooked on the bed, and she lifted the corner. Still nothing. No! Wait! Lying atop the webbing that supported the mattress was a piece of torn newspaper.

She sank down on the bed, and as she perused the little scrap, a disbelieving horror settled in the pit of her stomach. The words seemed to leap at her in disjointed chunks.

"Lord Justin Belforte . . . treason . . . body identified . . . decorated hero . . . escape of French general."

She read the piece again, and then once more before she finally grasped its contents.

Dear God, the name of her mysterious guest was Lord Justin Belforte! The man she had kissed with such abandon just a few hours ago was a wanted felon. A traitor!

A trembling seized her as she tried to assimilate what she had just learned. Apparently, the authorities thought that Belforte was dead. Had his French conspirators done away with the wrong man when they attempted to kill a pawn for whom they had no further use? Or had Belforte killed the man himself, hoping to avoid retribution?

As these and other even more chaotic thoughts whirled in her brain, Catherine grew numb with disbelief. She was sickened with the sense of betrayal that seemed to seep into every corner of her being like an ugly fog, creating a despair such as she had never known—even when she had discovered Francis's perfidy.

It must be just as she suspected. John—no, Lord Justin—had deceived her. He had no more lost his memory than she had. And the why of it was perfectly clear. My lord desperately needed a bolt-hole in which to lie hidden until he could contrive an escape to—where? America, perhaps. What better place could he have found than the isolated solitude of Winter's Keep? And to compound his good fortune, his little haven was guarded only by a parcel of gullible, foolish, single women, ripe for his blandishments.

One single, foolish woman in particular, she thought bitterly.

What was she to do now? She could not allow Jo—Lord Justin to remain at the Keep. She must be rid of him. Not only must she be rid of him, but she must see that he was made to face his punishment for betraying his country.

She paced the floor in furious circles. She would say nothing to the perfidious snake, but first thing in the morning, she would go to Sir Reginald Selwyn, the area's justice of the peace. Her brow wrinkled in concentration as she recalled snippets of information that had been dispensed in other newspaper stories about the escape of the French general. Apparently, Lord Justin had not actually been charged with a crime, but that was only because he was thought to be dead. Surely, Sir Reginald would know who to contact in the Foreign Office.

Yes, that's what she would do. Within a day or two Lord Justin

Belforte would be hauled away from the Keep in chains to meet his just reward.

Carefully, Catherine replaced the newspaper scrap beneath the mattress, then made her way back to her own bedchamber. She did not return to bed, however, but stood by the window for a long time. Vainly, she tried to quell the nausea that rose like a tide within her. Surely, she was overreacting to what she had just learned. Yes, she had every right to feel the indignation that surged through her. Lord Justin had played her—played them all a scurvy trick. His kindness to Grandmama, his quiet sympathy for Mariah, even his yeoman efforts in the fields had been part of the trickery. All false, all purposeful. Yet she felt more than indignant, more than betrayed. She felt used and violated, as though something deep within her had been soiled beyond redemption.

How could she have been such a fool—again? How could she have succumbed to the practiced blandishments of a lying, traitorous villain? Was she so pathetically starved for masculine attention? Was she so desperate for the touch of a man's hand? She had thought of herself as self-possessed. She believed she had raised an invincible barrier around her heart and her emotions.

She shook herself. She was behaving as though she had given her heart to the man, when in truth, she had only given in to a moment of madness in his arms. She had certainly not relinquished anything more important. She would see Lord Justin Belforte hanged and not shed a tear. She was still whole of heart and inviolate of spirit.

She drew a deep, shuddering breath and returned to her bed. Try as she might, however, she could not return to sleep.

"I am sorry to be the bearer of such tidings, my boy."

Charles Rutledge spoke gruffly from his place across the desk from Justin. Once again, they sat in Charles's candlelit study, where Charles had just imparted the news that, according to his informants, the Duke of Sheffield's health had worsened considerably in the days since Justin's return to England. He was not expected to live out the month.

Justin reached inside himself for the insouciant smile he kept in readiness for when the subject turned to his family.

"I've already told you, Charles," he said carelessly. "The duke's health is of no concern to me."

"But he is your father," expostulated Charles, shocked. "It occurs to me that I advised you badly in suggesting that you not visit

Sheffield Court. To be sure, your brother is in a position to do you a good deal of harm, but at a time like this . . ."

"Look, Charles, I am sorry to hear the old man is in such bad skin, but I feel no worse than at such news of any one of my acquaintances. It was Father who decided long ago that he'd just as soon forget I'm his son. It took me some years to get the message, but I finally came to terms with the fact. And now it's too late. If you are envisioning a dramatic death-bed reconciliation, you will have to look to Drury Lane."

Justin drew a deep breath. "I have not yet decided whether to confront St. John as yet, but please believe me when I say that the state of the Duke of Sheffield's health will have nothing to do with my decision. Now, have you any news for me concerning my little predicament?"

Charles sighed. "Not much, I'm afraid. I have discovered that, as we had already assumed, it was an Englishman who reported to Captain Bassinet of your mission to Huerta and provided him with a dossier on your background."

"An officer?" queried Justin sharply.

"Apparently."

"Was there a description?"

"Nothing very specific. The information came from a Spanish guerilla who had attached himself to the captain's camp. He speaks little English and said only that the man visited Bassinet in the dead of night. He was a big man and wore a dark coat. Does that strike any notes with you?"

"Mmp," growled Justin. "Perhaps." As far as it went, it described Roger Maltby to a T. Particularly, if the coat was the uniform of the Light Bobs.

"It appears to me," said Charles, an oddly hopeful note in his voice, "that the attempt on your life was not personally motivated, but sprang simply from a need to get you out of the way before you were able to complete your mission."

Justin rubbed his jaw dubiously.

"Thus, assuring there would be no troops guarding the bridge at Huerta? Possibly. However, that doesn't explain the good captain's comprehensive knowledge of my background—or the paper covered with St. John's handwriting."

Charles made no response. Indeed, mused Justin sardonically, what could the man say? "There, there, lad, I daresay a hundred reasons might be found for your brother's written words to find their way into a set of lethal instructions detailing your immediate demise."

Shortly thereafter, Justin left Charles in the shadowed study, and some time later he found himself again in the murky depths of the Pig and Whistle facing Jack Nail over a heavy wet, reflecting on his conversation with Charles. Could his friend be right? Was St. John far removed from his problem—even now hovering in filial solici-tude at their father's bedside?

Justin was surprised at the depth of what he very much feared was a futile wish that such was the case. He clutched at the table, digging his fingers into the rough wood as Jack's words served only to confirm his nightmare suspicions.

"It weren't easy findin' a position at yer pa's place," Jack whis-pered, the words sliding from the corner of his mouth like escaping prisoners. "Lucky I ran inta a stable boy at the village alehouse one night who 'asn't been with the family but a few months. I figgered 'e wouldn't be likely t'run t'the 'ead groom with any tales if I was ta offer him some temp'r'y employment elsewhere."

"And you were able to take his place?"

"Slick as a peeled eel, sojer. Can't say as I enjoyed the work," Jack continued meditatively, his eyes squinting almost shut. "Seems t'me as—since I didn't hire on with ye t'muck out stables, ye owes me a bit more than was pre'v'sly agreed on."

"I think not, Jack," Justin replied simply, but in a tone that effec-tively quelled any further negotiations on the part of his henchman. "Now, what have you learned."

"Well, there ain't much comin' and goin' at Sheffield Court, what with yer pa bein' laid up, but there's been a coupla callers now and then from Lunnon. They come late at night and leave early the next morning. I found out one of 'em's called Cyrus Bentick, and 'e works in the Foreign Office—over t' the 'Orse Guards."

"Yes, he is known to me," replied Justin, recalling a small, incon-spicuous man who apparently spent his days shuffling paper from one corner of his desk in a dim area of the Top Floor to another. "He works for—well, that is of no consequence. But why would he be visiting my father?"

Jack snorted. "Dunno. But, judgin' from the prad 'e was ridin', I wouldn't say 'e's wot you'd call a prime spoke at the 'Orse Guards. Now, the other fella—I recognized 'im. Name of Snapper Briggs, an' I know fer a fact 'e's done some work fer Jasper Naismith, a wery unpleasant fella, if ye take my meanin'. Big as a goriller and just as ugly and twicet as mean. Nobody's ever knowd Jasper t'be up t'any good."

"I see. In other words, if you were of a mind to do someone a bit of harm—"

"Aye. Jasper'd be yer man."

From the Pig and Whistle, Justin moved on to Gardiners Lane and Jerry Church. Here, he added a little more to his growing fund of information.

"Cyrus Bentick!" exclaimed Jerry. "By all that's holy, Justin. I think perhaps we've found our man. I investigated all the forgers I know of who might have been used for Rivenchy's identification papers and struck metal with one Frank Borritch. He did it! Said he'd been told to draw up papers in the name of a Sergeant Major William Waters of the Light Bobs. And who d'you think it was put in the order and paid him a bundle to do it? *And* to say nothing about it?" Jerry was fairly dancing in his excitement.

"Cyrus Bentick," replied Justin, his own heart beating fast. By God, it looked as though he had his man!

Jerry had little else to report, but Justin, declaring the information worth a hundredweight in gold, thanked him profusely and left with a promise to visit again in a few nights' time.

Still later that night, Justin paid his last call of the evening. One of the lesser bits of information imparted by Jerry was that Robbie had been wounded at the hands of a French column just outside Burgos. It was a shoulder injury—not serious, but enough to cause a possibly permanent impairment of movement. Thus, he had been transferred to courier duty and sent to London for an indeterminate length of time.

As it happened, this time, Robbie was home, just accepting a brandy from his manservant when Justin tapped at the window.

"Don't you ever use the front stairs?" he asked plaintively as his man crossed the room unhurriedly to assist Justin into the room.

"Only occasionally," replied Justin. " 'Evening, Henry." This to the bulky gentleman who, evincing little or no surprise at the visitor's unorthodox arrival, took coat and hat from him.

" 'Evening, Major," responded that personage. "It's a pleasure to see you again. I'm sorry I was abed when you called before. If you had rung," he continued reproachfully, "I should have been happy to provide you with refreshments."

"God forbid I should disturb your beauty sleep, Henry," replied Justin with a grin. "But, I'll have a drop of whatever you're peddling there."

Justin had learned some years ago that he might repose the same trust in Robbie's batman that he bestowed on Robbie, thus had no compunction in revealing his presence to the gentleman. Henry smiled benevolently, an expression that sat oddly on a face more accustomed to a certain belligerence of aspect.

"So what's toward?" asked Justin, seating himself in an easy chair opposite his friend. "How's the wound?"

Robbie flexed a broad shoulder. "Oh, tol'lol. Nothing more than a bit of a nuisance, particularly since it's kept me here in London instead of in Spain, where I could be doing more good. It's hard gleaning information that has to cross the Channel by smugglers' boat."

"But you do have something?" Justin asked with barely restrained impatience.

Robbie grimaced. "Oh, yes. It appears that the Spanish officer who was left in charge of the bridge at Huerta failed to receive orders to keep men posted at the bridge—which was your mission, of course. He was given orders—from an officer fitting your description—to abandon the place, thus leaving it wide open for all the Frenchmen fleeing the field at Salamanca—particularly one French general."

"The same fellow, I presume, supposed to be me, who ended up dead in a ditch."

"Precisely. Also—" Robbie shifted in his chair. "I've been over to the Horse Guards once or twice. I have to tell you, old man, mention of your name brings nothing but a cold, hard stare."

Justin made no response, but sat in silence for a long moment. "Tell me," he said at last, "are you acquainted with a Cyrus Bentick over there?"

Robbie's brandy paused almost imperceptibly in its progress toward his lips. "Bentick? I don't think—" He sighed. "Actually, he was the one man who seemed inclined to discuss your case with me. He's an officious little chap—screwed-up face—looks like he's been constipated for several months. I don't really know what he does over there—has a small desk littered with papers in a cubicle off in a corner in the dark. When I brought up the matter of General Rivenchy's escape, he was loud in his assertion of your guilt, and he expressed at some length his regret that you'd been snuffed before you could be brought to justice. What's your interest in the little toad?"

Justin related his recent conversation with Jack Nail, as well as the information he'd received from Jerry Church, to which Robbie responded with a low whistle.

"Good God, do you really think Bentick is behind the plot? Not just the treason, but the attempts on your life?"

"There seems little doubt of it—except—"

"Except what?"

"Except that our Cyrus doesn't seem like the type to mastermind a scheme like this."

Robbie, in the act of lifting his drink to his lips, stilled. "Oh, I don't know," he said at length. "He might have unsuspected depths. At any rate, there don't seem to be any other candidates." He paused. "Unless . . ." He stared before him. "Does it occur to you that it was awfully kind of Jerry Church to go to so much trouble on your behalf? To say nothing of the risk he must have braved to get that information?"

"Yes, it occurred to me almost immediately. However, as I said, he owes me a debt and—and he rather has it in for his superiors. Ever since he was accused—apparently falsely—of dipping his hand in the till over at Procurement, he's held a jaundiced view of everyone in authority. Seems to think he was robbed of any chance he might have had for advancement, and he's an ambitious young chap. At any rate, I believe him to be sincere in his efforts on my behalf. Not that the idea of St. John working with Bentick is incredible."

Robbie grunted. "Vengeance, like politics, makes strange bedfellows."

"But—My God, how could St. John possibly have joined forces with someone like Bentick? How would he even know Bentick?"

"It's hard to say how anyone meets anybody—at his club, perhaps, or at the theater, or—oh, I don't know—" Robbie threw up his hands. "Feeding the pigeons at St. Paul's, perhaps. If Church is to be believed, it seems obvious to me that somehow St. John got wind of Bentick's plot and decided to create an advantage for himself."

"An opportunity for the revenge he's sought for so long?"

"Well—yes."

Justin sighed. "It seems abysmally far-fetched. There must be some other connection—someone higher up known to both Bentick and St. John. Bentick must be working for someone. But who?"

"I think you're wrong," said Robbie heavily. "I think Bentick's our man."

Justin's eyes narrowed. "We need more information before we can make a case, however." He finished his brandy in a single gulp. "I think I shall have to repair to the Court, after all. It's time I had a talk with St. John."

"You don't think you ought to wait until you have some sort of proof?"

"I think proof is going to be hard—if not impossible—to come by. No, I need to talk to St. John. I believe I'll learn all I need to know when I confront him face-to-face."

Justin rose. Robbie also stood and walked with him to the window. "By the by, how do things stand with you and your lovely hostess? Does she still believe you to be non compos? Have you made your way into her bed yet?"

Justin flushed. "She still thinks I have no memory of my past," he said stiffly, "and she is not the sort of woman who entertains stray confidence tricksters in her bed."

Robbie gave a low whistle. "Sorry, old man. Like that is it? Well, well—the age of miracles is upon us."

Justin suppressed the surge of irritation that rose in him. "I don't know what you're talking about, you ass. I'm simply saying that some women are susceptible to liberal applications of butter from the sauce boat and some are not. Miss Meade is one of the latter. Nor is she worthy of such treatment. And now, if you don't mind, the hour grows late, and I'd best wend my way homeward. Keep me posted," he added, swinging his leg over the window ledge.

As he made his way through the silent streets of London toward the Cambridge Road, Justin pondered further on his conversation with Robbie. He had been unwontedly vehement in his defense of Catherine Meade's virtue. Particularly since he had mounted what could only be termed an assault on that virtue some hours earlier.

He had been astonished at the depth of her response to his kiss. He was gratified, of course, and he would willingly have plundered further the delights of her softly curving body if she had not drawn back. For, of course, he would not pursue a female against her will. Usually, he did not find it necessary to do so. He had learned many years ago to discern which women would welcome his advances and participate enthusiastically in their own seduction, and which would not. He never attempted to overcome the defenses of the latter, for that way lay all sorts of unpleasant repercussions. If the affections of the lady in question were seriously engaged, it usually meant the painful end to a liaison. Lord, he sounded like the veriest coxcomb! He knew himself to be an uncaring cad, but it was no part of his intention to inflict a hurt on anyone, either. He certainly was not prepared to give his own heart—if he had one to give, that is—but he had no wish to damage anyone else's.

What was the state of Catherine Meade's heart? He rather thought she had her own barriers firmly in place, but the fire she had displayed in his embrace made him wonder. He had a good idea that she had virtually seen through his deception and that she had recognized him for what he was—a thoroughly bad man, in his father's words. If this were the case, she probably stood in no danger of succumbing to his devastating charm.

Laughing at this absurd conceit, Justin turned into Coppersmith Street on the outskirts of the city. The area was a warren of narrow lanes and alleys that eventually led into the Huntingdon Road, and Justin was glad of the three-quarter moon that illuminated his passage.

His musings continued. At any rate, he thought, his relationship with the beauteous Miss Meade had just taken a new turn, and it would be interesting to see how things developed. He must admit, he was somewhat taken aback by his own reaction to the kiss. He had, not unsurprisingly, experienced a surge of desire as her lips had parted under his and her body had pressed into him. But there had been something else—something he had not experienced with any other woman. He had felt a sense of joining with her, just as he had felt an odd connection with her from the moment he had looked up from his bed to fall into that incredible emerald gaze of hers. It was as though when he had covered her mouth with his, their two halves had been united to make one whole, and when she had pulled back so suddenly, it was as though a part of his very soul had been wrenched from him.

Which was ludicrous, of course. Catherine Meade was a part of the world of Winter's Keep, which was, in turn, merely a wayside stop—a temporary haven. The day would soon come when he would leave its serenity and peace to take up the sordid chaos of his own life. By then—

Justin felt the bullet enter his body before he heard the shot. He ducked when he heard the crack, but it was too late. For a moment, he felt nothing, but as his searching fingers encountered the wet, stickiness that oozed from his side, the pain hit him like a searing knife stroke, and he fell forward against Caliban.

By a monumental effort, he remained in the saddle. He knew that to fall now would expose himself to another effort by his would-be assassin.

Winter's Keep. He had to get to the Winter's Keep. Halting when he reached an open area past the cluster of buildings that marked the outer limits of the town, he shrugged out of his coat and balled it into a large pad. Tearing his neck cloth from his throat, he bound the coat tight against his side. He urged Caliban forward then, struggling to maintain consciousness. He had a long ride ahead of him. He must not give up. He must not fall. He must get home to the Keep—and to Catherine.

Chapter Twelve

Catherine did not know how many times that night she paced the perimeter of the small rug that lay near her bed. For some hours she attempted sleep, but, giving up at last, she had taken up her peregrination, her steps marking the passing of the endless minutes. Finally, like a piece of driftwood tossed on a beach, she stood once more by the window. It was almost dawn, she noted abstractedly. Treetops could be seen silhouetted against the lightening sky, and the grass was losing its mantle of dappled silver to return to its customary color.

Wearily, she began to turn away toward her bed, but a flicker of something dark caught her eye. Yes, there—just beyond the copse of trees that marked the boundary between the parkland and the Home Farm, a horse and rider made their way slowly toward the house.

He was back!

She fought the urge to run from her bedchamber to intercept Lord Justin—to scream her rage and pain at him. She would do nothing of the kind, of course. As she had promised herself, she would remain silent. In the morning she would notify the magistrate of the traitor's presence in her home and then—and then matters could take their course.

She turned away once more, and once more was brought up short. There was something odd about the way Lord Justin and Caliban progressed. The great horse was not precisely trotting, but he was moving at a speed too hasty to be called a walk. His rider seemed to be having difficulty maintaining his position on Caliban's back. Why, he was not returning to the stables, but had turned toward the front of the house. Good God! He was hurt! She could see clearly now that his face was as white as the bit of shirt that could be seen under his tattered coat.

Unthinking, she whirled about and ran downstairs. Flinging open the front door, she raced down the shallow flight of steps just as Justin approached the house. Her feet scarcely touching the gravel she flew to Justin's side as he slid from Caliban's back. She realized immediately that he had not dismounted, but simply fallen from the horse. She could not hold him upright, but fell with him to the ground, her hands and the front of her dress covered with his blood. At her gasp of horror, he opened eyes that had fallen shut some miles ago.

" 'Lo, Catherine." He smiled muzzily. "I seem to . . . I seem to be in a . . . a spot of trouble . . . again."

His gray eyes clouded like the sky on a dull day, and his lids drooped closed again as he slumped against her breast.

"Well, I'll have to say," remarked Adam some hours later, snipping thread from the last suture in Justin's side, "the advent of this fellow in the neighborhood has done wonders for my medical skills. I've had more opportunity to practice on him than I've had in a year of dosing all the rest of the citizens of Hertfordshire put together. He must be luckier than anyone else in the county, too. If the ball had entered a hair's breadth to the east, it would have hit his intestines, or something else equally critical. As it was, it passed right through, sparing him any nasty excavation work. No, he's not going to die, Catherine," he concluded testily. "You can relax. You and Mariah and Lady Jane, as well."

Catherine sank back against her chair, feeling completely boneless. After Justin had been brought upstairs, his form a deadweight in the arms of the footmen who bore him, Mariah and she had been unable to wholly stop the river of blood that poured from his wound. Adam had arrived a good hour after that to sew him up—during which Justin had not regained consciousness. At times his breath was barely perceptible as it sighed through bloodless lips.

"Are—are you sure, Adam? He is so pale—and still. And his breathing—"

"I didn't say he's ready to spring up and dance a reel," retorted Adam austerely. "I said he's going to live. At least it looks that way, if nothing untoward occurs. He's lost a lot of blood, and the ball tore up a great deal of muscle and tissue. I believe it's too much to hope that he won't run a fever, but he's young—and healthy as that misshapen horse of his. If we can control the fever, he should come around."

Catherine, limp with relief, drew in a long, shuddering breath. She berated herself for this show of weakness, particularly since she did not, she told herself once again, care if Lord Justin Belforte lived or died. In fact, in calling for help to scoop him into the house to save his worthless hide, she had probably been simply postponing the inevitable. She experienced an unpleasant start at the thought.

Still, she could not leave him lying in front of the house while his life's blood drained away into the gravel. She had, she reminded herself sourly, done nothing about contacting Sir Reginald. Well, she supposed she could wait until Lord Justin had regained consciousness before turning him over to the law.

Her fingers clenched in her lap. She might as well be honest with herself. She did not want to contact Sir Reginald. She wanted to confront Lord Justin, to vent her spleen and to see if he had any explanation for his perfidy. Yes, that was it, wasn't it? she thought in a wave of self-disgust. She wanted to give his lordship an opportunity to exonerate himself, to somehow exculpate himself in her eyes.

Dear God, she must harden herself. There was nothing he could say that would excuse his villainy. Why must she—?

"What?" she asked vacantly, aware that Adam had addressed her.

"I said, my dear, that you may safely leave your visitor in the care of one of the maids now."

He rose and held out his hand to Catherine, but her hands remained in her lap.

"No!" she said explosively. "I shall tend him myself."

Adam's mouth tightened. "But that is highly improper, Catherine. Lady Jane—?"

He turned to the older woman for support, but she merely smiled placatingly. "I think we need not worry about propriety, Adam. Mariah and I will be here most of the time to help with the work of tending Mr. Smith. Now, don't worry," she admonished. "You know that once Catherine has her mind set on something, she can't be moved with blasting powder."

Adam frowned but made no response. He turned on his heel and stumped from the room. After a moment, Mariah rose from her chair and hurried after him.

Observing her approach, Adam slowed his pace down the corridor until her steps matched his.

"Really, Adam," she gasped a little breathlessly. "Catherine is merely reverting to her ministering angel mode. She would behave so to anyone who lay injured under her roof."

Adam snorted. "Seems to me her concern for that fellow is nowhere close to angelic."

Mariah placed a hand on his sleeve. "Truly, Adam," she said

anxiously. "I do not think you have anything over which to concern yourself."

"I'm not concerned," he responded in a stiff voice. "It is only that—" Catching sight of the dismay in her gaze, he halted suddenly, a painful smile curving his lips. "I think you have a touch of the ministering angel in your own makeup, my dear. Thank you for caring." He sighed. "I had not thought myself so obvious, although perhaps it is only so to one who takes the trouble to look. I sometimes wonder if I keep on trailing after her out of sheer habit, for I certainly seem to be making little headway."

"Oh, Adam, don't say that. I know Catherine is fond of you!"

"I somehow don't find that very encouraging," replied Adam. "She is fond of the vicar, too, but I do not believe she nourishes a deathless passion for him in her bosom. Catherine knows me to be her friend, and I think she values that—but, if she feels anything stronger, I'd be willing to eat that tapestry." He gestured vaguely toward the wall.

"Perhaps it will come with time," Mariah insisted.

Adam laid his hand over hers, his fingers tightening. "Thank you, Mariah. You are a great consolation to me."

She lifted her gaze to his as though seeking a hint of irony in his words. Finding none, she lowered her eyes in confusion and urged him hurriedly to the front door.

In Justin's bedchamber, Catherine sat alone with her patient. Lady Jane had taken herself off some minutes previously with the admonition to her granddaughter not to wear herself to flinders caring for the young man.

Justin had not moved since he had been brought into the room by two footmen and laid solicitously on the bed. His clothing, except for his drawers, had been removed, and now he lay silent and pale, looking unwontedly vulnerable under the coverlet. His latent strength was still apparent, but now he looked less an animal of prey and more a lost child. His breathing came slow and shallow, but steady.

As she gazed at him, unblinking, the thought came to her yet again. Why? Why had Lord Justin chosen to deceive her so? Why had he set about to attract her? Would it not have been enough to trick her and her little family into providing a haven for him? Surely, he must have sensed that he had fallen in with precisely the sort of menage who could be counted on to give a stranger safe harbor. But no, he had wanted more. He had wanted her heart.

And she had damned near given it to him.

Now she sat like a maiden chained to a rock, waiting for an explanation. For what little good it would do her. All she'd get would be more lies. At least, this time, she would have her guard in place—although, to be truthful, she'd thought it in place long before she had given herself to Belforte's embrace such a short time ago. Odd, the encounter in the corridor had taken place just hours ago, but it seemed like a lifetime.

Abruptly, she sat forward in her chair as Lord Justin's head turned restlessly on his pillow and his breath caught suddenly. His eyelids fluttered and opened. His eyes, darkened to the blue-steel of a rifle barrel, stared into hers, and once again she had that eery sense of communion with him as their gazes locked. With a physical effort, she turned away.

"Catherine?" he whispered.

"Yes—my lord," Catherine replied evenly.

Another phrase had begun to form on Justin's lips, but he stopped abruptly. His eyes widened, and for a long moment, he watched her as a number of emotions displayed themselves on his mobile features. Catherine wondered what was going on behind those gun-metal eyes. Was he concocting another story for her edification? Was he working up a convincing explanation for his behavior?

At last, he raised a hand to her. "So you know," he whispered weakly.

"Yes, Lord Justin." Catherine was pleased that her voice showed no sign of the turmoil that raged within her. "I know who you are and what you've done."

"I see." He did not ask how she had come by her information. "And now?"

"And now," she continued in a colorless tone, "it remains only to turn you over to the authorities." So much for her decision not to confront him with his crimes.

"Catherine, please . . ."

She carefully schooled her expression to one of stony implacability.

"You must do what you think you must," he said at last, his voice a papery rasp, "but please, give me an opportunity to tell you what happened . . . to tell you—"

"More lies?" she interrupted harshly.

To her surprise, he grinned, although by now he was growing visibly weaker. "No, the time for lies is past. Anyway, I have pretty much run out of the good ones. I promise you—for whatever that's worth—that I will tell you the truth. I never lie, you see, when I have promised not to." The smile dropped from his lips. "I will tell you everything . . . if you will let me. I am not a traitor, Catherine . . . but there is one . . . a traitor . . . lurking about somewhere . . . and I must find out . . ."

His voice faded to little more than an attenuated sigh. "Please, wait, Catherine, before you throw me to the lions. Let me . . ." Lord Justin's hand fell back on the coverlet, and his eyes closed.

Damn him! she thought savagely. He knew she would do as he asked. Despite her best instincts to the contrary, she would wait to hear him out before she went to Sir Reginald. What kind of wizardry did the man possess to make her go against everything in her that screamed, "Beware!" He had already caused her more heartache than she would have thought possible. Why was she ready to give him the opportunity for more?

She peered at him more closely. Though his eyes were closed, and he was obviously no longer conscious, he had not fallen back into a peaceful repose. He continued to move restlessly under the coverlet. She placed a hand on his forehead. It was very warm.

It grew warmer. Despite liberal doses of the drafts left by Adam, which Catherine and Mariah got down him only with a great deal of difficulty, Justin's fever rose, until by that evening he was burning with it. His eyes, when they opened occasionally, glittered in an unfocused stare, and two flags of bright, unhealthy color flared in his cheeks.

The heat raged in his body all that night and the next day. For hours, Catherine, and sometimes Mariah, sat by his bed bathing him with cloths soaked in cool water. On the evening of the second day, he became delirious. He mumbled incoherently, at times becoming distraught.

"I can't breathe," he gasped at one point, as Catherine laved his face for the thousandth time, while Mariah attempted to still him as he thrashed against his pillows. "I'm drowning!"

Lady Jane stood at the foot of the bed, her hand at her throat, her face a mask of distress.

"Behind you! Look out, Ned! It's an ambush!" Justin fought wildly to sit up. "The French! Huerta . . . must tell . . ." He fell back again on the bed, momentarily exhausted. "Rivenchy . . ." he whispered brokenly.

"What is he talking about?" whispered Mariah as she attempted to straighten the bed clothes and move him into a more comfortable position.

Catherine bit her lip. Lord, would the man condemn himself with his own tongue? She turned swiftly to the other two women.

"Why don't you two seek your beds? I'll watch our patient for a while," she continued over their incipient protests, "and you can come spell me later. There's no point in all of us wearing ourselves out at once. A fine parcel of wet noodles we shall be in the morning."

Mariah and Lady Jane exchanged dubious glances, but in the end Catherine had her way. Alone with Lord Justin once more, she contemplated him silently, once again chiding herself. She really did not know why she had sent the other two women from the room, or why she felt the need to stop him from accusing himself. Or why she knew an urge to press her fingers to the spot on his temples where his pulse could be seen beating wildly in faint blue lines under his skin. His lashes, absurdly long for a man, swept over his cheeks in ashy smudges, and his mouth was a thin slash in the sharp planes of his face.

His delirium grew in intensity over the next few hours, and several times Catherine was obliged to throw herself atop him to prevent his flinging himself from the bed. At others, he muttered gasping pleas and imprecations.

"Please—stop! Papa! Don't—no more. I'm sorry—I didn't mean . . ." He flung an arm over his eyes, which had filled with tears. "My God—Father—you can't believe . . . St. John . . . Don't . . . don't say any more! I can't . . . Sinjie!"

As he struggled and raved, there were more references to Father and to St. John, as well as to someone named Robbie and a Charles. He spoke to men who were evidently officers in the army of Wellington. Once or twice, in a softer tone, he breathed her own name among a tumble of words she could not make out.

Just before midnight, he grew quiet, and Catherine dozed in a chair at his bedside. Her fingers were clasped in his as they had been since the moment some hours earlier when, crying out in some private anguish, he had seized her hand in a fierce grip and refused to let go.

Now, his fingers relaxed, bringing her instantly out of her light sleep. Automatically, she brought her own hand to his forehead. She almost sobbed with relief to note that it was cool and filmed with a light sweat. His cheeks had lost their febrile glow and he breathed normally.

Like a tired child, Catherine placed her folded arms on the bed and leaned her head on them. Cradling Justin's hand against her cheek, she fell instantly into a dreamless sleep.

When Justin awoke, he felt as though he were being stabbed between the eyes by the shaft of sunlight that streamed in through his chamber window. He squeezed his eyes shut for another moment before cautiously opening them once more. He peered around the room. It was empty except for a familiar, plump form sitting in a chair next to his bed. He frowned. She was knitting! Why was Mariah knitting in his bedchamber? Why was he still in bed with the sun high in the sky? And why did he feel as though every inch of his body had been dragged through a particularly rocky bramble patch?

He made an experimental move toward sitting up, which brought such a wave of pain that he grunted aloud with it. Instantly, Mariah lifted her head. Setting aside her work, she rose to approach the bed.

"You're awake!" she exclaimed. "Oh, thank God."

Wondering why the Deity should be thanked for such a mundane happenstance, Justin attempted a smile. "What—what happened?"

"Why, you were shot, Mr. Smith. Catherine found you outside early yesterday morning. You were covered with blood!"

"Good God!" Memory returned in a flood. "Where is Ca— Miss Meade now?"

"Oh! My goodness—of course. She will wish to know right away that you have waked." She whirled about and ran from the room.

Painfully, Justin tried to recount in his mind the events of— yes, it must have been the night before last. He remembered the journey into London, and the people he had met with there. And his return home . . . He had turned into Coppersmith Street, and . . . My God, he had been ambushed yet again! Who was it who kept trying to kill him? No one knew he was alive! Except, of course, for those few persons whose aid he had enlisted. But it couldn't . . .

The effort to make sense of the calamity that had befallen him proved too much, and after a moment, his eyes closed and he drifted into the comforting darkness that still hovered close by. Thus, when Catherine entered the room a few minutes later with Mariah, it was to find him fast asleep once more.

"At least, he's resting naturally now," remarked Mariah. "See how he's turned on his side. That's a good sign."

Adam declared himself in agreement when he stopped in to visit, a few hours later. Justin awoke at the doctor's entrance and bestowed on him a sleepy smile.

"You have an excellent trio of nursemaids," said Adam jovially, and after a brief examination, announced judiciously that his patient was on the mend and might have a little gruel for luncheon were he so inclined.

"That's generous of you, old man," replied Justin, who was obviously feeling much stronger, "but you see before you a man on the verge of starvation. I was thinking along the lines of a beefsteak—or two."

"No, no. I'm afraid not." He turned to Catherine. "If he retains the gruel, he may have a bit of boiled chicken for dinner with, perhaps, some toast dipped in tea, but nothing more elaborate than that."

Justin groaned dramatically, but made no further protest.

Later, as Adam left the room, he hustled Catherine out of the door before him. "All right," he said firmly. "Now that he seems to be firmly planted once more in the land of the living, perhaps you'll be good enough to tell me what the devil's going on."

Catherine returned a blank stare.

"Don't give me that, young woman. I want to know how that rapscallion happened to turn up here at the crack of dawn with a bullet hole in him. He must have been out all night—probably in London. I'll grant you, Catherine, that he's a personable rogue. Everyone likes him. *I* like him. But the operative word here is rogue, and I want to know what he's up to."

Catherine maintained her air of bewilderment. "How could I possibly know what happened, Adam? I have not spoken to him, except very briefly, since he was brought in feet first."

Adam harrumphed. "You must know this is a matter for the magistrate, my dear. Will you notify Sir Reginald, or shall I?"

"Really, Adam," retorted Catherine in some irritation, "I appreciate your solicitude, but I think you take too much on yourself. It is Lo—Mr. Smith who was wounded, and it seems to me it is up to him to go to the authorities. After all, what can any of us report except the fact that he was shot? Sir Reginald will surely want to know more than that."

Adam scowled. "Yes, I suppose he will . . . but something must be set forward."

"As soon as Mr. Smith is a little stronger—tomorrow, perhaps, I will speak to him about sending for Sir Reginald. That is all I can promise, old friend."

"I cannot be satisfied," sighed Adam, "but I suppose I have no choice. All I ask is that you don't simply let the matter slide. It is high time you discovered just who your visitor is and what he was doing on your property in the first place."

"Indeed," replied Catherine soothingly. "I agree with you completely, Adam, and I shall do my best to unravel the puzzle with all possible speed."

"And you will send for me if . . ." Adam trailed off, unable to put into words what he was warning her of. "If you need me," he concluded, rather red-faced.

"Of course, I will. I always do, do I not?" Catherine reached to brush his cheek with her lips. "You know I don't know how I would go on without you."

Adam smiled rather painfully. "I only wish that were true, my dear."

By that time they had reached the hall, and after Adam had accepted hat, gloves, and walking stick from Timkins, he bade Catherine good-bye, promising to look in on John Smith again in a day or two.

For a few moments after his departure, Catherine stood in the hall, staring at the door. Then, thoughtfully, she returned to Lord Justin's bedchamber.

He was dozing when she entered the room, but his eyes flew open at her advent. His gaze followed her warily as she approached his beside. She said nothing at first, simply seating herself with folded hands, but he soon began to shift uncomfortably under her gaze.

He cleared his throat at last. "I expect you are waiting for an explanation."

She still said nothing, but continued to look at him with an unmistakable air of condemnation.

"All right," he sighed. "I shall freely admit I have used you very badly, Catherine, and I don't know if I can ever make it up to you, but I will tell you the truth about myself now. I may be putting my head in a noose by doing so, but I owe you this. I will give you a round tale—the unvarnished history of my misdeeds—and I will answer—factually—any questions you may have." He drew a long breath. "As you already seem to know, my name is Justin—Lord Justin Belforte, that is, and I am the second son of the Duke of Sheffield.

"And I am, as you also seem to be aware, an accused traitor to king and country."

Chapter Thirteen

Catherine drew in a sharp breath. The son of a duke! How in the world had the offspring of a peer fallen so far as to become a traitor to England?

As if reading her thoughts, Justin uttered a sharp, bitter laugh that sounded loud in the room. "Sounds rather exalted doesn't it? However, even great oak trees can produce rotten acorns." He smiled at her expression of startlement. "Yes, I will freely admit, my dear, that you are right. I am a perfect villain—in as much as any of us is perfect. Well, in light of my behavior since I met you, I can hardly claim to be anything else, can I?"

Catherine smiled thinly. "Very clever, my lord. You are apparently a devotee of the theory that the best defense is a good offense, but, in this case, do you think it a wise approach?"

Justin nodded in appreciation. "Possibly not, but if I'm going to tell the truth, I'll do best to dish it up cold. I can think of little to say that will give you a good opinion of me."

"Tell me something of the duke—your father. And St. John."

Justin's head snapped up. "St. John? Who told you of him?"

"You did, in your fever. You—you seemed to be pleading with your father. And remonstrating rather strongly with St. John. Your brother?"

Justin nodded curtly. "Yes, however we will not discuss my family, if you please."

"But why did you not turn to them in your trouble?"

Justin sighed impatiently. "My mother died when I was born. My father and my brother think I am dead," he said flatly. "In any event, I have not spoken to the duke in more than ten years. I see St. John from time to time, but only when necessary or in chance encounters."

Catherine's hand flew to her throat. "Ten years! But, that's—that's—"

"—Only to be expected given the relationship between my father and myself."

"But how did things come to such a pass? My own parents and I do not communicate, but up until the time I—that is, I offended them grievously—as they did me, but—"

"Oh, I offended my father all right—by being born. You see, my mother died in giving birth to me, and he simply never forgave me."

"But that's ridiculous! How could anyone blame an infant for such a tragedy?"

"Believe me," said Justin with a cold smile, "I had ample opportunity to ponder that question, with no appreciable results."

He raised his hand in a dismissive gesture. "However, I did not bring the matter up to wallow in recollections of my misspent youth. I merely wish to explain how it was that I became a spy."

"A s-spy?" asked Catherine faintly.

"Yes. You see, matters between my father and myself reached such a dismal pass that after I was sent down from Oxford in disgrace—no, I am not going to explain that, either. Suffice it to say that the offense was genuinely heinous, and the bagwig had no choice but to ban me from the hallowed halls of Brasenose. At that point, my father informed me that the doors of my home would in future be locked against me, and he would no longer be responsible either for my debts or my actions."

"Dear God," breathed Catherine, almost gasping at the freshet of pain that welled in her. The memory of her own abandonment rose in her mind.

Justin glanced sharply at her. "I really cannot blame him. I was an unsatisfactory son in every sense of the word. I am only surprised he did not give me the boot years before. In any event," continued Justin, "I crawled to London with my tail between my legs to my friend, Charles Rutledge." Briefly, Justin described his relationship with Charles. "He did not condone what I'd done, but he was not unkind, and he told me that if I gave my word to him that I would try to make something of myself, he would start me on a career in the army."

"He believed you would keep your promise?" asked Catherine skeptically.

For the first time that night, Justin's smile held a genuine warmth. "Yes, he did. And I held to it. Oh, I did slip up a little now and then, but if I do say so as shouldn't, I became a credit to my regiment—which was the Light Division, by the by. The famous Light Bobs," he explained pridefully. "Fortunately for me, early on in my military career, I more or less slid into the intelligence branch. The skills required there are practically tailor-made for one with a broad streak of villainy in his makeup, and I was a resounding success at sneaking and skulking, to say nothing of deceit and treachery."

"I see. But, tell me, my lord, how it is you happened to be accused of treason. After your protestations of service to your country, I presume you are going to assure me that it is all a vile calumny."

For a moment Justin whitened. He opened his mouth as though to hurl a stinging retort, but instead merely stared rigidly at her for what seemed like an eternity.

Catherine drew herself up defensively. "Yes, that's all very well. I can see you'd like nothing better at this point than to drive me from the room with a fiery sword, but the fact remains that you still need me. You still need a place to hide away until you're strong enough to leave the country—or whatever it is you have planned."

"I am not going to leave the country," growled Justin through clenched teeth. "That's the whole point of what I'm trying to tell you. I am not guilty of treason! Will you listen? Please?"

Catherine knew an urge to beg his pardon for the cruelty of her words, but the pain he had caused still rose fresh and raw in her breast. She nodded coolly. In a voice that was growing weak with fatigue, Justin recounted the events that had brought him to Winter's Keep at the moment of her shed's collapse.

Catherine was fascinated, despite herself. "So there was treason committed. Someone contravened Wellington's orders and aided General Rivenchy to escape."

"Yes, but that someone was not me. Whoever it was covered his tracks well and went to a great deal of trouble to make sure I'd be blamed. And he went to even more trouble to make sure I wouldn't be around afterward to cause problems."

Catherine experienced a sick feeling in her stomach as she contemplated Justin's words. "Do—do you think there was just one man involved?" she asked. "I mean, if you were supposed to be racing toward Huerta—who was in Salamanca, helping the general escape?"

As she spoke, Justin's heart lightened infinitesimally. Did Catherine believe him, then?

"I don't know," he responded slowly. "I have considered that possibility, but there would have been time for Rivenchy's release just before I set out. We were camped just outside of Salamanca, and Rivenchy was interned not five miles from our post. He was first missed, apparently, not long after I left for Huerta. The same man could have accomplished both the escape and the journey to the bridge at Huerta, although I should imagine he would have required some help."

A long, thoughtful silence ensued. Justin stared intently at Catherine, but she found that she could not return his gaze.

"Do you believe me?" Justin asked at last, his voice a harsh croak.

"I don't know," Catherine replied baldly. "You have deceived me about so many things, it's hard to discern the truth from your expert lies, particularly when you lie so charmingly." She bent a penetrating stare on him. "Even now, I feel there is something you are not telling me."

Justin reddened. God, she was doing it again. In his brief narrative, he had omitted mention of the paper covered with St. John's handwriting.

"I am truly sorry, Catherine—" he began, but Catherine held up her hand.

"Please spare me, my lord. I don't think I could take any more self-serving apologies. Let us just take it as read that you would not have lingered at Winter's Keep any longer than it would have taken to get your clothes repaired if you hadn't required a bolt-hole at the moment."

Her words were so close to the mark that once more Justin felt his cheeks go hot.

"Yes, but—"

"It's all right. Your actions were eminently reasonable. You could not very well reveal your identity to us, so your supposed amnesia was a master stroke."

Catherine spoke coolly, but Justin had no difficulty in discerning the anger that trembled in her voice.

"You're right, Catherine. It was necessary. I am not proud of trying to dupe you, but—"

"Oh, not trying, my lord. You were supremely successful. If it were not for your habit of sneaking off to London in the dead of night, I never would have found you out."

"Ah, I've been wondering about that."

Briefly, Catherine related her sightings of the cloaked, mid-night rider, and her subsequent search of his room.

"So you are not above a little sneaking and lurking yourself, my dear." His eyes lit with momentary laughter, instantly quelled by the indignation that flared in her gaze. "What do you propose to do now?" he concluded quietly. "You have me at your complete mercy."

"I very much tend to doubt your entire story," Catherine said. "The evidence against you is overwhelming, and my brief experience of you is such to make me believe that nothing is beneath you."

She was aware as she spoke that she was fueling her anger, and giving vent to it at the same time. She wanted to see him wince, to make him pay in some small part for her own foolishness in nearly succumbing to his charm. And his wiles. She was fully rewarded, for he went white, his eyes hard and flat as slate. She knew a moment of compunction, which she suppressed instantly and with great firmness.

"However," she continued austerely, "I do believe a man should be given the chance to prove his innocence. On the slight possibility that you are telling the truth, and on the premise that you are not likely to scarper off to the West Indies or to the Antipodes in your present condition, I shan't notify the authorities—yet."

Justin let out the breath he had been holding for what seemed like the last half hour. "Thank you," he said simply.

"Don't thank me yet," she commented in a sharp tone. "The time for duplicity is over. I must insist that you tell Mariah and Grandmama what you have told me."

Justin sat upright in bed, causing him to gasp with pain. He fell back against his pillows, shaking his head to clear it. "No! You must not tell anyone. It will mean my death! Or"—a sardonic gleam lit his eyes—"do you mean to have your revenge, after all?"

Inside her palms Catherine's fingers turned to rakes, but she maintained her pose of detachment. "Not at all. Mariah and Grandmama will remain silent, if I ask them. They will not betray you."

Despite another fifteen minutes of rather desperate cajolery, Catherine would not be moved from this position. Indeed, it was only with a great deal of difficulty that Justin dissuaded her from revealing his identity to Adam, as well.

At last, Justin sighed heavily. "Very well. I suppose I must consider myself lucky that Sir Whatsit, the magistrate, is not even now waiting in the wings to pounce on me." Glancing up at her, he suddenly grew serious. "I do thank you for your forbearance, Catherine. Were I in your position, I would not believe a word of what I have told you, and if I were in a position to be giving you advice, I would tell you that you should probably take immediate steps to see me into the hands of the law." He reached to take her hand in his. "But thank you for not doing so."

Flushing hotly, Catherine pulled her hand away. "Your advice seems eminently sound, my lord. I cannot think why I do not avail myself of it. Suffice it to say that at the slightest hint of any further duplicity on your part, I will send for Sir Reginald so fast it will make your ears spin."

Affixing a suitably chastened smile to his lips, Justin recalled a maxim related to him by a horse trader of his acquaintance. "When you've made the sale, stop selling the merchandise." With this in mind, he closed his eyes as a very real wave of fatigue swept over him.

"Thank you, my dear," he murmured. However, just before he sank into a laudanum-induced slumber, his eyes snapped open.

"Ah—Catherine?" He cleared his throat. "There is just one more small favor I must ask."

A week or so later, Catherine, immersed in her account book, was called to the morning room to greet a guest. The gentleman who rose from the chair at her entrance to the room bowed with surprising grace for one so rangy in build. Eyes of a peculiar shade of blue-green gazed down at her from an alarming height, and when she held her hand out to him, it disappeared in his grasp like a bird flying into a cavern.

"Mr. McPherson," she said, smiling. "Thank you for coming so promptly."

"How is he?" asked the gentleman, without further preamble.

Catherine laughed. "A great deal better than he was when I wrote to you. In fact, now that you are here, you may help us keep him lashed into his bed."

"Thank God." At Catherine's gesture, he sank again into his chair as she took one opposite. "I expect he is giving you no end of trouble. It—it is good of you to—to give him succor, ma'am. I know it looks bad, but Justin could no more betray England than I could fly to the moon. As you can see"—he chuckled, extending legs that were long and lanky and thickly muscled—"such a feat would be pretty much beyond me."

Catherine smiled faintly. "It appears Lord Justin has chosen his friends wisely, Mr. McPherson. He has been anxiously awaiting your arrival."

A troubled expression crossed the Scotsman's craggy features. "Ah—something has come up since I last saw Justin. I wonder— that is, I apologize for being so abrupt, but may I see him now?"

Puzzled, Catherine rose immediately, and with her guest at her heels, led the way from the morning room.

"Good God, if you don't look like something the cat threw up on Aunt Tillie's best carpet," were Robbie's first words on beholding Justin sitting up in bed.

"Why, thank you, you miserable reprobate. It's good to see you, too."

These amenities out of the way, Robbie perched on the edge of the bed and subjected his friend to a minute scrutiny. "Hmm," he drawled at last. "It appears you'll live."

Indeed, thought Catherine, Justin looked markedly improved from the day when he had emerged from his fever, and it was apparent that he was reposing in bed very much against his will. He was propped up by innumerable pillows and his coverlet was strewn with books, newspapers, and an open notebook in which could be discerned pages of slashing handwriting.

"Yes," he remarked, "thanks to Miss Meade and her family, I have been snatched from death's door and will probably make a full recovery."

The smile that accompanied his words was a model of courteous gratitude, but Catherine sensed the plea that lay behind it. Lord, did the man still require some sort of assurance that she believe in him? Why, for heaven's sake? He had what he wanted. She had promised not to turn him over to the law. Surely, her good opinion could not matter to him.

Hardening her sensibilities, she returned the smile with a noncommittal stare and turned toward the door. "I know you two gentlemen have much to discuss," she said. "I shall leave you to it."

"No!" Justin uttered the word with an odd urgency, and Robbie shot him an inquiring glance. "Please stay. I—I want you to be aware of what I shall be doing, and your counsel will be most welcome."

Catherine hesitated a moment before moving back into the room. She perched on the edge of a chair some distance from the bed.

So far, so good, thought Justin before turning to Robbie. He realized, to his intense irritation, that his relief at her decision to stay in the room was out of proportion to his request. Why he cared so much that Catherine believe in his innocence, he could not say. She had promised to keep his secret, and he believed she would hold to that—at least until he healed. Over the past few days, however, she had rejected, in the politest way possible, all his overtures.

Well, what else had he expected, for God's sake? She must be weary in the extreme of being betrayed by the men who entered her life. He could only hope that her agreeing to stay in the room signaled a thaw in the offing.

"It was the damn—most peculiar thing," he said to Robbie. "I was riding along and—"

Robbie lifted his hand uncomfortably. "Wait, Justin. I am most interested in this latest attack, but I have something I must tell you first. I was at Horse Guards yesterday, and stopped in to see Charles. He told me he had just received word that—I'm sorry, Justin. Your father is dead."

Chapter Fourteen

It seemed to Justin that the room dimmed, almost imperceptibly, and the air around him chilled just a little. For a moment he simply stared at Robbie, uncomprehending. Then, with a slight start, he passed a hand over his forehead.

"He's gone? Really?" he murmured, forcing a smile to his lips. "I suppose I have been expecting it. It appears I have fulfilled the prophecy he made so many years ago that I would be the death of him."

"Justin—" began Robbie, but Justin forestalled him with an uplifted hand.

"No, no, never mind. I would be lying if I said that I feel any grief for the old man. I did rather wish—But, no. Death is a melancholy subject, and I should prefer to think about living." With an effort, he widened the smile he had finally been able to contrive. "And if I wish to continue doing so, I'd best confine my thoughts to the problem at hand."

To his relief, Robbie made no remonstrance, but said quietly, "Very well, then, tell me what happened. In Miss Meade's note, she said only that you arrived here early in the morning a few days ago with a bullet in your side."

"It was the most peculiar thing." Justin related the events that had occurred after he left Robbie's house five nights before.

"I don't understand," Robbie said some minutes later from the large easy chair in which he was now ensconced. "How could anyone have known you'd be in Coppersmith Street at that hour of the night?"

"The obvious answer, I suppose," he continued, answering his own question, "is that someone was following you. But who?" He steepled his bony fingers before him.

In her chair some distance away, Catherine bent over fingers clasped tightly in her lap. She listened to the two men, but her mind persisted in drifting to the news Justin's friend had just imparted and the manner in which Justin had responded to it.

Catherine had nearly cried aloud in her shock at Justin's posturing, for she was sure that was what it was, but a glance from Robbie had silenced her.

She sighed. It had been almost a week since she had sat in this same chair in confrontation with Lord Justin. Why, she wondered for the hundredth time, could she not admit to him that yes, she believed with all her heart that he was no traitor. Was it pride that had caused her to maintain a cool aloofness from him in the days that had followed? Even to Mariah and Grandmama, she had been unable to express her belief in his innocence, as deep as it was instinctive.

Oddly, she had not been obliged to convince either of those ladies of the necessity for keeping his identity a secret.

"Treason!" Mariah had exclaimed. "What a daft idea. Mr. Smith—or Lord Justin Belforte—is no doubt something of a rogue, but I'd be willing to wager my best Sunday tucker that he's no traitor."

Lady Jane echoed these sentiments and proclaimed herself ready and willing to do all in her power to assist "dear John" in exonerating himself.

Neither lady, however, was on hand to help greet Mr. McPherson on his arrival, and once Catherine had brought Justin's visitor to his bedside, she had felt very much de trop. It was not as though she had anything to contribute, she reflected pensively. None of the persons discussed by the two men were known to her, and the theories propounded one after another were meaningless to one unfamiliar with the workings of the Depot, whatever that might be.

Catherine lifted her head, realizing that a silence had fallen between the two men.

"In any event," Justin said at length. "It appears I must go to Sheffield Court."

"To attend your father's obsequies? But you won't be fit to travel until after—"

"No," interposed Justin sharply. "To confront St. John."

Catherine's ears pricked up. St. John? Ah, yes, the mysterious brother with whom Justin was apparently on no better terms than he was with his father. But—

"What does St. John have to do with anything?" she said aloud.

Robbie and Justin glanced at each other before Justin replied slowly. "You were right when you sensed I was leaving something out, Catherine." A knot formed in his throat, and he swallowed hard, angered that the words were so hard to speak.

Clenching his fists, he told Catherine of the paper, its image now burned in his memory, bearing Sinjie's handwriting.

"Good God," whispered Catherine. "Your own brother? You intimated that you were estranged, but—but, does he hate you, then?"

"I did not think that was the case, but it appears I was wrong. Now," he said, sitting upright preparatory to throwing back his bedclothes. "If someone will hand me my breeches and shirt—"

Justin's countenance had by now grown so forbidding, that Catherine refrained from questioning him further, nor did she dispute his efforts to leave his bed. Robbie, however, apparently had no such compunction.

"Hold up, laddie," he said. "You'll be going nowhere for a while."

"Nonsense." Justin turned a glowering countenance on him. "I've been wallowing here for days, and I feel fine."

Thrusting his feet over the side of the bed, he attempted to stand, only to crumple into Robbie's waiting arms. Catherine flew from her chair and ran to his side as well.

"Now, you see?" she scolded, her voice rising to cover her fright at his labored breathing. "You will tear Adam's stitches."

Justin sank back on the bed, appalled at the results of his small effort. "At least," he said at last, "you must help me to a chair, so I can start regaining my strength. And"—he turned his scowl on Catherine—"I must start eating something besides that dam—wretched pap you've been feeding me. No wonder I'm weak as a cat."

"But, last night, you had a broiled chicken wing—and this morning some nice toast and—"

"Tchah!" responded Justin succinctly. "That stuff is barely enough to keep Lady Jane alive. Now, please send me up some real food. Please," he added, his expression softening. "I cannot simply lie here while my fate hangs in the balance."

Catherine felt herself weakening under that gray, supplicating gaze. "Actually," she said grudgingly, "Adam said we might prepare something a little more sustaining for you, starting today."

"Good," Justin replied promptly. "And I shall come down to join you for dinner."

"Oh, I don't think—"

"Sounds like just the ticket," interjected Robbie smoothly. Placing a shoulder under Justin's arm, he assisted him to a chair by the window. "I'll volunteer to help tote him around. He can retire directly afterward if he begins to swoon in our laps."

Catherine shrugged in resignation.

"Very well, I shall give orders to cook to set two extra places." She turned to Robbie. "How long will you be staying with us, Mr. McPherson?"

"I must return to London tomorrow," replied Robbie. "I'm sorry, old man," he continued in response to Justin's grunt of protest. "I gave them a tale at the Horse Guards of having to dash off to see my ailing Aunt Leastow, and I don't want anyone sending me messages there. I'll try to return here every few days or so, but—I think I'm being watched."

"Well, I wouldn't be surprised," remarked Justin. "Anyone who knows either of us well would assume I'd try to contact you."

"Indeed. I'm pretty sure I managed to get out of London this time without being followed, but I don't want to push my luck. Nor do I want to appear as though I'm trying to shake off anyone who might be trailing me."

Justin nodded.

"I shall leave you two gentlemen to plan your strategy," said Catherine, making her way from the room. "Mr. McPherson, when you are ready to be shown your room, please ring, and one of the servants will find me."

"Please, Miss Meade, since we seem destined to be coconspirators, could you call me Robbie? We Scots, you know, cannot bear formality."

Catherine smiled. "I was unaware of that particular national trait. Very well—Robbie, if you will call me Catherine, as well."

"Humph!" interposed Justin in a tone of great affront. "I don't recall your inviting me to use your first name."

"That is because you blithely usurped that prerogative without my permission—Lord Justin." She bent an impudent smile on him and swept from the room, rather pleased with herself.

It was an hour or so later that a maid found her in the stillroom with a message that their guest was ready to leave Mr. Smith's bedchamber. She hurried upstairs to find Robbie awaiting her in the corridor.

"I fear I wearied Justin," he said worriedly. "He dozed off in the middle of a sentence, so I thought I'd better leave him."

"Yes, he thinks he is ready to go out and conquer the world, but his wound was grievous, and he has a long way to go before he can return to normal activity. Or at least what he considers normal activity." Catherine glanced up at him tentatively. "He is, of course, fretting himself to flinders over—this business, which does not help his recovery."

Robbie smiled, and Catherine thought she had never met a man with such an ability to convey a sense of security and reassurance. She led him to a room a few steps down the corridor. "I put you in the room closest to his. That way you won't have so far to travel to your war councils."

Robbie smiled briefly. "That's as good a comparison as any, I suppose. Whoever has framed Justin for his own iniquity has covered his tracks well. We're going to have the devil's own time exposing him."

"He is fortunate in his friends," said Catherine carefully. They had by now reached the doorway to the chamber allotted to the guest, and she showed him inside.

"We will be going down to luncheon soon. I suppose you would prefer to take a tray in Justin's room—" Robbie nodded. "But, I hope you will stop first with us so that I may introduce you to my cousin and my grandmother, both of whom are eager to meet you."

"A pleasure, ma'am," said Robbie, with another nod and a bow.

"In the meantime," concluded Catherine, "please ring if you need anything."

After a swift glance about the room to assure herself that everything necessary had been provided for their guest's comfort, Catherine took herself off.

Robbie was no more seen until, as promised, he appeared in the sunny chamber designated long ago by Lady Jane for the informal luncheons she preferred. Catherine presented him to Mariah and Lady Jane, who pelted him with questions about Justin's contretemps. Unfortunately, he could provide little information either on the actual perpetrator of the treason of which Justin was accused or the strategy he and Justin would implement to bring him to justice.

Excusing himself as soon as he had eaten, Robbie left the room to visit his friend.

"Well!" exclaimed Lady Jane querulously. "He seems like a very nice young man, but not very forthcoming."

"I'm afraid he simply can't be of much help, Grandmama. He and Lord Justin have a hard road ahead of them. Right now they seem at a standstill." Catherine hoped that the chill her words brought her was not reflected in her voice. Dear God, what if they never found out the identity of the real traitor? Justin could not stay in hiding forever, and as soon as he showed his nose outside Winter's Keep, the authorities, gleeful that their prey had not escaped them in death, would pounce on him like wolves. Unless, of course, he fled the country. Somehow the thought of this solution brought her no comfort.

She reminded herself yet again that she did not care what happened to him. She would not like to see an innocent man punished for a crime he had not committed of course, but other than that, the fate of Lord Justin Belforte meant nothing to her. Then a thought struck her. An innocent man? Why was she so sure Justin was incapable of treason? Everything she knew of him pointed to instability of character, not to say pure wickedness. Despite his kindness to her family, he had deceived her cruelly. He had forced his attentions on her. Well, perhaps "forced" was not quite the proper term. He had kissed her, and she had turned to flame— and—and it had meant nothing to him. Lord, she almost wished she could believe him guilty of betraying his country. Then, at least, she could abandon him to his fate with a clear conscience.

She realized her reflections were becoming more convoluted and confused by the moment. She should just stop thinking about him. Yes. Just go on with her life as though he had never plunged into that shed to rescue her and her luckless dog.

She rose to leave the room, only to be halted as Lady Jane, who had been frowning thoughtfully, lifted her hand.

"You know, my dear," she said, "I have been wondering where I heard the name Justin Belforte before, and I just remembered . . . It was some years ago, in London. His brother, St. John, I think his name is, Earl of Haddington he was then, was betrothed to one of the Season's beauties. When Justin came to town, he and Lady Susan created quite a scandal, practically living in each other's pockets. Everyone assumed they were lovers, in fact."

Catherine paled, but she simply inclined her head in courteous attention.

"The day came when the young earl came peltering down to London from the family estate, where he had been staying for some months with his father. It was said that he and his brother had a terrific row. It was also said that Lady Susan was enceinte. In fact, she admitted as much to her closest friends and said that Justin was the father. The betrothal between Haddington and the girl was severed, and Lady Susan left town precipitously, with the family putting it about that she was visiting a distant aunt.

"The next thing we heard was that she had miscarried. Some

time later she married an obscure baronet, who subsequently put her from him. She hied herself to the Continent after that, and every now and then someone would comment that she had been seen with Count This or the Baron That. I believe I heard recently that she died."

"Dear God," whispered Catherine. "How could he—?"

"We don't know the truth of what happened," said Lady Jane sharply. "It's my belief the girl was no more than a slut gowned in silk and lace."

"Perhaps," said Catherine stonily, "but to have abandoned her in such a fashion when he had made her pregnant . . ." She shook her head, sickened.

"As I said, we don't know what really happened. As I understand it, young Justin denied—quite vehemently—that he was responsible, and—"

"Well, he would, wouldn't he?" retorted Catherine. "Is that not the way of the world? At least the way of charming men with a penchant for ruining young women?"

She jumped from her chair and hastened from the room, unable to continue the conversation.

She repaired to her study, where she sat for some moments, staring blankly before her. Dear Lord, had Justin truly betrayed his brother with the man's own fiancée? It was hard to believe he could be guilty of such monstrous behavior, yet there must have been some grounds for such a story. On the other hand, the rumor mill of the *ton* ground exceeding fine, but was not known for the truth of its output. After all, no one knew better than she the wounds that could be inflicted by the careless cruelty of gossip.

Yet it seemed that the more she learned of Lord Justin Belforte, the more he stood convicted of being a scoundrel of the first water.

She shook herself. She had told Justin that she believed him entitled to a chance to prove his innocence of the charge of treason. She was prepared to grant him that chance. No more, no less. She had, she told herself once more, no real interest in his character, or his past, or his future.

With this thought clutched firmly to her bosom, she settled once more to her accounts, and it was here some two hours later that she was discovered by Robbie.

"Oh, no," she said with a laugh in answer to his query. "You are not interrupting in the least. I am always glad to drop my book work like a hot chestnut at the least encouragement. Do sit down while I ring for tea. How is our patient?" she asked a moment later as she settled into a comfortable chair opposite Robbie near the fireplace.

"Not in the best of spirits, I'm afraid. This confinement could not have come at a worse time for him, for he is fairly raging to be up and doing something about the calamity that has befallen him."

"Tell me, Robbie." Catherine grew serious. "Do you have any idea at all as to the identity of the real traitor? The person—or persons—who are trying to kill Justin?"

A shadow passed over Robbie's face, and he lifted a hand as though to ward off something unpleasant.

"No." He said shortly. After a moment he continued slowly. "We don't know the motive behind the crime, you see. It may have been committed not by an evil man, but by one who found himself in a set of circumstances that—" He broke off abruptly and uttered a short, awkward laugh. "But I don't know why I am speaking so. Everything is sheer speculation at this point. I must tell you, however, that I am pleased to hear that you believe in him."

Catherine glanced at him, conscious of the odd thought that Robbie McPherson was keeping something from her—something that very much troubled his mind.

"Mr. Mc—Robbie," she said at last, hating herself for what she was about to ask. "Tell me something about Lord Justin Belforte. If I'm to give him the sanctuary of my home while he tries to wriggle out from under a charge of treason, I would like to know him better. He has not been very forthcoming."

Robbie chuckled. "No, I suppose not. Justin is not given to talking about himself."

"Frankly," continued Catherine, "what I know of his lordship makes me doubt my wisdom in believing his story—which you must admit is not wholly probable."

Robbie's brows lifted. "How so?" he asked, rather frostily.

"Simply, that from what he's told me, and—and from what I've heard from others—he's not a very nice man. In fact, his activities to date seem to indicate that he's a complete villain."

"I see. He has told you of his work in military intelligence?"

"Yes, and that work seems to consist of every sort of trickery and deceit—the same sort of thing he practiced on me, in fact."

"Catherine, the gathering of intelligence, by its very definition, requires a certain degree of deception. All of us who serve in this capacity have done some things that we're not proud of."

"That's just the point. Justin seems as though he's very proud of his chicanery."

Catherine's voice was stiff with accusation, but Robbie merely shrugged.

"Is it not nice to know that one is good at one's job? Without the knowledge of the enemy's movements, strengths, and weaknesses that we have brought to Wellington on a daily—sometimes hourly—basis, he would not be enjoying the success in the Peninsula that has been his these past months. Many more Englishmen would die without our efforts on their behalf. Some of the men have lost their lives in the pursuit of this duty."

Catherine felt shamed. Who was she to point her finger at those who risked life and limb in the performance of a function so vital to the war effort? Her thoughts must have been reflected in her face, for after a moment, Robbie's voice softened. "But you are right. Many of us have done a great many things in the name of England of which we cannot take particular pride."

"Such as duping a witless spinster?" asked Catherine sharply.

Robbie sighed. "No, that was not well-done of him—and I know he is sorry for it, but, as he has explained to me—and no doubt to you—he had little choice."

"Oh, yes, he did explain that. Most reasonably. I just don't think I believe him."

"Believe him, Catherine," said Robbie earnestly. "I know he paints himself in a very bad light, but—well, there is a reason for all that."

"His father?"

Robbie glanced at her sharply. "You know about him?"

"A little. Justin told me something of his background before he entered the army. You knew him then, did you not?"

"Oh, yes. I used to spend school holidays at Sheffield Court. Those were good times, for the most part—except for Justin's father. Henry, that is, the eighth Duke of Sheffield."

Catherine was startled at the sharpness in Robbie's voice, and her gaze dropped to her lap. She pleated the skirt of her blue muslin morning gown. "I understand Justin and his father did not get on very well."

"That's putting it mildly. In old Harry's eyes, Justin could not put a foot right. He was constantly railing at the boy about his behavior, or his appearance or—" Robbie drew a deep breath. "I often thought that getting sent down from Oxford was the best thing that ever happened to Justin, for otherwise he might not have ended up as one of the best of Wellington's agents."

"And did Justin's father condone that?"

"As a matter of fact, the duke knew nothing about what Justin did in the army. He knew only that he had purchased a commission. Of that, I think he did approve, since a military career is so eminently suitable for a younger son. However, by that time he had unburdened himself of any responsibility for Justin's actions, and he claimed to be supremely indifferent as to the manner in which path his son chose in what he categorized as his unswerving journey to perdition. According to St. John, that's how he put it."

"Ah, yes, St. John."

"Justin's older brother. His only brother, the son of the duke's first wife. You see," Robbie continued after a moment, observing Catherine's blank stare. "The Duke of Sheffield first married Lady Emily Derwent, the daughter of the Marquess of Marchinton. As I understand it, it was the premier match of the season—possibly even the decade. Nothing could have been more propitious than the union of the two ancient, honorable, and horrifically wealthy families. St. John was born a year later to much fanfare and general satisfaction. Unfortunately, Emily contracted a virulent fever the following year and within three days had passed away."

"How terrible," murmured Catherine.

"Yes, wasn't it? And unfortunate, too, since, although the duchess had dutifully produced an heir, she departed this vale of tears before cranking out the requisite spare, a lack which the duke evidently felt he must address."

Catherine was chilled at the crudity of his words, but said nothing, merely lifting her brows so that he would continue.

"As you may infer from what I've said, up to this point in his life, the duke had never strayed from the path of propriety. From all reports, he had done what was expected of him for all of his six and twenty years—participated in the right sports as a boy, indulged in a judicious display of high spirits as a youth, joined all the right clubs as a young man—well, you see what I mean. Upon the death of his lady, however, something snapped. Oh, it was a brief, uncharacteristic slipping of his leash, and one that he would come to regret bitterly, but apparently the duke fell in love—and with a most unsuitable young woman.

"Her name was Amelie de Brissac. She was the daughter of an émigrée, and she was a lady's maid! She was a tearing beauty by all accounts, and Harry was dazzled out of his well-ordered wits. For the first and only time, he ignored the conditioning of a lifetime, as well as the loudly anguished strictures of his family, and took the 'foreign tart,' as she was termed by one of Justin's aunts, to wife."

By now Catherine was feeling physically assaulted by the man-

ifest indignation that flowed through Robbie's narrative like a hot
current.

"At least," she whispered, "the duke was given a chance at happiness. Was it a good marriage?"

"No, indeed. They were miserable! Within a few months,
Harry apparently came to his senses, waking to the realization
that he had made a truly ghastly blunder. Everything in his
duchess that had caused him to fall in love with her—her beauty,
her wit, her impulsive vitality—he now loathed as a reminder of
his momentary aberration. He made her life a living hell with his
criticism and his caustic tirades."

"How—how do you know all this?"

"Mostly from Justin, in bits and pieces. And some of it from St.
John—saintly, insufferable St. John. He, as the fruit of the good
and pure Emily, could do no wrong. The duke petted him like the
favorite son that he was, and regaled him with tales of Justin's
mother's general unworthiness. The failings of her son, of course,
were only to be expected and duly elaborated upon for Sinjie's
benefit. By the time I knew Justin, he fully realized that Sinjie
and his father existed in another universe, far removed from the
one inhabited by his own unacceptable self—a world of mutual
esteem and satisfaction."

"Are you saying the duke turned Justin's brother against him?"

Robbie frowned. "I don't think he did so purposely. Such behavior would have been beneath him. It was more a case of, 'Boy,
why can't you be more like your older brother? He knows what is
expected of him and never disappoints me.' Or, 'You deliberately
took that sword down from the wall, after you were told not to
touch the armaments? St. John would never have done such a
thing. But I suppose it's only to be expected from—' " Robbie
broke off. "Lord, I don't know how many times I watched him
whittle Justin down to a sullen lump of unhappiness. And then,"
he continued a moment later, "Sinjie would take up the thread.
Taking Justin aside, he subjected him to lecture after solemn lecture on his shortcomings and his tainted background, his lack of
anything approaching an appreciation of what was due his station.
He would generally conclude with a blanket indictment of
Justin's character."

"Good God," gasped Catherine. "He would humiliate his
brother so? In front of his friend?"

"Indeed. I think my presence lent a certain spice to the occasion for St. John."

"What a dreadful young man!"

"Mmp. At any rate, one can't say that Justin did not try to measure up to his father's ridiculous expectations. I believe he thought if he could accomplish that, his father would love him, and St. John would—well, at least tolerate him. But, as might have been expected, his efforts failed at every turn. With the best will in the world, he managed to feature in a veritable parade of disasters, from overturning his boat in the lake to scaring all the broody hens into nervous prostration one day when we were practicing ambuscades, to allowing his dog to commit an indiscretion on Lady Pimfret's skirt."

"But surely those were all boyish mishaps."

"Not in the duke's eyes. It seemed to me as though Justin was taken to task at least once a week for some solecism or other."

Catherine sat silent for a moment. "And St. John never got into trouble at all?"

"Never. He was Justin's shining example and he never let the boy forget it."

Catherine expelled a long, shuddering sigh. "But the duke finally washed his hands of Justin. How did that come about?"

"Ah. Well, over the years, Justin's transgressions became more, er, purposeful. I think he rather began to enjoy his wicked reputation and found a certain degree of fulfillment in his increasingly reprehensible pranks. He began to take a certain perverse pleasure in displeasing Harry and in scandalizing St. John, although by now Sinjie had pretty much given up on reforming Justin, particularly since on one occasion Justin nearly put a period to his existence when he opened his mouth once too often.

"In his teens, he got into some serious trouble from time to time, involving magistrates and constables and other minions of the law. He got into fistfights, he devised pranks that were borderline destructive, and on one occasion, he was caught stealing money from the church poor box."

"No!" exclaimed Catherine, shocked.

"Oh, yes. I understand that an old woman in the village wanted a new hat for her grandson's christening and could not afford it. The woman had been kind to Justin, and, as he told me later, it seemed to him she was as deserving of a new hat as the town drunk was of money for a pair of boots—money that would probably only have gone for a monumental bender."

"Oh, dear," said Catherine, suppressing a smile.

"At any rate, all during our days at Eton, Justin was constantly immersed in hot water, and when he went up to Oxford, despite my best efforts to the contrary, he fell in with an extremely undesirable set of youths. They were the sort that might have been designed to lead an unhappy, headstrong lad directly to perdition. They drank themselves into oblivion every night, seduced every female who would allow it, regularly boxed the Watch—that sort of thing. Old Harry finally warned Justin that the very next time he was notified by the bagwig that his son had been up to no good, he would abandon the boy to his own devices.

"I was not on hand to observe what happened next, but Justin described the whole thing to me later. The very next night, he and a group of his compatriots drove their curricles through the streets of Oxford. It was late, of course, but they caroled merrily at the top of their lungs, mostly bellowing out obscenities. When they entered a particularly narrow street, one of them discovered that by flicking his whip to the right and to the left, he could reach the windows on either side. It was the work of a moment to wager on who could break the most glass in a single pass down the street. Justin won, of course."

"Of course," murmured Catherine.

"They thought the whole thing glorious fun at the time, but as you can imagine, the bagwig took a dim view of the escapade. The residents of Cricklade Lane were clamoring for Justin's hide, and he was only too willing to give it to them. To Justin's unbelieving horror, his father not only refused to pay for the damages, but sent a message that his son would no longer be welcome at Sheffield Court. I went to the old man myself to plead for Justin, but I was turned out of the house before I could even begin my carefully prepared speech.

"Justin had no money of his own, of course, so he spent a wretched few weeks in the parish clink. Being a duke's son, even one who had become a persona non grata in his own home, he was not punished any more harshly than that."

Catherine blinked to dispel the unwelcome tears that welled in her eyes. "And that's when he went to London to seek his friend's assistance?"

"Yes, and he and the duke never spoke with each other again."

"Dear God," whispered Catherine. She could not help but note that Robbie, for all the length of his discourse, had not shed any light on the matter of the seduction of St. John's fiancée, but so many other things had been made clear to her now.

Chapter Fifteen

"Aha. Very unwise of you, my dear, to put your queen in such jeopardy." Justin nudged a rook into a new position on the board.

He and Catherine sat opposite each other on the secluded little terrace that lay just outside the library, engaged in a sanguinary game of chess. He watched the play of sunlight on the tendrils of Catherine's hair that had managed to escape her muslin cap, and realized that he had rarely spent a happier two weeks. If it were not for the cloud that hung over him in such persistent malevolence, he might have imagined himself died and gone to heaven.

Catherine had unbent remarkably since Robbie's departure for London the morning after his arrival. She had added her support to his pleas to Adam to include a trifle more mobility into his daily routine, and had ordered several footmen to place themselves at his disposal for the purpose of carrying him to a chair placed in some sunny spot just outside the house.

He no longer needed carrying, of course. He had started walking about the house and grounds on his own over the last few days, and had spent a number of clandestine hours in his bedchamber, exercising. He had made rapid progress in his recovery, and knew he was now strong enough to make his way to Sheffield Court. He had not spoken to Catherine of this.

"Aha, yourself, my lord. Check."

Justin came to with a start and glanced at the board in some confusion. Catherine had completed her play and was gazing at him in pleased anticipation, mixed with an unmistakable smugness.

"Escaped your doom, have you?" he asked lightly. He leaned forward to contemplate his situation, taking her hand for a moment as he did so. Smoothly and firmly, she removed it from his grasp. He laughed ruefully to himself as, with great precision he obliterated the knight Catherine had set up to protect her king. Catherine may have unbent, he thought, but she was still wary of him. She was cordial and helpful and seemed truly interested in his plight, but she rarely allowed herself to be alone with him and she conversed with him on only the most general of subjects.

Which was all to the good, of course. Whatever had befallen her in the hands of Francis Summervale, she had obviously emerged from the encounter with her moral standards intact. No dalliance for Miss Catherine Meade with feckless strangers. In addition, she had very properly taken him in a certain dislike. Such being the case, he was loath to force his attentions on her.

Still, he missed the discourse they had shared in the days before she had discovered his true identity. They had not talked of anything of import—their favorite poets, their differing tastes in art—but they had laughed a good deal and she had genuinely seemed to enjoy his company. As he had hers.

And now, even though he had forfeited the easy confidence she had granted him before, he still liked being with her. She was an unusual woman, restful and stimulating at the same time. He liked to watch the play of emotions over her face as she talked and the grace of her movements as she served tea or reached for a book high on a library shelf. If the memory of the kiss they had shared in a darkened corridor returned all too often to haunt his dreams—both waking and sleeping—he considered that he was dealing with the situation with his usual dexterity.

He shook himself. At any rate, this idyllic interlude would soon end. He was much stronger now. As a matter of fact . . .

He lifted his eyes from the board to Catherine's face.

"My dear," he said abruptly. "It is time for me to leave."

Catherine's heart gave an unpleasant lurch at his words. She had known this moment would arrive—realized it was getting closer with each passing day—but now that it was here, she had difficulty in assimilating the idea.

"But—your w-wound," she stuttered. "You are not well enough. You need—"

"I am well enough. My walks about the estate have grown longer, and yesterday Caliban and I rode to the village and back with no ill effects. It is time I faced my problem, and whatever is to come of it."

She was obliged to admit the truth of what he said. She rose from the table, the chess game forgotten.

"But do you not wish someone to go with you?"

"Robbie offered to accompany me—after trying to dissuade me from making the trip—but I must do this alone."

"I see." Catherine attempted a smile, with only minimal success. "Very well, then. You will come again, will you not? Afterward? Mariah and Grandmama will want to know the outcome of your visit to your brother."

"And you?" Unknowing, Justin held his breath.

Catherine flushed and dropped her gaze. "Of course, I would like to see you again as well. In fact, you are welcome to stay with us for a while. Even if you discover your brother has—or— that is, no matter the outcome of your visit with him, you will need a place to stay."

"After I have seen St. John," replied Justin gently, "my secret will be out. I shall return to London—if I am not summarily tossed into prison to await trial—and will hire lodgings of my own—or perhaps I shall billet with Robbie. However—" Almost without will he moved closer to her.

"Yes?" Catherine whispered.

"I hope that we will remain—friends. The time I have spent here at Winter's Keep is precious to me. You—and Mariah and Lady Jane—have been a lifeline."

Dammit all, he thought, perspiring. What did he think he was doing? It had, of course, been necessary to make a pretty little speech of farewell to the mistress of Winter's Keep, but why had he grasped her hand as though it was, literally, the lifeline he had mentioned earlier. He noted in passing that Catherine had not wrenched it away from him, but stood staring as though she, too, were locked in some sort of paralyzing spell.

"I—" he heard himself continue. "You—" Her jeweled eyes seemed like green ocean pools, pulling him into their mysterious depths. He drew a deep breath. "Catherine—" His hand, seemingly of its own volition, reached to tuck a stray tendril of honey-colored hair into the cap from which it escaped. The next moment his arms encircled her, and he pulled her to him.

A slight whimper of protest broke from her when he brought his mouth down on hers, but her lips opened under his. Her arms crept around him, and she pressed the incredible softness of her body against him. For an instant, they seemed transported to another time and place—somewhere he'd never been before—and he ached with a yearning to remain there forever with this uniquely special woman and her lovely, womanly curves. He caressed the sweet length of her back and felt her responsive shudder. Her full breasts moved against him, and he gasped with his need for her.

A sudden burst of laughter from servants approaching from beyond the hedge surrounding the terrace brought him to his senses. He released her abruptly, but not before she had already placed both hands on his chest to thrust herself away from him. For an instant, she stared at him, her gaze wide and startled.

Justin's mouth curved in a rigid smile. "It appears I must apologize—again. The trouble is, my dear, you are too damnably attractive."

When she did not return his smile, he continued, the merest hint of strain in his tone. "Catherine—this has been a pleasant idyll. I have enjoyed your company more than I would have believed—that is, you almost make me wish I were not such a wretched prospect for a gently bred maid. But I am, you know. With the best intent in the world, I am one of life's born destroyers of happiness. I would not want to ruin yours."

Still she did not respond, but continued to gaze at him, her emerald eyes dark.

"I—I must go," she whispered at last. Whirling about, she hurried through the French doors that gave access to the library. She paused on the threshold and turned back.

"When?" she asked brokenly.

"Tomorrow morning," Justin replied, his own voice a harsh rasp.

Catherine turned once more and hurried into the house. Blindly, she made her way to her study, and, because her knees would no longer hold her up, she sank into a chair by the window. You fool! she berated herself. She had done precisely what she had determined she would not. She had allowed all her resolutions to be swept to the winds in the circle of Justin's arms. At his first touch, she had simply melted into a puddle of acquiescence, and the warmth of his fingers on her cheek had created such an ache of wanting deep within her that she'd wished nothing more than to bury herself in him. Dear Lord, she had opened herself to him completely. And she had reveled in his kiss; a kiss that, while gloriously satisfying, left her yearning for so much more.

She tried to tell herself that it was only because she was growing into spinsterhood and had never lain with a man that she had responded so wantonly and so completely, but—no, it was more. When his mouth had come down on hers, she felt, along with the urgency of her need, a union with him of body and spirit. It was almost an extension of the connection that seemed to join them with every word they spoke to each other and every glance exchanged.

Why should she feel this bond with a man she could not even let herself like? He had duped her once, and every instinct warned her that he was not to be trusted. He had as much as told her that he was not prepared to lose his heart to her. Good God, even he had warned her that he was a villain, and there was no real reason why she should not believe him. All the evidence showed him to be a user of people for his own ends, and a seducer of his own brother's fiancée, to say nothing of that most vile of creatures, a traitor to his country. Yet when she looked into those polished-pewter eyes, she saw a man of decency and honor.

In fact, the more she came to know him, through his own actions and the words of his friend, the more she was convinced that his unworthiness lay in his own vision of himself, fostered so cruelly by his father—and his brother. Was she being foolish beyond permission? Was she allowing herself to be deluded yet once again?

She sighed heavily. Not that her feelings for Lord Justin Belforte were of any importance. He would be gone tomorrow.

The words echoed mournfully in her mind. Oh, she might see him again. If he were successful in his quest to exonerate himself from a charge of treason, surely he would visit Winter's Keep in the future. If he were less fortunate—well, she could always visit him in prison—at least until he was hanged.

The thought made her almost physically ill, and she rose abruptly. Lord, she must get on with her life and stop dwelling on what lay ahead for Justin. Moving to her desk, she pulled her rent book from the pile of papers there and, seating herself, began a distracted perusal of its contents.

Justin departed Winter's Keep early the next morning under threatening skies. He drove the curricle Catherine had insisted he take rather than endanger his wound on horseback. Caliban trotted behind the vehicle, tossing his tether and whiffling angrily, as though proclaiming this arrangement unacceptably beneath him.

Justin covered the miles for the most part unseeing. His wound troubled him very little, thus there was nothing to distract his mind from the turmoil that raged within him. His mind was filled with thoughts of Catherine. What was there about the green-eyed witch that had so captivated him? He had known many women. He had made love to many, and even developed an affection for some of them. But never had he plunged into the shattering maelstrom of emotion he had experienced at the first slight pressure of her mouth against his. When she had responded to his kiss, he had wanted nothing more than to lose himself in her lovely feminine warmth. What would it have been like to continue that magical embrace to its natural conclusion? What would it be like to take

Catherine Meade to his heart and to his bed, to keep her and hold her for the rest of his life?

A wave of chill realization spread through him. He had come to the knowledge long ago that love was not for him. How could he ask a woman to commit herself to one such as he—a failure at everything he had ever attempted that did not involve knavery and deceit?

Not that he wished for any sort of commitment at all, of course. But he knew that whatever the outcome of his quest for exoneration, he must not see Catherine again. She could not be part of his future, wherever it lay.

But he would miss her.

He made good time on the road to Barkway, despite having to stop to rest more frequently than he would have liked. By late afternoon, he was within ten miles of Sheffield Court. His thoughts turned to his father and St. John.

What would Sinjie's reaction be when he turned up at the Court? he wondered. No doubt his first move would be to send for the magistrate. After that, he would either try to throw him out of the house or lock him up in one of the cellars to await retribution.

Well, he was welcome to try either of those avenues, but, by God, he would answer a few questions first.

As he rode, he endeavored to work up a lather of indignation over St. John's supposed iniquities. All he could produce, however, was a cold, desperately unhappy quivering sensation in the pit of his stomach. Justin still found it hard to believe that St. John would resort to attempted murder to wreak the vengeance on him that he had harbored all this time. On the other hand, outside of the animosity between them, Sinjie had no motive to employ such drastic measures. St. John as the heir—no, he amended with a pricking behind his eyelids, St. John was now the Duke of Sheffield with all the honors and status and wealth the title embodied. Justin counted for nothing in the well-ordered pattern of St. John's life. He posed no threat either to his brother's well-being or his life of privilege. It was also well-nigh impossible to imagine St. John as being privy to treason.

But there was that paper in the possession of Le Capitáin Paul Bassinet.

It was eight of the clock in the evening when Justin arrived in the village of Barkway, less than a mile from the Court. He dismounted stiffly before a small inn, one that had rarely known his custom in the distant days when he frequented the local watering spots. He instructed the ostler to have the curricle drawn to the back of the yard and the horse that had pulled it stabled. Then, after tethering Caliban outside, he entered the little hostelry. Gratefully, he sank into a padded settle near the hearth in the public room, and, ordering a tankard of ale, he glanced at his surroundings. The place did not seem to have changed much since he had seen it last. The same crudely fashioned tables and benches squatted under the same low, smoke-stained beams, all illuminated by a few sconces and the light from the meager fire that crackled in the hearth.

Good, the place was thinly attended. Only three men could be seen: sons of the soil from the looks of them. They sat in a group at one of the tables, looking as much a part of the decor as though they'd been in situ since the place was built. They eyed him curiously when he entered the room, but apparently the inn was close enough to the highway so that the sight of a stranger was not unusual. One of the men, bald as a cantaloupe, was caught in a fit of laughter.

"Eee," he gasped. "And then t'vicar lost his spectacles. Only young Fletcher grabbing 'em saved 'em from tumbling into the grave."

One of the other men, whose bushy pate more than made up for his companion's lack, joined in the laughter. He gestured with the pipe he had been cleaning out with some industry. "Wouldna that ha' been somethin'? Wi' all the nobs standin's about. What a send off fer the old duke!"

Justin's ears pricked up.

"Ay," interposed the third man, the oldest of the three and so thin his bones almost protruded from beneath his skin. "We an't had such a collection o' swells around these parts since t'young master—that is, His Grace now—was christened. Ah, ye want t'talk o'grand gatherin's. This was a piddlin' affair by comparison."

"Weel now," responded Baldy, "what would ye expect? T'old gaffer weren't exackly sociable of late."

The Bush snorted. "Couldn't face any o'his grand friends, what wi' his boy wanted fer hangin'."

Bones shook his head. "Now, waren't that a queer stir up? Imagine young Master Justin doin' the dirty to 'is own country."

"He allus was a bad 'un," remarked the Bush, inhaling a noisy draft of ale.

"Oh, I dunno," Baldy responded judiciously. "He was used to spend a lot o'time with my Seth—took his mutton in our cottage dunnamany times. He was an imp, no question about that, but I never saw any real evil in 'im."

The Bush tapped the dottle from his pipe. "'Pears he musta changed some, then."

"I sorta liked the lad, too." This from Bones, shaking his head lugubriously. "He allus seemed all by himself most o'the time. Used ta come around my shop, askin' if he could help out."

The Bush snorted. "That is as may be, but they got him dead t'rights helpin' that Frenchy general escape. I say, it's too bad the Frenchies killed 'im off. I woulda like to a seen 'im hanged fer what he did."

After a moment, his companions nodded in ponderous agreement, then Baldy rose with a monumental sigh. "Ee, I'd best be on me way. Rain's comin'. I told the missus I'd be home early. She'll comb me hair with a joint stool if I don't bustle about."

The other two stood as well, and with much scraping of chairs and regretful calls of farewell to the innkeeper, they made their way unsteadily into the deepening twilight outside.

For many moments, Justin sat motionless on the settle, his tankard untouched on his knee. It seemed some of the inhabitants of Barkway had not forgotten him, or at least the boy he had been. Vague memories of afternoons spent in the tinker's shop—its owner a little more plump and a great deal more supple than the cadaverous specimen he had become. As for Seth, he remembered him well—a tall, gangly youth, not overbright, but willing to while away the occasional afternoon with a younger boy aching for company.

Justin waited another few minutes until full dark had fallen before leaving the inn. As he left the building, the rain that had threatened all day began to fall, spattering into the dust of the inn yard. Walking to the curricle, he pulled a voluminous cloak from his portmanteau and wrapped it about him, just as the clouds burst above him in a blinding torrent.

He mounted Caliban, keeping the great stallion to a walk. He was darkly pleased that the rain veiled the surrounding countryside, for he had no wish to relive the memories that lurked behind every hill and tree. Nor had he any wish to encounter any of the other denizens of the village. At the sight of a rider approaching him, he made to pull aside. A big fellow, he was, his face, hidden by the heavy, hooded cape he wore against the weather. The stranger swerved abruptly into a side lane as though—but surely, thought Justin, startled, the man had not wished to avoid him. No doubt, he had merely reached his turn, although, as he recalled, that lane led only to a small pond, far removed from dwelling or shop.

A mile or so down the road, Justin reached his own destination and left the road at a patch of overgrown shrubbery that nearly hid a narrow, forgotten entrance to the estate of Sheffield Court. The gate had rusted open many years before, and Justin carefully urged Caliban through the aperture.

Some fifteen minutes later, he was able to make out the manor house through the rain. At first, he could discern no illumination in the interior of the house, but as he swung toward the rear, a single panel of light emerged through the gloom. Justin halted. Dismounting, he ordered Caliban in a whisper that was not quite steady to remain where he was.

Ascending the terrace that surrounded the house, he stood for a moment, gazing through the French doors that, he knew, opened into the duke's study. A figure sat at the desk, pouring over several documents scattered on its surface. Very quietly, Justin tried the door handle, which opened noiselessly under his fingers.

The man at the desk did not look up until Justin had entered the room. After a startled instant, he lurched to his feet, his mouth open.

Justin smiled coldly. "H'lo, St. John. How've you been?"

Chapter Sixteen

"J-Justin!"

St. John grasped the edge of his desk as though to keep from falling. He lurched toward Justin.

"My G-God. Justin!" he gasped again as Justin moved casually into the room.

Instinctively, Justin thrust his arms before him to ward off St. John's progress. Lord, he thought, his brother had changed greatly since their last encounter. Though he was only some four years Justin's senior, he looked a good ten years older. He was a tall man, heavily built, with a square, shadowed jaw and eyes of a light, piercing blue. A sparse covering of graying dark hair drifted over the expanse of exposed scalp that glinted palely in the candlelight.

To Justin's astonishment, St. John did not halt as he approached, but stretching his arms wide, threw them around his brother.

"Justin!" He was almost sobbing now. "My God, you aren't— you're alive!"

"As you see," Justin remarked dryly, disengaging himself from St. John's embrace. He stepped back. "Doing it too brown, Sinjie. You cannot mean to try to convince me that you're pleased to see me."

"Good God," said St. John, unheeding. "You're soaking wet. Here, let me help you . . ." With astonished grunts, he assisted Justin in divesting himself of the dripping cloak. Tossing it over a nearby chair, he moved to the bellpull on the wall. "I'll ring for—"

"No!" said Justin sharply. "Do not call anyone, Sinjie. I crave some private conversation with you. A few moments only, then I shall be on my way. May I sit down?" Without waiting for a reply, he lowered himself carefully into a leather chair near the fire. Despite his insouciant attitude, he was desperately tired from his journey, and his side had begun to ache badly.

"Of course," St. John said dazedly. "Good God," he said again, almost uncomprehendingly. "I can't take this in. We—I thought I'd never see you again."

"No, I don't suppose you did."

By now St. John seemed to have assimilated Justin's unexpected return, and he returned to a more normal demeanor. Marking the astringency in Justin's words, his features pinched into the disagreeable lines so familiar to Justin.

"Well, how could we have expected otherwise? Where the devil have you been? You must have heard that Father was desperately ill. Since you have apparently survived your, er, adventures intact, could you not at least have come home before he passed away?"

Justin shrugged. "I suppose so, but I had no interest in seeing him, you know. No more, in fact, than I should imagine he had in seeing me."

St. John's mouth fell open. "Not interested in seeing you? My God, Justin, he knew he was dying. He knew you were being accused of treason! Of course, he would have wanted to see you."

"Do you seriously think I was about to expose myself to what would no doubt have been the finest tongue-lashing he ever delivered—to say nothing of being handed over to the authorities—merely to gratify his desire to collect his progeny together for a deathbed scene?"

"The authorities! But he—"

Justin interrupted him with a slashing motion of his hand. "Cut line, Sinjie. I did not come here to discuss my lack of filial devotion. I want to have a word with you about a certain piece of paper."

"What?"

"Yes, brother of mine. You see, I am determined not to swing for a crime I did not commit."

"Well, of course—"

"Thus," Justin continued, unwilling to be deterred in an interview that, so far, was developing even more unpleasantly than he had anticipated, "I am prepared to expend considerable effort in bringing the real culprit to justice. It appears," he concluded in a flat tone, "that you might be able to shed some light on the circumstances that led to my appearance on a very short list of suspects."

St. John, sinking slowly into a leather arm chair near the fire, goggled at him.

"Wh—what the *devil* are you talking about?"

"Oh, very good, Sinjie. I spent a long time perfecting an expression of bewildered innocence—I've had recourse to it many times—but I bow to a master. Allow me to enlighten you."

In a voice raw with suppressed emotion, Justin related the events that had brought about his ignominious return to England some three weeks earlier. St. John listened without comment, but when Justin spoke of the paper on Captain Bassinet's desk, his jaw tightened in a manner strongly reminiscent of their late father. For a moment, Justin was transported to one of those interminable, accusatory sessions with the old duke that had so haunted his memory.

By the time he had finished his narrative, St. John had stiffened into what appeared to be a pillar of outraged indignation.

"Are you intimating—?" he began, scarcely able to speak from between lips that seemed composed of some sort of nonmalleable metal. "Do you actually think that I—that *I* had something to do with your being accused of treason?"

Justin's heart pounded in his chest. His breath seemed to choke him as he forced himself to answer coolly. "Bewildered innocence phasing into moral dudgeon. Very impressive, but not quite credible, Sinjie. You have disliked me since we were both in short coats. You have hated me since your beloved played you false. I must say, I was unaware of the depth of your displeasure with me; but it appears you are prepared to go to some length to remove me from your personal universe."

For a long moment St. John said nothing, and Justin watched him dispassionately. Why had everything gone so wrong between the two of them? A silent, bitter laugh curled in his mind. God, it had been years since he had asked himself that question. And he was no closer to an answer than he had been when he had asked it of an uncaring deity so many years ago.

The wish that Catherine were here skittered across his mind like a streak of the lightning that flashed outside. Much as he was loath to admit, he needed bolstering at the moment. He very much would have liked a friendly hand to grasp, a sympathetic presence at his side. It was the height of presumption to think of Catherine in this connection, but still, he—he needed her.

He turned his attention back to his brother. St. John might protest his innocence in the matter of treason and attempted murder against his brother, but he could not deny the years of unremitting hostility he had displayed toward his younger sibling or the cries of vengeance he had hurled at their last meeting. His thoughts sank into a morass of dark memories from which he was pulled abruptly, aware that St. John was speaking.

"I cannot express to you," he said awkwardly, "my—my appalled dismay that you would believe me capable of such a thing, and—"

He halted as Justin snorted inelegantly.

"Just as father believed me incapable of treason?"

"As a matter of fact—what is it?" he asked as Justin began to rise, only to fall back into the chair.

"Nothing. I am still suffering a few twinges from the bullet I took in London last week."

"Last week!" St. John leaped to his feet to hurry to Justin's side. "Look here, you young fool, we cannot continue this discussion now. You're white as milk."

"Your concern touches me beyond words, brother, but—"

"Never mind my concern," St. John said harshly. "If you collapse at my feet in a relapse, you'll no doubt blame me for that, too. Now, do be quiet and let me think."

The absurdity of the situation combined with his increasing weakness caused a bubble of amusement to rise within Justin. My God, nothing had changed. His brother was still taking him to task.

"You are right," continued St. John. "You must not be seen. However, all the servants are abed, so that should not be a problem. I shall assist you upstairs, and you may sleep in your old room. Tomorrow, I'll get Mrs. Abercrombie to do the bed. I shan't explain anything to her, but if she puts two and two together, she'll keep silent. You always were a favorite with her."

Justin lacked breath to argue with this program, and, after a long pull at the brandy St. John poured for him from a decanter on the desk, he allowed his brother to help him upstairs. This, despite an insistent voice within him, pointing out that this was a very bad idea. He was virtually putting himself at Sinjie's mercy, but he was so very tired.

By the time he had navigated the stairs, with St. John's help, he could hardly see, and his last thought as he drifted into a bottomless sleep in the bed that had been his for so many years, was that Sinjie must have doctored the brandy.

He did not know for how many hours he slept, but when he opened his eyes, it was still dark and someone was shaking his shoulder. It hurt like hell.

"Justin! Wake up! For God's sake, open your eyes!"

Blearily, Justin attempted to rouse himself to consciousness. St. John was frantically pulling on him, urging him to rise. With great effort, Justin lifted his head.

"Wh—wha—?"

"We've got to get out of here! The whole bloody place is on fire!"

In her bedroom at Winter's Keep, Catherine's eyes snapped open, and she sat up abruptly in bed. After some hours of a restless thumping of her pillow, she had fallen into a fitful doze, only to be awakened by—Something was terribly wrong. Danger! She must warn Justin. She had swung her feet over the edge of the bed before she came fully awake to realize that the night was calm and quiet. Justin was not in the house and could not be in danger from anything here.

What was it, then, that had brought her to such horrified consciousness? Dear God? What was happening at Sheffield Court?

The fact at last registered with Justin that the room smelled strongly of smoke. Unable to shake the grogginess that clung to him like the fumes themselves, he clung to St. John, who, coughing and panting from the effort it took to breathe, pulled him from the bed.

In the corridor outside, the voices of approaching servants could be heard, and St. John half dragged Justin to another room, some distance away. Dropping him roughly on the bed, he growled. "For God's sake, stay put. I'll return as soon as I can."

He ran from the room, leaving Justin to inhale great lungfuls of untainted air. He supposed he should be out helping to put out the blaze, but in this instance, discretion seemed much the better part of valor. His head was beginning to clear, and he realized that the fire did not, apparently, threaten the house. He had glimpsed flames in his bedchamber as St. John hustled him from the room, but apparently they had not spread. Thoughtfully, he took up the tinderbox that lay on the bedside table and lit the candle that rested close to hand. He listened. Judging from what he could hear of the uproar in the corridor, things were already under control. It appeared that St. John's prompt action had saved him from being roasted in his bed like a Christmas goose.

Busy with the implications of this fact, Justin did not heed the ensuing commotion taking place almost within arm's length. It was only when his door latch lifted softly that he raised his head to observe St. John's entrance into the room. His nightshirt was begrimed and badly stained with smoke, as was his face, and his hair stood up in dusky tufts about his head. He flung himself into a chair near the bed with a profound sigh.

"All is well, then?" asked Justin.

St. John passed a hand over his forehead, leaving a streak of white that was somehow ludicrous against the black of his face. "Yes," he replied, sighing gustily. "The fire had only progressed as far as a couple of chairs in your room—not even that far in mine."

"Yours?" asked Justin, startled.

"Yes." St. John frowned. "It was just pure damned luck. I tossed about for some time after I retired." He shot a glance at Justin. "I had a great deal to think about. I think I must have just fallen asleep, when I was wakened by I knew not what. I had the impression of someone slipping from the window over the balcony outside. Almost before I was full awake, I noticed the smell of smoke. Imagine my surprise to discover that someone had set the hangings alight."

Justin almost chuckled at St. John's expression of disgruntled indignation.

"I rose immediately, of course, and rang the bellpull—and then I'm afraid I rather lost my head. I rushed out into the corridor shouting for the servants. I ran back into the room and began throwing water from my basin and pitcher onto the flames, as well as from the carafe by my bed. Naturally, it didn't take long to accomplish this, and it was only then that I thought about you in your room just a few doors away. Well," he added in an exculpatory rush, "I had rather a lot on my mind at the moment."

Again, Justin knew an illogical urge to laugh.

"At any rate," continued St. John, "the fire is out now. I sent some of the footmen to check out the premises to make sure that nothing else is alight, but it appears that all, as you say, is well."

"Except," murmured Justin, "that someone is apparently prowling the hallowed grounds of Sheffield Court with the intent of killing off the entire Belforte line."

"Yes, there is that." St. John rubbed his chin. "Shall we repair to my chamber? I think I could stand a nip of something."

"Righty-ho," said Justin, climbing from the bed. "As long as it isn't laced with laudanum."

St. John had the grace to look shamed.

"Ah. Well, I had a bit of it in my desk, left over from Father's medications. I didn't want you waking in the middle of the night and haring off before I had a chance to talk to you."

The two men exited the room and Justin instinctively turned to the left. St. John laid a hand on his arm. "I'm in the master's suite now," he said awkwardly.

"Of course, you are," responded Justin smoothly, turning.

Entering the duke's sitting room, he looked about him curiously. So far, Sinjie had made few changes. The same massive chairs that he remembered from the previous occupant, dotted the room like upholstered boulders, and the other furnishings—several tables, a commode, a wardrobe, several cabinets, and a small desk—were fashioned of some species of dark, malevolent-looking wood. Hangings of a heavy dark green damask shone dully at the windows and the bed that could be seen in an adjoining chamber.

"Yes, it's all just the same," said St. John, following his brother's gaze. "I—I plan some changes, but . . . It seems so soon."

Justin said nothing, merely nodding as he settled into one of the boulders. St. John went to a cabinet and brought forth a bottle and two glasses. Pouring a liberal splash into both, he handed one to Justin and took the other to a nearby chair.

"It appears I owe you an apology," said Justin at last.

St. John raised his brows.

"I accused you of evil intent on my life. I was evidently wrong."

"Yes, you were, and what I want to know is why—"

He was interrupted by the sound of voices raised in acrimony in the corridor outside the master's suite, followed almost immediately by a thunderous pounding on the door. Exchanging a glance with St. John, Justin leaped to his feet and hastened from the room to the bedchamber, where he paused, out of sight of whoever might enter.

Whoever proved to be a pair of stalwart footmen. Sandwiched between them was the struggling figure of Robbie McPherson.

What the devil—! thought Justin, gaping unbelievingly. What was Robbie doing here?

Shoving Robbie ungently into the room, one of the footmen approached St. John.

"We caught this feller lurking about outside, my lord. Sneaking toward the west terrace, he was. He says—"

At this point, Robbie wrenched himself from the hands of his captors. "I was not sneaking," he said testily. "I saw smoke, and I was running toward the house." He bent a significant stare on St. John. "I am a friend of a rather close relative of yours, and I want to know what you've done with him."

"What!" exclaimed St. John. "What have you got to do with my—with my relative."

"If you'll send these fellows about their business, I'll be happy to discuss the matter with you—Your Grace."

"Ho!" interposed one of the footmen. "Send us away, would ye, ye—ye miscreant?"

St. John glanced toward his bedchamber, where Justin stood in his line of sight, but not that of Robbie or the footmen. Justin nodded frantically.

"No, it's all right," said St. John curtly. "Leave us."

The footmen, obviously feeling their master had taken leave of his senses, backed slowly from the room, muttering barely concealed objections to this plan. As the door closed behind them, Justin emerged from the bedchamber.

"Robbie! For God's sake, what possessed you—? How did you know I was here? Why did you—?"

"Justin! Are you all right?" asked Robbie, ignoring his friend's sputtered greeting. "You look like a death's head on a mop stick. Though"—he shot a glance toward the duke—"at least you don't appear to be in durance vile."

"Do you two mind?" interposed St. John with some asperity. "Justin, it appears this person is known to you . . . ?"

Wearily, Justin waved his hand. "St. John, this is Robbie McPherson, meddler extraordinaire and thruster of spokes into wheels. I think you must remember him?"

"McPherson." St. John frowned. "Yes, I do recall him. Scruffy little brat who talked too much. Always abetting your escapades. But what the devil is he doing here?" St. John's voice cracked in bewilderment.

In reply, Justin merely turned to fill a third glass from the bottle in St. John's cabinet. He handed it to Robbie with a gesture toward another chair and indicated firmly to St. John to return to the one he had been occupying before the interruption by the footmen.

"Now," he growled to Robbie. "Speak."

"Well," began Robbie after a long pull at his glass. "I visited the Keep early this morning and was told by Catherine that you'd gone tearing down here—against everyone's advice. I decided to come down and look in on the proceedings, just in case you—" He glanced at St. John. "Just in case you ran into any trouble."

At this, St. John rose abruptly once more. "I fail to see," he said in a strained voice, "why everyone seems to be laboring under the ludicrous delusion that I wish to put a period to my brother's existence."

"Considering the fact," retorted Robbie, "that you and your fa-

ther made life a living hell for his entire boyhood, and the fact of
your loudly stated intentions later on to make him pay for ruining
your life, I don't think such an assumption is anything like ludicrous. You have always hated Justin. We have only to discover
how—"

"You insolent cur!" St. John had gone quite pale, and the hand
that was raised to Robbie trembled with a rage that could not be
doubted as sincere.

Justin rose to intervene.

"This is getting us nowhere. Robbie, St. John just saved my
life. Sinjie, Robbie has been my friend for a very long time. A
disaster has befallen me, and he's merely looking for answers.
The fact that a paper covered in your handwriting showed up on
the desk of a French officer who was interrogating me with some
severity, caused some, er, misgivings for both of us."

"Anyway," continued Robbie hastily without giving St. John
the opportunity to voice the protest that bubbled almost visibly on
his lips, "I reached the court just after dusk, and I was reconnoitering, when I almost ran into you."

"That was you on the road!" exclaimed Justin. "Why did you
slink off into the shrubbery?"

Robbie shifted uncomfortably. "Because I knew you didn't
want me there. I just thought to avoid any unnecessary, er, discus-
sions on the matter."

"I see," remarked Justin dryly. "Go on."

"I saw you enter the house, and I just waited around for a
while. Getting soaked to the bone, for all the thanks I got," he
added in some dudgeon. "After a while the rain stopped, and I decided at last to find an inn. I planned to come back later for more
reconnoitering. I was some distance away from the house when I
saw smoke coming from an upstairs window. I hustled back to investigate, only to be set on by those two young behemoths."

"Serves you right, cloth head," commented Justin unfeelingly.
"If ever I heard such a birdwitted scheme. Once I was inside the
house, what did you think to accomplish, prowling about the
place like a villain in a gothic novel?"

Once again, Robbie squirmed in his chair, but lifting his chin
replied pugnaciously, "I got here in time to save your bacon, did I
not?"

"Yes, you did, dear boy," replied Justin, "or, at least you would
have if Sinjie had not already brought the situation under control."

Robbie sneered. "Did he, now? Or did circumstances arise that made it imperative to call off the attempt and make it look like he was saving your bacon? Have you forgotten the existence of his midnight visitors?"

"No I have not, and—"

"Midnight visitors?" interposed St. John querulously.

"No, I have not," continued Justin, holding up his hand to stay St. John's further questioning. "And I intend to get to the bottom of all of it."

He turned then to St. John. "You see, brother, it was not just the existence of that paper that encouraged my unseemly suspicions. When I returned to England and began investigating your activities, I discovered that you had begun keeping some very strange company. Perhaps you can explain the presence at the Court—at some very odd hours—of a pair of specimens who ordinarily would never have made it through the front gates had they shown their faces here in daylight."

Justin searched St. John's face, but could find nothing beyond blank bewilderment there.

"Specimens?" he echoed. "I don't—oh." His cheeks flushed as comprehension crept over his features. "You mean Bentick. And the other one—Briggs." He began to pace the floor. "Look here, Justin, I don't know why you could not have just come home and faced me—and father."

"Of course," interjected Robbie savagely. "He should have just strode in and said, 'Excuse me, Father, Sinjie, but it appears one or both of you is doing his best to see me hanged. And taking potshots at me to boot.' "

"Potshots?" St. John swiveled to face his brother. "You told me of being shot. What—?"

"I was just getting to that. Robbie, I would like to speak to St. John alone. If you would not mind—"

"Yes," chimed in St. John irritably. "Tell the fellow to go away." He moved toward the bellpull. "I'll have you shown to a room. One relatively free of smoke and flames, although I'm not yet convinced you had nothing to do with the fire."

Despite Robbie's roar of indignation, it was obvious that St. John was merely venting his spleen with this accusation, and once more, Justin held up his hand.

"Please, let us have no more recriminations. Robbie, do as St. John asks. He is hardly likely to do me in now, particularly with a suspicious friend hovering on the premises."

For some moments, Robbie growled inarticulately, but when, at last, a footman appeared—not, fortunately, one of his erstwhile captors, he left the room with reasonably good grace.

"Strange fellow," murmured St. John as the door shut behind him. "What the devil did he mean by my hating you? And Father?"

Astonished at the question, Justin did not answer, but merely goggled at his brother. St. John peered at him in growing consternation before finally taking a seat near him.

"My God, Justin, do you really think—?" He drew a deep breath. "I thought you knew—that you understood. Justin, Father loved you. He loved you more than anything else in the world—as he did your mother.

"And it was a love that utterly destroyed him."

Chapter Seventeen

Justin felt as though the universe had suddenly skewed in its ordered progress. For some moments he gaped at St. John. He opened his mouth, but could form no words.

"What the devil are you talking about?" he said at last in a harsh growl. "To Father, I was lower than a cur he might have found in the streets. Surely, you must remember. You reminded me often enough of his loathing for me."

"Oh, God," said St. John tiredly. "Yes, I treated you badly, but I thought you knew—" He uttered a long, shuddering sigh. "I thought you must know why."

As Justin continued to stare at him, stupefied, St. John spoke again. "First of all . . . ," he began awkwardly. "About Lady Susan. She's dead now, did you know?"

Wordlessly, Justin nodded.

"When she knew she was going to die, she apparently got religion. She came to me and confessed that you were not responsible for her pregnancy. Justin, she was having affairs with three men at the time! She told me that you and she had never—that is, she said that you were more interested in tweaking my nose than pursuing a romance with her. I should have written to you, but it—it seemed more the sort of thing I should say to your face. And I did not know how to find you at the time. So, you see, it is I who owe you an apology."

Justin was silent for several minutes. For some reason, he felt like crying. Surely, he should have experienced some pleasure at his vindication, but he felt only a deep sadness.

"Yes, you do," he said at last, forcing his tone to lightness. "However, having just pulled me away from a fiery death, I suppose we can consider the account square."

St. John sagged in his chair and remained so for several seconds. He shook himself at length.

"Well, then," he continued in an unsteady voice, "getting back to Father. You must know the story of how he met your mother.

He never spoke to me of her until his later years. She was beautiful beyond imagining, he said, and floated through life as though wrapped in a bubble of warmth and wit and sparkle. One had but to look at her to become enchanted. Despite the fact that she was abysmally unsuitable, and over the violent objections of his family, he married her."

"From all accounts," interposed Justin harshly, "he had an odd way of showing his love."

"Well, that was just it. You know how he was, a veritable pillar of duty and conscience. In the end, he could not reconcile his standards with what he'd done, and as a result he made both your mother and himself utterly miserable.

"He could not simply accept his feelings for her and enjoy them. No, he found it necessary to find fault with her. I suppose somewhere in his twisted sense of morality, he came to believe that by constantly belittling your mother, flagellating her—and himself—with her unworthiness, he could somehow assuage his guilt in falling under her spell."

Justin snorted. "There are so many flaws in that reasoning that I don't know where to start unraveling them."

"I agree, but who looks for reason in an obsession? And that's what his failure in his duty became to Father. When you were born, his guilt was compounded. Because you were the son of her body, he loved you." St. John paused. "More than he ever loved me," he added in a low voice. "But, again, he could not allow himself to admit it. To hide his affection, even—or perhaps, especially—from himself—or possibly to try to kill that affection, he meted the same treatment to you that he had to Amelie. In later years, I think he'd managed to convince himself that you really were worthless. In the end, however, the spark of affection that remained in him for you, blazed once more into an inferno."

"Except in the little matter of treason. He evidently had no difficulty in believing that."

"Treason!" exclaimed St. John, startled. "He never thought for an instant that you were guilty of treason. Nor," he added brusquely, "did I."

It seemed to Justin that he had ceased to breathe some fifteen minutes ago, and he now expelled an explosive gust of air. He could not take in what St. John was telling him. He wanted so badly to believe his brother that he could fairly taste the words as they rolled around in his mind. His Father had really loved him?

No. Impossible. No man who loved his son could have reviled

him so thoroughly over the years. Justin twisted his mouth into a smile.

"You make a lovely story out of it, Sinjie. And your own contribution to my boyhood wretchedness? I am breathless with anticipation of your explanation of that."

A dark crimson flooded St. John's cheeks. "I suppose I can't blame you for finding this beyond belief, but it's true. I know it is. As for me—" He rose to pace the floor. "In the beginning—when we were small—I was jealous of you, but I admired you. You were so many things that I was not—bold and quick of wit, with the gift of making people love you."

"With one glaring exception," murmured Justin.

St. John dropped his gaze "In the beginning I prated at you from an honest desire to change your ways. I thought that if only I could make you understand your failings in Father's eyes, you would make an effort to fit his idea of what you should be like. As I grew older, however, I began to realize that Father was covering his true feelings for you. You see, in conversations with him when you weren't around, he spoke of you far differently. His love for you and his pride in your strength and intelligence—even the daring of some of your pranks—was as evident to me as though he had painted them on a sign. I—I grew to resent you—and yes, for a while I hated you."

"For the first time," interposed Justin dryly, "I believe you."

"He told me later," said St. John, seating himself once more, "that it nearly broke his heart when you appeared to be fulfilling all his prophecies of disaster for you. Oddly, he professed a complete mystification as to why you should be turning out so. By the time you left for Oxford, he believed there was no hope for a reconciliation between you, and that your general wickedness had reached a point where he could no longer control you. That, of course, is when he decided to cut the connection.

"I have never seen a man so despondent. A hundred times after that, he began a letter to you, only to toss it into the fire. His pride would not allow him to admit any wrongdoing on his part—in fact, I believe all he ever had to say on the subject was, 'Perhaps I was a little harsh on the boy.' In any case he could not bring himself to apologize. It was only when word hit the newspapers that you were suspected of treason that his world truly came crashing down on him. You did know of his illness, did you not?"

"Of course. The news that my perfidy had caused him to suffer a paralytic stroke was brayed in every journal in the country."

"It was not your perfidy, it was the accusation of it that brought about his collapse, and, of course, the news of your supposed death. To the very end, he believed in your innocence."

"I thought you said he had come to believe I was truly depraved and vicious and altogether rotten to the nub."

St. John rubbed his nose. "Not that rotten, apparently. 'Sinjie,' he said to me over and over, 'there was hardly a limit to the boy's wildness, but, by God, I know he would never stoop to betraying his country.' "

Hearing the echo of his own words, Justin felt tears pricking at the back of his eyes.

"All very touching, I'm sure," he growled.

"He set about trying to prove your innocence, you know."

"What?" Justin sat up very straight.

"He went to the Horse Guards and pounded on every desk there. He tried to see Charles Rutledge, for he knew you two were particular friends, but Rutledge was not about. Someone said he thought he was temporarily out of the country. So Father made do with one of the other high-ranking personages there. He made a bloody nuisance of himself, declaring the impossibility of the reports of your crime. He got nowhere, of course, and in the end, no one there would so much as talk to him. Later, he hired a clerk from the Intelligence department to dig up the facts."

"Cyrus Bentick!" Justin fairly leaped from his chair and began pacing the floor in the same route taken earlier by St. John.

"Yes."

"What about Snapper Briggs?"

"How did you know he and Bentick had been here?"

Briefly, Justin detailed his instructions to Jack Nail to keep tabs on the residents of Sheffield Court.

"My God," gasped St. John. "You set someone to spy on us?" His strong, thick fingers formed into fists, only to relax a moment later.

"I suppose I cannot blame you," he said heavily. "If you suspected me of trying to do away with you, it behooved you to, er, take steps."

"Yes, I thought so, too. And I'm not sure I still don't."

He sighed heavily, and for an instant he simply wished the world and all the problems that seemed all at once to overwhelm him, would just go away, leaving him alone with—with Catherine in this candlelit bedchamber.

What the devil . . . ? Was he actually lusting after a woman at a time like this? But, no, it wasn't lust that caused her to appear suddenly in his thoughts or prompted this peculiar, immediate yearning for her. He just wanted to talk to Catherine. To mull aloud with her over St. John's astonishing revelations. My God, Sinjie was asking him to reverse the hurts and slights of a life-time—to completely rethink his feelings for his father and his brother. It was all, he thought dizzily, too much. He had never in his adult life felt the need to turn to someone for advice and sup-port—but, if he could only talk all this out with Catherine, per-haps he could make some sense of it all.

He jerked his attention to St. John, who had begun to speak again.

"It was not until after Father had suffered his stroke and we had removed from London to the Court that Bentick showed up. He was aware, he said, of Father's efforts on your behalf, and he said he might be of some help. Frankly, I didn't trust him, but Father was desperate. He paid the little toad a thousand pounds to garner information for us. It didn't take me long to perceive the fellow was a complete fraud. He crept in periodically with reports cast-ing suspicion on everyone from your commanding officer to Wellington himself." St. John chuckled dryly. "He mentioned several officers in your unit—even that McPherson chap, and at one time I think he even dragged in Castlereagh."

He shook his head. "At any rate, after Father passed away, I gave him his walking papers.

"As for Briggs, we hired him at Bentick's insistence. He seemed to feel he needed some backup in prying information out of various people he thought might be helpful. Smugglers, for in-stance."

"Smugglers!"

"Well, yes, Bentick said that in any plot involving people on both sides of the Channel, some way must have been found to transmit messages quickly and secretly."

"Ergo, smugglers." Justin stared thoughtfully at the fire. "I sup-pose that makes sense."

"In any event," said St. John, "I got rid of him, too. He wasn't providing anything useful, and it made me uneasy just having him around. I could all too easily envision us waking up one morning with ice picks in our backs."

To Justin's surprise, the chuckle that rose to his lips was un-forced. He realized that St. John's monologue was having an ef-fect on him. It was too much to say that he accepted all that he'd been told this extraordinary night, but he was appalled at how badly he wanted to believe it all. He had thought any feelings he'd had for the old man dead beyond redemption. But, God, how he wanted to let himself be immersed in the tale, to let it soothe away the hurt and humiliation of all his growing-up years.

"Did you not get my letter?" asked St. John.

"Letter?" echoed Justin, still staring bemusedly at the fire.

"Yes. Father had a series of strokes, you know. After the last one, he realized that he was about to turn up his toes, and he dictated a letter for me to send to you. In it, he spoke of some of the things I've told you tonight. In addition . . ."—St. John paused, seemingly for dramatic effect—"he wished to inform you that he was willing Longbarrow to you."

"Longbarrow!" exclaimed Justin.

"Yes, he knew you loved the place, and he wanted you to have a home of your own. And, I think, he wanted to make amends somehow for his mistakes."

"When did you send this letter?" asked Justin, his heart pounding so that he could hardly speak.

"It must have been about a month ago, I suppose. You never received it?"

"I think I might have," said Justin slowly, "and not even known of it. I think it must have been delivered to my tent and subsequently stolen."

Enlightenment sprang to St. John's broad features. "The paper! The one with my handwriting all over it!"

"Yes," replied Justin musingly. "At least," he amended hastily, "it may be. At any rate—Longbarrow is mine now?"

"All yours. 'Should've done it long ago,' were his words, as I recall. And he bequeathed a healthy fortune to you, as well." St. John rose again to stand before his brother. "Justin, I must know. Do you believe me? You cannot think I was ready to commit treason and have you blamed for it! And tried to have you killed in the bargain?"

Justin lifted his eyes. "God knows, I've tried, St. John. It would have been the easiest route, and such a neat solution to my problem, but I cannot . . . No, I do not—and never did, really—believe you tried to ruin me—or kill me."

For an instant, Justin thought St. John was going to throw himself at his feet. Instead, after an abortive gesture toward Justin, he straightened slowly, as though he had just rid himself of an intolerable burden.

"Thank God," he whispered. "Thank God." His expression lightened, and Justin realized for the first time that there was a striking resemblance between himself and his brother.

"What will you do now?" he asked, returning to his chair. "I wish you would remain here, now that you've finally decided to come home."

"But I am not home," replied Justin softly. "Thank you for your invitation, however, right now no one here knows of my existence, and I think it best to keep it that way. At any rate"—he smiled, albeit somewhat painfully—"Sheffield Court has not been my home for a long time. My home lies at Longbarrow now. Although, right now it's as dangerous for me as the Court. No, there is only one place I can think of where I can remain safely hidden."

A small, bright flame lit within him that soon spread its warmth into every corner of his soul. "I'm going back to Winter's Keep—and to Catherine."

Chapter Eighteen

"Ah, this is good," sighed Justin, waggling into his chair.

He and Catherine sat opposite one another at the breakfast table in Winter's Keep. Justin had arrived there late the night before, long after Catherine had retired for the evening. She had heard the rattle of his vehicle on the gravel, however, and had hastened downstairs to greet him outside the front door as he pulled the curricle to a halt.

She was dismayed at how glad she was to see him. She had not expected that he would return—at least not so soon. After ushering him into the house, she propelled him to the kitchen, where she prepared a midnight meal with her own hands of cold meat, cheese, and bread, washed down with liberal drafts of the estate's home-brewed beer.

Justin informed her almost immediately that he no longer regarded St. John as a suspect. He also told her a little about the fire and of Robbie's appearance at the Court. A hundred questions bubbled in Catherine's mind, but observing that Justin's eyes were closing of their own volition in weariness, she held her tongue and instead bade him sharply to remove himself to his bedchamber before he fell into his plate.

"Excellent advice, as always," Justin had said, and brushing her cheek with his lips, he did as he was told.

Now she watched him consume a large portion of eggs and York ham, aware that her gaze devoured him just as ravenously. Lord, what was the matter with her? she wondered, a panicky flutter rising within her. Not that the answer wasn't obvious, of course. He had played her false, and he had as much as admitted he had done the same with countless others. He had apparently seduced his brother's fiancée and then refused to marry her. Not that she was one to talk of marrying to avoid scandal, of course, but still . . . The man was a self-admitted villain, and she had fallen in love with him.

She turned the idea in her mind slowly, examining it like a rare jewel. She should be appalled, she supposed. She should consider an attachment to such a rogue a disaster. She could not account for the little rockets of happiness that burst at intervals within her, expanding in waves until she thought she might burst. Perhaps love brought joy to a woman, no matter the pitfalls that lay ahead.

Justin had declared himself an unworthy candidate for a life-long commitment. He had insisted that the kisses shared between them had been but part and parcel of a brief, albeit pleasant idyll. But her toes curled inside her jean boots as she recalled the way his body had melted against hers at their last encounter. She was convinced the man was not immune to her. Furthermore, something deep and sure within her cried out that he was not simply looking for a fleeting seduction. The warmth in his eyes, she was certain, sprang from an honest affection rather than from lust.

Well—she grinned to herself—perhaps just a touch of lust.

She reached to touch his wrist lightly. "I am so pleased that you and your brother have reconciled. It must be a great weight off your mind to know that whoever has been planning your downfall so assiduously, it is not a member of your family. It is unfortunate that you did not get the opportunity to speak to your father."

Justin laughed shortly. "You are being diplomatic, my dear. I had plenty of opportunity to see my father, and I do not think I would have changed my mind, even knowing what I know now."

Catherine glanced at him in surprise.

"St. John can maunder on till his eyes bubble about Father's awful feelings of guilt, but I cannot stir much sympathy for him in my breast. He may not be wholly to blame for the way I turned out, but I can't help feeling he was at least partly responsible. He was an unlovable, curmudgeon who took out his self-pity on his son. As for St. John, I believe he, too, was a victim of Father's obsession, but—"

"But he apparently did not hold you in such contempt as you thought. I never did understand," she continued tentatively, aware that she was treading in territory that might be best avoided, "why you felt he bore you such enmity."

"As to that . . ." Justin lifted his head to gaze at her. His eyes were like a rainy sea. "There was an incident—when I was much younger—for which St. John blamed me. And not without good cause."

"You need not tell me about it," said Catherine hurriedly, "if you'd rather not."

"No, I would rather you hear all this from me. You see, there was a young woman named Lady Susan Fairhaven . . ."

The telling of the story did not take long, and when Justin reached the part about the lady's confession to St. John, Catherine felt a tide of joy and relief well up in her. She had not really believed him capable of such cruelty, she told herself, but it was good to know the facts bore out her instincts.

"I can't say that Sinjie and I have fully come to terms," Justin concluded, "but we at least have something of an understanding of one another."

"I hope it will grow into more than an understanding," said Catherine with a smile.

Justin grinned. "At any rate," he said, deftly changing the subject, "I want to thank you for allowing me to return to the Keep to regroup. I wish I did not have to leave again so soon."

"So soon?" she echoed in dismay.

"I have work to do in London. I cannot be skittering back and forth in the dead of night any longer. I must find lodgings in town."

The idea flashed into Catherine's mind full-blown, and before her better judgment could snatch it from her, she spoke.

"Ahhh . . ." she began.

Justin glanced at her questioningly.

"It may be difficult for you to maintain your anonymity if you hire lodgings yourself. Or were you planning to stay with Robbie? Or Mr. Rutledge?"

"No," Justin replied emphatically. "Whoever is on my tail is watching them as well, I am sure. I would not put them in further jeopardy. I shall just have to take my chances that I can find a snug ken. That is, house," he explained hastily. "Forgive my lapse into thieves' cant. I shall use a false name, of course, and—"

"What you need," interposed Catherine austerely, "is a snug fortress. To say nothing of a supply of funds. Forgive me for speaking plainly, but you cannot apply to your bank for a draft, after all, and I do not believe you will wish to borrow from either Robbie or this Mr. Rutledge."

Justin stared at her blankly. "Are you suggesting that I accept money from a woman?"

"Not 'a woman,' " Catherine snapped. "Me. And this is a loan. I have more money than I know what to do with, and I know you will repay me." She lifted a hand to stem the torrent of protest she could see forming behind his eyes. "Now, please, just hear me out."

Justin opened his mouth, but closed it again almost immediately and flung himself back into his chair. He thrust his hands upward in a negative gesture as Catherine continued.

"I propose to hire a house for a sojourn there for myself and Mariah and Grandmama."

"What?" Justin's expression could not have contained more astonishment had she announced her decision to set sail for Antarctica.

"They have been after me for years—as has Adam—to visit London, and I have come to admit to myself that it has been the most arrant foolishness on my part to have stayed away so long." She drew a deep breath. "You see, it was not merely an aversion to city life that drove me from town."

Struck by an unaccustomed compunction, Justin said hastily, "My dear, it is not necessary—Just because I chose to bare my soul to you a few minutes ago, you do not—"

"No—no, it is not an incident of which I am particularly proud, but locking it away as I have for so many years has merely lent it a wholly unwarranted importance."

In a cool, even tone, she told him of her brief indiscretion with Francis Summervale and the cataclysmic upheaval it had caused in her life.

As he listened, Justin's hands clenched into fists. My God, he had no right to condemn any man for dishonorable behavior, but—the bastard! Summervale had ruined the life of a beautiful young girl, whose only crime was a passionate nature and a giving heart. He had taken her innocence—no matter that he had left her physically unspoiled—all for his own greed. He wished that he had come to know Francis Summervale in the Peninsula well enough to take his measure. By God, he would have trumped up a reason to slay him. He wished the snake were available right now for having his guts strung out to dry in the knacker's yard. He wished—

He came to himself with a horrified start. What he wished was that he could take Catherine in his arms and murmur that none of it mattered, that she was inutterably precious—the sweetest, loveliest, finest woman he had ever met and that any man would be both humbled by her perfection and proud to make her his own if she would so much as deign to look in his direction.

My God, he had never spouted such drivel in his entire life.

Swallowing hard, he spoke in a tone so dry it could have been served crumbled in soup, "You are right. You have been foolish beyond permission."

At the startled expression in her eyes, he continued harshly.

"Do you really think your little escapade occupied the minds of the ton for longer than it took some idiot to spawn a new tidbit? I would be willing to wager that if someone were to have mentioned your name the following month, it would have produced nothing but blank stares. In other words, my dear Miss Meade, you have immured yourself in this admittedly pleasant little cocoon for naught."

Catherine, prepared for every reaction from commiseration to condemnation almost gasped. She felt as though Justin had thrown a glass of cold water in her face. A moment later, she was forced to smile. Perhaps an icy shower was precisely what she needed. At any rate, the astringency of his speech caused her to straighten abruptly, her eye kindling.

"That is easy for you to say, my lord. I daresay you have grown quite accustomed to being held up for public pillory. Oh!" Catherine gasped at the thoughtless cruelty of her remark. "I am so sorry! I didn't mean—"

Justin merely chuckled. "Not to worry," he said, waving an airy hand. "I have developed the skin of a tropical reptile. And you are quite right. Just because I have learned to thumb my nose at the vagaries of public opinion, does not mean everyone should be so uncaring. Where would we be, after all, if no one quailed before a leveled quizzing glass?"

Catherine was forced to laugh. "Civilization would no doubt quiver on its foundations."

"Precisely. Now, getting back to your generous offer—"

"Yes," interposed Catherine. "The thing is, I plan to hire a house in a respectable but completely unfashionable part of town. Hans Town, perhaps, or the area near Russell Street. I shan't know anyone. You will be yet another distant cousin. Perhaps Mariah's brother! Come to visit us from—oh, Canada, perhaps. I shall bring only one or two of my most trusted servants with me, and the rest will know nothing of my background, or yours. Among the staff, however, we shall number several very large, very unpleasant footmen, with strict orders that our privacy must be guarded at all costs. You see? You can come and go as you please, but while you are in the house you will be unassailable. Thus, there is no possible reason—"

"Say no more, Generalissimo," replied Justin, laughing. "I never turn down an offer of largesse, regardless of the gender of the offerer, and I shan't start now. Please accept as read my bottomless gratitude. But"—he hesitated for a moment—"I have to ask myself—why? We are not related—we are not old friends. I believe—that is, you seem to have formed a reasonably correct assumption of my character—or lack of it. Much as I appreciate your concern and your help, I cannot help but wonder about its source."

Catherine could feel herself flushing, and she dropped her gaze. "I must say, I wonder myself. I think it is because, particularly in light of the events you related concerning your visit to your home, I have come to believe you are innocent of the charges leveled against you. It goes very much against the grain with me to see an innocent man suffer for something he did not do. Ergo, I wish to help you. Tell me," she continued hastily, searching urgently for a safer topic, "have you any further thoughts on who the guilty person might be?"

"As a matter of fact," began Justin, but, apparently changing his mind, he finished regretfully, "No, I'm afraid not. I'm hoping that once I take up residence in London, Robbie and I can put our heads together and—what?" he asked, at her slight intake of breath.

"Nothing," she replied quickly, but as he continued to gaze at her questioningly, she continued. "It's just that I have been wondering about Robbie. I know he is your best friend in the world and you've known each other for donkey's years—and you trust him, and—and all that." She faltered as Justin's expression grew dark. "But just think of the sequence of events. Do you not think it remarkably coincidental that it was Robbie who urged you to leave for England, and then on your first night in this country—when no one else knew you were here, you were ambushed? Then, on another night, you were shot just after you left his lodgings. And, finally, there is the matter of the fire at Sheffield Court. Who else knew you were there last night? No one but St. John, who rescued you from the flames—and your very good friend, who was found skulking around the grounds immediately afterward. In addition—I can't help feeling at times that he is hiding something."

By now Justin's expression had grown thunderous. "That's enough, Catherine," he fairly barked. "Robbie would no more betray England—or me—than I would him."

"Even for a great deal of money?" she asked. "It is my impression that Robbie, not being the son of a peer, has no private income."

Justin nodded unwillingly.

"He is an officer, however," continued Catherine, "and as such is constantly in the company of the sons of wealthy men. Such a lifestyle is expensive, and—and there are many men who will, even against their inclination, sacrifice the principles of a lifetime for money."

"But not Robbie." Justin's voice was a harsh growl. The recollection flickered in him of Robbie's newly acquired wealth—his improved accommodations, his more fashionable wardrobe, all through the supposed benevolence of an aunt previously unknown to Justin. He drew an unsteady breath and continued. "The operative word in your theory is, 'coincidental.' Naturally, Robbie has been aware of my movements because I have included him in all my comings and goings. Whoever is behind the attempts on my life also apparently is making it his business to keep abreast of my travels. It is probably not too difficult to do so if he has the time and money and the will to keep a watch on both Robbie and Charles. Which is why, of course, your offer of a haven in the heart of London is so welcome. Tell me," he finished, obviously no more comfortable with the subject than Catherine had been, "how do you think Mariah and Lady Jane—and Adam—will respond to this startling volte-face on your part?"

As it turned out, both ladies were loud in their support of the notion. Even Adam, after a moment's hesitation, added his voice to the chorus of approval.

"I—that is we—All of us in the neighborhood will miss you, of course. We will miss all of you," he concluded, red-faced, glancing at Mariah and Lady Jane.

Indeed, thought Catherine, she rather thought it was not her own, precious self the good doctor would be missing. Adam had taken to visiting the Keep with even more frequency than usual, but now the object of his attentions appeared to be Mariah. He was ostensibly interested in the nostrums her cousin prepared in the stillroom, which had gained a reputation throughout the area for their curative powers. However, Catherine had noted that the two spent an inordinate amount of time simply wandering the gardens or seated on the terrace, their heads bent together in earnest conversation.

Lady Jane dispatched a note to her man of affairs, one Thomas Silchester, who responded in a suitably gratified manner that, although Lady Jane had had no need of his services in recent years, he was more than happy to arrange matters for her in a manner with which, he assured her, she would be pleased.

Thus, less than a week later, a large, elegant traveling coach wended its way into London, bearing the inhabitants of Winter's Keep. The coach was followed by a second vehicle, just as large if not quite so elegant, carrying Timkins, the butler, and Mrs. Jameson, the housekeeper, the only two servants from the Keep to make the journey. They were followed, in turn, by several wagons filled with the provisions deemed necessary by these worthies for a sojourn in the wilds of London.

The house chosen by Mr. Silchester was located in Caroline Street, a quiet cul-de-sac just off Bedford Square. They were greeted at the door by the gentleman himself, spare of face and figure and endowed with a pair of spectacularly bushy eyebrows, who, if he was surprised to note that the Lady Jane's household had been expanded to include a gentleman previously unknown to him, kept any untoward surmise to himself.

The ladies declared themselves enraptured with the house, which included a small garden between the rear entrance and the stables, and Justin noted with satisfaction that the location of the place was such that it was within a few minutes ride of such locales that might be necessary for him to frequent in his pursuit of his quest.

Justin also noted with approval the small army of footmen hired by Mr. Silchester. Not a one of them was under six feet tall, and they all looked as though they could have wrestled bears. In fact, it was more than likely they had been brought in from the ranks of the pets of the Fancy.

Justin's first night in the house on Caroline Street was a busy one. His first stop was a call on Charles, who spent the first ten minutes of the visit upbraiding Justin for his visit to Sheffield Court.

"You might at least have told me of your intention," he said, barely managing to keep his voice low enough to avoid an interruption from one of his staff. "I'll accept your conviction that St. John is not the man we're looking for. I never thought that dog would hunt, anyway. But to bolt down there without protection—"

"Robbie was on hand," retorted Justin unrepentantly.

"Yes, but you did not know that. Which brings me to another point," he continued. "I gave you explicit instructions that you were not to get in touch with Robbie. Now you tell me that you've been in contact with him almost from the day you returned to London. How do you expect me to help you if you do not follow orders? You always were an insubordinate whelp," he grumbled.

"Charles," said Justin gently. "You have been working on this for weeks now, with no appreciable results. No, no"—he held up a hand as a flash of pain shot into Charles's eyes—"I know you have been doing everything possible. However, I realize you have a great many other matters to attend to. I cannot expect you to devote your every waking minute to my problems."

"But, I have been doing just that!" exclaimed Charles. "I can do none other. My affection for you—" He halted abruptly, apparently embarrassed as would any good Englishman at almost giving vent to a mawkish display of emotion. "I have hardly stirred from my desk since Rivenchy escaped. That situation alone was enough to demand my complete attention, and when your name came up in the matter, I redoubled my efforts.

"And, in fact," he continued, "I have come up with something that may be useful. A very good friend of that private in the Rifles—the one who went missing just about the time your supposed corpse was found floating in a ditch—did come into some money in the days prior to his disappearance. He put it about that he had won it at cards, but it appears to have been a rather large amount to have been staked in a game among fellows of such low rank. Indeed, if any such sum had been won, the others in the game would surely have talked of it for days. Yet no one in the 95th seems to remember such a high flyer. The private, by the by, one Hieronymous Kemp, never did show up again."

"This is something like, Charles!" Justin exclaimed. "It's certainly the most valuable piece of information we've had to date on the Peninsular end of the situation."

"Yes, however, the fact that we don't want your enemy to know that we're investigating makes it difficult to do any extensive nosing around."

"Mmp. Perhaps I can manage something on my own, or Robbie might be able to—"

Charles stood abruptly. "For God's sake, don't involve Robbie any further."

Justin's eyes widened. "He's already involved, Charles. He's the only one who knows my situation, and he's the one man who could garner the facts about Private Kemp without arousing suspicion. I don't understand," he concluded, "why you are so reluctant to bring him into this. It seems to me, he's one of the few assets I have—besides you—in this whole mess." He hesitated. "Is there some reason you want to avoid using Robbie's expertise?"

"No, no," replied Charles hastily. "Of course not. I just don't want to see anyone else put in danger. And since he's your best friend—In addition, this is an extremely delicate matter. Robbie is the best of good fellows, of course, but he is not an operative, and it has been my experience that the more people you have mucking about in any given situation, the more chance there is of making mice feet of the whole thing."

"Yes, I see your point," said Justin softly. "But Robbie isn't just people."

The discussion between the two men continued for some minutes without resolution, and when Justin left Charles's house a few moments later, as usual by the French doors that led directly from his study, it was with his friend's admonitions still ringing in his ears.

As he made his way through the silent streets around Lincoln's Inn Fields toward a seamier section of town, however, he whistled thoughtfully. As much as he might decry the misgivings conveyed by Charles, he found it necessary to admit that yes, it appeared Robbie was not being completely honest with him. He would, of course, be willing to wager his life that Robbie had not lied, precisely, but a still, small voice within whispered that there was something his good friend was not telling him.

And, come to think of it, Justin thought with an unpleasant sinking sensation in the pit of his stomach, he was wagering his life, was he not?

Chapter Nineteen

"It seems to me the next logical step," said Robbie in an argumentative tone. The hour was much advanced, and he and Justin were seated in Robbie's dining parlor. Justin had arrived at Robbie's digs an hour or two ago, after leaving Charles's house for a visit to Jerry Church. From there, he embarked on a rather extended foray into several dubious establishments in London's Dock area, as well as in other equally unsavory neighborhoods. There, he had interviewed a scattering of individuals with whom he'd had dealings in the past on a variety of matters. He'd asked a few questions and made a few requests, and now he was glad, he reflected, to be away from the sights and smells of the city's underbelly.

The remains of a substantial meal lay scattered on the table before him, and two or three empty bottles lying abandoned before them gave evidence to the length and intensity of the discussion underway.

"But," said Justin for what seemed like the hundredth time, "you can't go haring off to the Peninsula. Since you're supposed to be here recuperating, you'd have to go in disguise, and that would mean all sorts of complicated arrangements—which would take time and money to put together."

"Not all that complicated, and not that much money," replied Robbie somewhat owlishly. "I can use the tinsmith's cover that you're so fond of. You already have the stuff for that, so it won't cost a penny. I can beg a place on Ben Jarvis's boat or with Clem or another one of our smuggler friends. There's a parcel of them that owe us favors."

"Yes, but—"

"No buts. Discovering that Roger Maltby was apparently paid handsomely and given false papers to get Rivenchy through English lines and that Private Kemp was handed over to a person or persons unknown just so he could be drowned in a ditch, could be the answer to everything. I need only a few minutes private conversation with Maltby. If I read him aright, he'll blow the whole whid with just a little persuasion."

Robbie bunched his fingers purposefully.

Justin sighed. "It's very tempting, to be sure. But it seems to me that if anyone should be bounding across the main to repair my fortune, it's me."

"Don't be daft. If anyone discovers you lurking about camp in disguise, you'd find your neck in a noose before the cat could lick her ear. If I'm discovered it would be, 'Oh, hullo, McPherson. What the devil d'you think you're got up as?' I might have a little explaining to do, but nothing I couldn't talk my way out of. In addition," he continued after a moment, "I have an interest in this, too, y'know. There's a traitor at large, and I wouldn't mind being the one to bring him to justice."

Justin fell silent, unable to think of a response to Robbie's argument.

"Right, then," concluded Robbie. "I'll be off tomorrow. I'll have my little chat with Maltby, and after he confesses what he's been up to, and who paid him to get up to it, I'll turn him over to Scovell. He can take it from there."

"Yes, and in the meantime, Jerry Church seems to think he's closing in on Cyrus Bentick as our main suspect. Says he's been behaving very strangely of late. It may be time I had a little chat with Cyrus. By God, Robbie!" said Justin exultantly. "It's possible that within a very short time, my name will be cleared."

Robbie sent him a shuttered look. "Yes, of course it will, laddie," he said at length, and once more Justin experienced the chill feeling that his friend was keeping something back.

The sun was gilding the tops of London's thicket of church steeples when he let himself through the garden door that led from the stables to the house in Caroline Street. To his surprise, he found Catherine waiting for him in the small breakfast room at the rear of the house.

"A fine time to be getting home," she greeted him, smiling. "The neighbors will think my cousin is a regular peep-o'-day boy."

"Good Lord! What are you doing up at this hour? Surely, you haven't been—"

"No, I have not been up all night waiting. I will confess, though, that I put in a restless night. When dawn came creeping into my room, I gave it up and came downstairs. You're just in time for breakfast," she said, gesturing him to a chair at the table.

"Coffee should be forthcoming any minute. Tell me, did you learn anything of value?"

Instead of following her direction, Justin moved to stand next to her, marveling at the lightening of his heart when he'd entered the room to discover her standing at the window. Her green eyes glowed in innocent invitation. She was garbed in some sort of filmy, silken thing, and she smelled like a sinner's dream of heaven.

Suppressing with difficulty an almost intolerable urge to gather her in his arms and kiss her till she was breathless, he turned away to take the seat indicated.

"Yes, I believe I may have. I set some inquiries in motion, and I'll know more in a few days."

He related the results of his visits to Charles and Robbie.

"Oh, Justin," she whispered. "Do you really think Robbie will pull it off?"

"Oh, I should think so. I don't believe Roger Maltby is the man to resist Robbie when he is in full persuasion mode."

Catherine eyed him thoughtfully. Despite his obvious fatigue, he stood straight and tall in a dark coat and pantaloons of an inconspicuous gray. How was it, she mused distractedly, that he managed to look so impossibly elegant in such unfashionable attire? For a moment, she reflected in some regret, she had thought he meant to kiss her. Why had he not? Particularly, since she had dressed in what she felt was her most becoming morning gown with just such an outcome in mind. For a self-declared scoundrel, he was remarkably slow to take advantage of a situation that had been virtually dished up to him along with his breakfast toast.

She shook herself, returning to the matter at hand. Evidently, she reflected, Justin still reposed full trust in his friend. Well, he certainly knew Robbie better than anyone—but she felt uneasy that Robbie had been allowed to take matters into his own hands—at least on the Peninsular end of the investigation.

"Did you uncover the evidence you had hoped to find of Cyrus Bentick's activities?"

Justin nodded noncommittally, and it seemed to Catherine that a shadow fell across his features. However, he said only, "I think I may have. I should know more in a day or two. Ah, did you say something about coffee?"

"Oh. Yes, it's so early the servants are not about yet. But I stopped in the kitchen and Mrs. Jameson was just getting out the breakfast china. We should—ah, here we are," said Catherine as one of the hulking footmen hired by Mr. Silchester lurched into the room bearing a large coffee urn. Behind him, a maid carried a tray laden with toast, muffins, and other assorted breakfast items.

"Cook said t'tell ye, mum," said the maid, gasping a little as she curtsied, "that the eggs and ham and kippers will be along in a moment."

"Thank you—Begley, isn't it?"

"Yes, mum. Thank ye, mum." The maid, having laid out the contents of the tray on the buffet table, curtsied once more and bustled from the room.

"And what are your plans for the day?" asked Justin, buttering a scone with a lavish hand.

"I am going to pay some morning calls," replied Catherine with visible satisfaction.

Justin paused, his scone suspended in midair. "Morning calls?" he echoed in surprise.

"Yes. I have maintained contact with one or two friends—real friends—who supported me throughout the scandal that erupted over my Francis Summervale episode. I wrote to tell them I was planning a visit to London, and they replied, insisting I come to see them while I'm here."

"Excellent." Justin smiled warmly. "I predict that by the end of the week you will be immersed in morning calls and balls and Venetian breakfasts and all the rest. You'll be promised to more routs and *soirées* than you can fit into your schedule."

Catherine's returning smile was tentative. "Your assessment may be a bit premature, but at least so far, I am glad to be back in Town." She paused. "Have you given any thought to your own future, once you've reclaimed your status as a law-abiding citizen."

Justin was startled. No, he had not. He had not been able to think past the mire of betrayal and humiliation in which he had been immersed for what seemed like an eternity.

"I suppose I shall go back to soldiering," he said slowly. "Although," he continued, an unconscious smile warming his eyes, "now that I am a man of property, I suppose I must give some thought to selling out—later—so that I may take up residence at Longbarrow." He turned impulsively to Catherine. "I can't wait to show it to you. I know you'll—" He halted abruptly. Good God, what did he think he was about? When this ugly mess had been settled, his first priority would be to remove himself from the tempting vicinity of Catherine Meade with all possible speed. "That is," he concluded stiffly, "I hope you—and Mariah and Lady Jane—will come to visit—someday."

Catherine, feeling his rebuff as though he had physically put up his hands to push her away, replied with great precision. "Yes, that would be very nice—someday."

An awkward silence fell between them, and Catherine almost sagged with relief when, a few minutes later, Mariah entered the room.

After an exchange of greetings, Justin yawned ostentatiously once or twice before bidding the ladies a courteous good morning and taking himself off to his bedchamber for a few hours' rest.

"Did he just come in?" asked Mariah curiously.

"Yes. He's been out combing the city for pieces of his puzzle."

"Poor man. What a dreadful situation to find oneself in."

"Yes," replied Catherine thoughtfully. "Particularly, when the pieces of the puzzle may include the involvement of his best friend."

"What!"

Briefly, Catherine related her suspicions of Robbie, to which Mariah responded in some indignation. She had met Robbie during his visit to Winter's Keep, and she had been favorably impressed with him at the time.

"Goodness!" she exclaimed. "I never heard of such treachery. What is Justin going to do about it?"

"Please, Mariah, we mustn't jump to conclusions. I may be entirely wrong about Robbie. I just wish Justin would at least consider the possibility that he may be—"

"Nurturing a viper in his bosom," finished Mariah dramatically.

"Well—yes," replied Catherine.

"At any rate, I hope we won't have to remain in London for a long period of time."

Catherine shot her cousin a surprised glance. "I thought you wanted to come. Really, my dear, if you wished to remain at home, you needed only to say so."

"Oh, no," said Mariah quickly. "I have long wished you to winkle yourself out of the hole you'd crept into at the Keep, and I've looked forward to a time when we could come down to town to enjoy the sights and the shopping, but—well—"

"Would your sudden attachment to the Keep have anything to do with a certain physician of our acquaintance?" Catherine asked archly.

"Oh, my, no!" Mariah flushed to the roots of her brown ringlets. "That is—oh, Catherine, do you mind? Adam and I—

that is, we have become much closer of late, and before we left the Keep—well, he asked if I would marry him."

In her agitation, Mariah had spilled coffee in her lap and now she addressed herself to it in some agitation.

"Mind!" Catherine set her own cup down with a clatter and reached to enfold her friend in an embrace. "Of course, I don't mind. I've been watching the good doctor fall under your spell and wondered when he would bring himself to the mark. Oh, Mariah, I am so happy for you! Have you set a date?"

"No. We thought next spring, perhaps. He wishes me to go to Scotland with him to meet his family." She laid a hand on her friend's arm. "Oh, Catherine, I'm so glad you're not overset by my news. I know that you and Adam—"

"Have been friends for a very long time," finished Catherine firmly. "And that's all we were. When Ann died, he turned to me for a time for solace and companionship. I think I became rather a habit with him—but that's all it was. Truly, Mariah. You and Adam are perfect for one another."

Mariah smiled mistily. "Thank you, O best of my relatives. I must say, I agree with you." She shot Catherine a sidelong glance. "In any event, I have no compunction about snatching Adam from under your nose, since that spot has been so admirably filled lately."

Catherine stared at her. "I beg your pardon?"

"Now, don't poker up. I'm talking about Lord Justin, of course, and there's no use your denying there's something going on with you two, the way you've been going about smelling of April and May."

Catherine forced herself to relax. She was not given to unburdening her soul to others, but this, after all, was Mariah. She smiled a little sadly.

"I'm not sure just what you'd call whatever is going on between Justin and me. He seems to regard any sort of commitment as nothing short of a prison sentence."

"Oh, but surely when he's cleared his name—"

"When he's disproved the charges against him, he plans to take up the life of a soldier again—alone."

"Oh. Well—" Mariah grinned. "You'll just have to change his mind, won't you?"

Catherine lifted her brows. "Do you think it will be that easy?"

"You love him, do you not?" Mariah replied, laughing.

Catherine hesitated before nodding slowly.

"And it's obvious he loves you. I see no problem here."

"You relieve my mind," responded Catherine dryly. She rose, feeling several years older than she had when she came into the room. "I must go now. Grandmama will be waking soon, and I promised I would take breakfast with her in her room."

Slowly mounting the stairs, Catherine reflected on her conversation with Mariah. Was her cousin right? Did Justin love her? Her heart lifted and seemed to turn over in her breast at the possibility. It returned to its customary position with a thud, however, as she contemplated his avowal that the brief embraces they had shared were only part of a few fleeting moments of pleasure. He had as much as said he wanted nothing more from her. He felt he was unworthy of love. Could she change his mind?

Catherine and Justin saw little of each other for the next few days. To Catherine's surprise, Justin's words proved true. She found herself embarked on what to one accustomed to a life of seclusion, was a dizzying round of social engagements and shopping. Her days were filled with trips to bookstores, museums, and modistes; her evenings were spent at glittering gatherings of the *ton*.

Justin's activities were almost solely confined to the nocturnal hours. He was now a regular customer of an establishment near the mouth of the Thames called by the singularly inappropriate name of the Angel, and he closeted himself by the hour with owners of certain small boats that made clandestine trips between the French and English coastlines. He was also spending an increasing amount of time with Jerry Church.

It was as he was setting out for this third visit in as many days to this gentleman when he encountered Catherine in the entrance hall of the house in Caroline Street, in company with Mariah and Lady Jane. She was in full evening garb in a gown of amber satin, trimmed with acorns embroidered in a glittering, golden thread, and the light from all the candles in the chamber seemed gathered in the waves of her honey-gold hair and in the depths of her jeweled eyes. She was so beautiful, thought Justin with a swift intake of breath, that it hurt just to look at her. However, he said only, "You're all looking very fine tonight. Where are you off to?"

Catherine laughed a little breathlessly. "Oh, Justin. We're going to the opera! Is it not famous? I have not attended in years! Lord and Lady Abingdon have asked us to share their box."

"Lord Whissenhurst has promised to be there as well, has he not?" asked Mariah innocently. "At least he said he would make it a point to attend if you were going to be there."

Justin had seen men grind their teeth, but had never had occasion to perform the act himself. Now he felt as though he must be fairly pulverizing his entire jawline. Pulling himself together, he bowed smoothly over the ladies' fingertips and murmured something suitably inane.

Later, as he rode Caliban through darkening streets toward Westminster, Justin wondered if he were not perhaps going mad. He admired Catherine Meade greatly. She was unlike any other woman he had ever met, and he was undoubtedly sexually drawn to her. But, when all was said and done, she meant nothing to him. She had been a welcome port in a storm, and he was surely indebted to her. He had already acknowledged the fact that he would miss her when he left her company to take up the threads of his life. In addition, he was pleased that she was renewing the fabric of her own existence. She deserved whatever happiness friends and beautiful clothes and the acceptance of the *ton* would bring her. And that certainly included the inevitable presence in her life of a male admirer or two—or even several.

Why, then, had Mariah's reference to Lord Whissenhurst come as such an unpleasant shock? Shock, hell. It had been as though something large and sharp had exploded just under his rib cage.

He stiffened in his saddle. This was ludicrous. Was he actually thinking of making some sort of declaration to Catherine? Declaration of what? His undying lust, at worst, he supposed. At best, his enduring affection. Yes, she would always have that. And that would have to be enough, for he had nothing else to give.

With a strong effort of will, he turned his thoughts away from Catherine and bent them toward Jerry Church. He pondered the revelations produced by the young man on his last visit. He had discovered that Cyrus Bentick, too, had evidently come in for a little windfall recently. He'd been seen about town squiring various high flyers, and a couple of weeks ago he had purchased a new, very stylish phaeton and pair. It now seemed certain that Cyrus Bentick was the man responsible for arranging Rivenchy's escape, as well as the attempts on the life of Major Lord Justin Belforte.

On the other hand, Bentick certainly did not appear to possess the intelligence to put together a scheme of such magnitude as the whisking away of a French officer of the highest rank out of an English encampment and through miles of enemy lines.

Absorbed in his thoughts, Justin almost missed the turning off Horseferry Lane, but in a few moments he pulled up before the bakery in Gardiners Lane. From habit, he assured himself that he was not observed before climbing the stairs to the second floor. The door opened at his first knock, and Jerry's cherubic face appeared around the jamb.

"What ho, Church?" queried Justin mildly. "Have you anything for me this fine evening?"

"As a matter of fact, guv'nor," replied Jerry, his voice cracking with suppressed excitement, "yes, I do. Something you'll find very interesting, indeed, or my name isn't Jeremy Church."

Chapter Twenty

Jerry urged his guest to a seat at a table cluttered with papers.

"Look here, Justin," he said eagerly. He picked up a bulky packet of papers, bound with tape. "I got these from Bentick's house."

"His house! Good God, you broke into his home?"

"Well—" Jerry grinned. "I wasn't having any luck with the material I found in his desk. Bentick went out of the country on one of his flying visits to the Peninsula recently, so I took the opportunity to do a little extra reconnoitering. And wait till you see what's in here! I spent almost all of one night copying it all from his own private papers."

Justin gaped disbelievingly at Jerry before slowly lowering himself into a chair at the table. Gingerly, he untied the tape and began to read.

"Good Lord!" he exclaimed after a few moments. He was apparently looking at a ledger. "These go back at least two years!"

" 'April 12, 1810—received, 300 guineas for services.

" 'June 7, 1811—received for expenses—packet sent to Borchambeau at Sinebucco.' Lord, that was just before Badajoz. My God, he was sending off Wellington's battle plans to—The devil! Borchambeau was Soult's aide, as I recall.

" 'September 25, 1811—200 pounds for trip to Brozas. See Maltby and others (Binns, Trooper, Budger)—need more money from Mac.' "

Justin froze for a moment. Mac? He hurried on, paging through a chronicle of treason written in Bentick's spidery hand. At last, he came to more recent events.

" 'June 30, 1812—for Simon Jarvis—12 guineas,' " he read. " 'Trip to Santander, July 3.' Mmm, there are several entries of payments to Jarvis, who, if I'm not mistaken is one of the smugglers hired frequently by the Depot.

" 'July 21—For Frank Borritch—200 pounds!' My God! That's the forger!"

"Yes! And look here," interposed Church. " 'Received from my man—500 pounds for expenses—Fry, Maltby etc.' Do those names mean anything to you?"

"Yes, indeed," replied Justin grimly. "At least—Maltby is known to me, but I don't know anything about a Fry. Perhaps he was the one who did in Private Kemp."

"Um," said Jerry. "And see here, again an entry noting more funds from 'my man.' Do you think he's the same person as the 'Mac' mentioned earlier? And look, another two or three more personal payments to Bentick. Justin, you were right, Bentick was not the organizer of the plot to free Rivenchy. He was working for someone else! Who the devil do you suppose this 'man,' or 'Mac' is?"

Justin could not speak. Only one name leaped immediately to mind, but such an assumption was unthinkable. Numb with shock, he thumbed through the rest of the file. Some of the pages were Bentick's personal notes on the progress of the plot, starting with the day he had been contacted by "my man" with the offer of a substantial amount of money for his help. Bentick, it seemed, enjoyed the good life, and he had invested unwisely to obtain the wherewithal for his pleasures. For years, he had gambled, drunk, and womanized far beyond his means, and now, as attested by other records shoved into Justin's hands by an excited Jerry Church, was deeply in debt.

The self-loathing initially expressed by Bentick soon gave way to long, rambling, exculpatory passages that sickened Justin. He scrutinized the papers in growing anguish. "Victory at Salamanca—Rivenchy captured!—Must be released or we all face ruin." Ah. So Rivenchy had known of the agents in place deep in the heart of Whitehall, spreading their ruinous tentacles. Justin could imagine the dismay that must have struck the conspirators at the thought that Rivenchy might reveal this knowledge.

Justin read further. "My man on-site, of course, near Salamanca now—says he will handle it."

It was a good two hours before Justin rose from his chair. Turning to Jerry, he put out a hand blindly. "I thank you for your efforts," he murmured, almost unable to form the words. "You may consider our debt canceled."

A few minutes later, he left Jerry's lodgings with the file tucked in his coat and made his way back to the house in Caroline Street. The ladies were not home yet from their night at the opera. Justin walked through the silent dwelling to the library, where he poured a liberal splash of wine from a handy decanter. Without bothering to light any of the candles in their wall sconces, he allowed himself to be guided by the fading light of the hearth to one of the room's comfortable leather chairs.

He gazed unseeing into the partial darkness. Somewhere, deep within him, exhilaration lurked. He had in his possession the means to redeem himself in the eyes of the world—at least, all of the world that he cared about. The men who served in His Majesty's Peninsular Army and those who commanded them— and one other, of course. She had said she believed him, but he relished the thought of putting proof in her hands. Would Wellington offer him an apology for his willing acceptance of his name as traitor? Probably not. Would Scovell welcome him back with open arms to the fraternity of intelligence gatherers? Possibly.

Withal, he was almost consumed by a profound sadness. Unthinkable as it seemed, it appeared that one of the very few people in the world whom he had thought was his friend had betrayed him. This man had been a light in the abysmal darkness that had been his life for so long. Now he must confront him with his treachery.

Justin did not know how long he sat in the gathering darkness of the library. The fire sputtered and died without his knowledge, and the clock on the mantelpiece chimed first one hour, then two. At last, he rose slowly and went to the desk. There, he lit a candle, and opened the packet once more. For another hour he read. As he neared the end of the file, his hands gripped the papers and his breath suddenly caught in his throat.

Dear God, he had it all now, and he knew an urge to lay his head on the desk and sob. Instead, retrieving pen and paper from a drawer, he scrawled a brief note. He folded it and, having written Catherine's name, withdrew a stick of wax from the drawer and sealed it, using the candle flame. He sat for another five minutes, staring at the letter before he finally stood and left the house. He was almost overcome with a weariness such as he had never known, but it was time to present what he had learned to Charles.

It was well after midnight when he rode into the mews in back of Portugal Street. Soundlessly, he dismounted in almost total darkness at the gate that led from the stable area to the small garden in back of Charles's house. He did not tether Caliban, but with a few murmured words of instruction to the stallion, he began to lead him through the gate.

He was given only a second's warning of his assailant's approach. In a silent lunge, the man was upon him. In the faint starlight that was the only illumination of the scene, the glitter of a knife blade swung close to Justin's cheek. Instinctively, he thrust his hand up in protection and felt a burning slash of pain along his arm.

The man instantly followed his advantage with another thrust. Again, Justin dodged, but the residual weakness from his earlier wound became immediately apparent. The knife again found its mark, this time in his shoulder. By now his defensive reactions, never far from the surface, had clicked into place, and pivoting on the ball of his foot, he delivered a stiletto kick to the man's mid-section.

The man staggered backward, but almost immediately bored in once more. Justin became aware his new wounds were making him even more sluggish. That kick should have disabled his assailant, but it had gone slightly wide. And now the man was on him again. This time, he grasped Justin from the back, clasping him about the windpipe with one arm while he pressed the knife to his throat with another. His vision darkening, Justin struggled in the man's grasp.

"No good your fightin' it, me lord," a voice whispered harshly in his ear. "I've got you this time. This time you're finished."

His strength waning, Justin lunged in the man's grip, but his effort was futile. Then, gathering the resources that had never failed him before, Justin whistled through his teeth. It was a pitiful effort, really, producing only a gasping squeak, but almost immediately a rushing sound filled the air, and a huge, dark shape hurled itself against the man. With a startled cry, he released Justin and staggered back.

Pressing his advantage, Justin flung himself against his assailant, grasping the wrist that held the knife. His would-be assassin was not large or well muscled, and ordinarily Justin would have had no difficulty in disarming him. However, the man was still in full possession of his faculties, while Justin was weakening rapidly. God, this must be finished in the next few minutes, or he'd be done for.

The two men battled in a ferocious silence. The knife moved closer and closer to Justin's breast, until he could feel its point pricking through his clothing to his skin. Summoning the last of his energy, Justin twisted the blade away from his own body. In one, final, almost maniacal burst of energy, he pushed with all his strength.

The man uttered a gutteral sound and sagged in Justin's grasp.

Gasping, almost unable to stand, Justin leaned against Caliban's sturdy flanks, willing some of the great beast's strength into his own body. He shrugged out of his coat. The slash on his arm was not deep, oozing a sluggish stream of blood. His shoulder, however, was another matter. The knife had thrust fairly deep, and he was bleeding profusely. It looked, however, as though the weapon had missed any vital spots. With a marked sense of déjà vu, he unwrapped his neck cloth with one hand and pressed it to the wound.

He examined the motionless figure at his feet, turning it over with the toe of his boot.

"Snapper Briggs, I presume," he murmured without emotion.

In the house in Caroline Street, Timkins swung the front door wide to welcome the return of his three ladies.

"Oh, that was lovely!" exclaimed Mariah, handing her cloak to the butler.

"Yes, it was, wasn't it? Just lovely," echoed Lady Jane.

"I do so enjoy Mozart," said Catherine, removing her own cloak. "I have never seen a performance of *The Magic Flute*, however. Was not Brimonda perfectly exquisite as Pamina?"

"Oh, ho," retorted Mariah with a grin. "I did not think you were paying much attention to the stage. What was going on in the box seemed of much greater interest to you."

Catherine flushed, and Lady Jane, observing her, chuckled.

"Indeed, Lord Whissenhurst seemed to find the conversation—or perhaps something else—in the box of equal fascination."

"If you two are going to start imagining things every time I speak a few words to a gentleman, you're going to have a busy time of it before we return home." Catherine could hear the smile in her voice as she spoke. Really, if truth be told, she *had* flirted with the rather weedy Lord Whissenhurst, but it was somewhat in the line of returning to an old game that one has not played for years. It was always a pleasure when one regained a skill long assumed gone forever.

It meant nothing, of course. Indeed, she was not sure she would recognize Lord Whissenhurst if she were to meet him on the street the next day, for all evening long another face had been superimposed on his features. How would Justin look in full evening dress? she wondered. Nothing less than magnificent, she would wager.

She hoped he would not be out all night again on his quest. He claimed to be completely healed from his wound, but, talk as he would, it was obvious his journey to his old home had set him back. The stress of his confrontation with his brother, even though it had turned out well, in addition to his brush with death in a burning bedroom, had all taken their toll. Tomorrow, she told herself firmly, she would insist that Justin spend the day resting.

"Are you coming up, Catherine?"

She turned to observe Mariah at the staircase, her foot on the first stair. Lady Jane was ahead of her and was already halfway to the next floor.

"Yes," replied Catherine, "I must stop in the study first. I left the book there lent to me by Squire Wadleigh. It's a copy of Pryne's thesis on marling, and I want to go over a little of it in my chamber before I retire."

"Good heavens, child!" exclaimed Lady Jane. "Can you not leave the Keep behind you? You should not be wasting time in London reading up on agricultural methods. Now, come up and get your beauty sleep."

"In a moment, Grandmama." Smiling, Catherine waved the two ladies on their way upstairs and proceeded toward the study. The volume she sought lay on the desk, but it was not until she had picked it up and was about to turn away when she noticed the folded paper on which was inscribed her name.

Opening it, she glanced at the signature and received an odd, tingling shock when she recognized Justin's name. It seemed strange that she had never seen his handwriting before and thus had not recognized it on the front of the letter. She scanned it quickly.

Dear Lord, she breathed when she had come to its end. Justin had acquired the proof he needed to clear his name! Her eyes went to the letter again. "On my way to Charles's . . ." she murmured. Why, he must be speaking to Mr. Rutledge right at this very moment. Perhaps by tomorrow, Justin would be in a position to reveal the fact that he was alive and that he was no traitor.

She hugged the thought to her, her joy dimmed only slightly by the knowledge that if all this were to come to pass, he would be leaving soon for Longbarrow to claim his inheritance. Well, she would face that when the time came. In the meantime—

Her reverie was abruptly shattered by a sharp rapping on the front door. She knew Timkins had retired immediately after their arrival home and would not hear the knock in the bowels of his butler's sanctuary, so she hastened across from the study to open the door herself.

"Robbie!" She cried in astonishment. "What are you doing here?"

She stared dazedly at him. She was sure Justin had told her that his friend was headed for Spain to discover what he could about Roger Maltby's activities.

Robbie brushed past her into the house without waiting for her invitation. "Good evening, Catherine," he said breathlessly. "Sorry to bother you so late. Is Justin here? I must speak to him."

His agitation was obvious, and his face, she noted, was white, almost pasty, even in the ruddy glow of the candles.

"N-no," she replied uncertainly. "He—he's out."

Robbie muttered something unprintable. "Do you know where he went? I must find him. I've discovered—that is, I have to tell him—The devil take it! Where is he?"

For a long moment, Catherine simply gaped, her mind seething. He was Justin's best friend in the world, but she did not trust him. If Justin were here, surely he would tell her to reveal to Robbie that he had gone to see Mr. Rutledge. On the other hand, if what she suspected was true, Robbie McPherson was the last person in the world to be told where Justin was at this moment.

"Well?" asked Robbie impatiently.

"I—I don't—" she began.

"No, I don't suppose he would tell you," he interposed. "Damnation! Sorry." He ran thick fingers through sandy hair that was already standing on end.

"Well," he continued, "I know one place he will no doubt stop. I'll go to Charles's house now and just wait for him."

"Charles!"

"Yes, Charles Rutledge. You've no doubt heard Justin speak of him."

"Yes, but—"

"I'm sorry, I have no time to speak further," Robbie said in a strained voice. "It is imperative that I find Justin as soon as possible."

"Oh, but—" Catherine put out a hand, but Robbie was gone, slamming the door behind him.

For a few moments, Catherine paced the hall floor in an agony of indecision. Everything in her insisted that Justin would be in grave danger if Robbie were to run him to earth at Mr. Rutledge's house. She must do something—but, what? At last, she drew a sudden, deep breath.

There was no way she could stop Robbie from finding his quarry, but she would, by God, do her best to prevent harm from coming to Justin.

Pausing only to throw her cloak about her shoulders, she fled toward the rear of the house in the direction of the stables.

In the mews behind Charles's house, Justin turned away from the lifeless body of Snapper Briggs. With Caliban at his heels, Justin entered the garden gate and proceeded toward the house. Making his way to the long doors that fronted Charles's study, Justin peered through the glass. He observed his friend, as usual, bent over his desk, all the candles in the room extinguished except for the few that stood about his immediate work area.

With a gesture, he bade Caliban to wait, and without ceremony he pushed open the door and stepped inside. He did not speak as Charles's head jerked up, but merely flung himself into the nearest chair.

"Justin!" Charles rose so abruptly that his chair was thrown to the floor behind him. "What—? My dear boy, you are hurt!"

He hastened to Justin's side and gingerly removed the reddening neck cloth from the younger man's wound. "Good God, what's toward?"

"It is not serious, Charles. My arm has already stopped bleeding, and I think, if you will lend me your kerchief, I can stop up the nick in my shoulder."

Charles produced a linen handkerchief from his pocket and unwound his own neck cloth as well. Carefully, he bound the kerchief in place around Justin's shoulder. "It's more than a nick," he growled. "Let us hope we have staunched the flow. Now," he said, pouring a glass of brandy for Justin and seating himself nearby. "Tell me what happened."

"I had a little run-in with Snapper Briggs," replied Justin levelly. "Apparently, he was watching your house, waiting for me to show up. Again, apparently, he knew I would come eventually."

"And you believe it was he who was responsible for the other attacks? I don't know any Snapper Briggs. Who the devil could have set him on you?"

"I believe I have the answer to that as well." He smiled a trifle painfully. "You see, quite a bit has happened since I last saw you."

Charles leaned forward in his chair. "Tell me."

Justin hesitated. "To begin with, I have been in touch with Jerry Church for the last week or so."

"Jerry Church." Charles rolled the name on his tongue. "I know him, do I not? Yes." His eyes opened wide. "By God, Justin, Jerry Church works on the Top Floor. He's some sort of clerk!"

"Yes."

"But why would you go to a stranger there, when you know I have been working on your case? Good Lord, Justin, how could you trust some minor functionary you don't even know. He may be preparing to turn you in even now. I don't—"

"I thought it necessary," said Justin quietly, "for a number of reasons. And my decision seems to have been proven wise. Jerry was able to provide me with some extremely valuable information. In fact—" Justin drew a long breath. "He has given me the answer, Charles. I know now who is the traitor in the Depot and the real traitor in the Rivenchy affair. And a bloody disgusting mess it is, too."

Charles's jaw dropped open. "You know? You know everything?"

Justin nodded. "It appears we were right. Bentick is a spy. He's been arranging for the shipment of information to the French for a couple of years now, and it was he who paid a forger to draw up identification documents for Rivenchy's escape."

"My God!" whispered Charles. "The man has worked under me for almost ten years! I can't believe this."

He sat down and drew a shaking hand over his brow.

"There is more," said Justin quietly. "Bentick was not working alone. In fact, he was merely a pawn. Another man supervised his efforts, and that man was in direct contact with the French."

"My God," said Charles again, rising abruptly. "Do you have any idea who—?"

"Bentick did not put a name to the man."

It seemed to Justin that Charles sagged at the news.

"However, in the file obtained for me by Jerry Church, Bentick listed names of contacts in the Peninsula. A few were underlings, but most were men from whom he took orders. At the top of this list was someone to whom Bentick referred as—as Mac."

"Mac!" repeated Charles explosively. He sat down again, heavily. "Dear Lord, Justin, I was afraid of this. I did not wish to say anything before, because I know of your long-standing affection for Robbie McPherson, but there were several indications—known only to me—that pointed directly to him. My dear boy, I am so very sorry."

"As am I, Charles." Justin's voice was a harsh rasp. "I, too, had perceived several signposts that led to the probability of Robbie's guilt. The sudden rise in his standard of living, the fact that it was eventually borne to me—as well as—to someone else—that he was hiding something. And Bentick's reference to 'Mac,' of course, but—" He drew a deep, shuddering breath. "I came to realize eventually that I was quite wrong in my suspicions. Not that those suspicions ever became full-blown. I know Robbie rather better than that. Of course," he added, in a barely audible tone, "I thought I knew you, too."

Charles, in the act of bringing his glass to his lips, paused. "I beg your pardon?"

Justin could hardly form the words. "I told you Charles, I know everything. It's over."

Slowly, Charles set his glass on the table at his elbow. He leaned forward in his chair, and his gaze narrowed. "Do I hear you aright, Justin? Are you saying . . . ?"

Justin sighed. "You know, Charles, when I visited you after my return from the Continent, one of the first things I noticed about this room was the absence of the clock that used to hang above the mantel."

His expression one of bewilderment, Charles said, "What? What has that to do with anything? I told you—"

"I know what you told me. It was out for repairs. However, I notice it is still missing. Those repairs are taking a rather long time, are they not?"

"Justin, I don't know what the devil—"

"And the Venus. Do you think if we were to retire to your drawing room, we would find it there—among a classical grouping? I think not."

Charles drew his hand over his face, once again trembling badly. But now, his face was heavily bedewed with perspiration.

"Justin, if you're saying what I think you're saying, I—well, I can't believe you would think such a thing of one who loves you like a son."

Justin winced. "Oh, God, Charles, please don't. I can hardly believe it, either, but yes, I am saying that it is you who are the traitor who has been passing secrets to the French for the past two years and the man who arranged for Rivenchy's escape. And it is you who has been systematically trying to kill me for the past month."

Chapter Twenty-one

For a long moment, the only sound in the room was the muted crackle of the small fire in the hearth and the soft rush of the breeze as it pushed in the curtains of the long windows of Charles's study.

Charles's demeanor had changed somewhat in the last few minutes. He had settled back in his chair, a small twisted smile on his face. His eyes were those of a swordsman fighting for his life.

"And on what do you base this absurd accusation?" he asked, all avuncular inquiry, an adult ready to listen to the prattlings of a child.

"Oh, I cannot say I attached any particular importance to the gradual disappearance of your knickknacks. In fact, with all that I learned from Jack Nail's surveillance and my own prowlings, my thoughts were—most unwillingly—beginning to turn to Robbie. Then, something you said awhile back clicked in my brain. You see, you told me that you had scarcely left your desk for weeks—since before Salamanca. Yet St. John told me that when my father tried to see you at Horse Guards, you were away—possibly, out of the country."

Charles waved a hand. "Well, of course, I may have been absent once or twice—It is necessary for me to visit some of our positions in Spain from time to time."

"But you were not in Spain, Charles," said Justin softly. "Jerry checked your whereabouts and reported that you had no journeys scheduled at all over the last month or so. A few questions, however, to the smugglers we use for clandestine dashes across the Channel revealed that you went across to Opporto in Portugal, just a few days before Rivenchy's escape and returned less than a week afterward."

Justin rose and began to pace the floor. "One or two of these gentlemen," he said meditatively, "also mentioned that you had for many months been making trips to Rambouillet, not far from Paris. I would be willing to wager that no one on the Top Floor, not even Wilkerson, knew anything about those."

Charles said nothing, but he seemed slightly diminished as he listened intently.

"Getting back to the tiresome subject of your missing possessions, once I learned of your mysterious excursions, I set Jack Nail to scouring all the shops in London that specialize in expensive curios. He, or one of his men, discovered that just such a clock had been brought in to one of those establishments by a gentleman whose description closely matches yours. It was sold not long afterward. The shopkeeper reported that the same gentleman had brought several other items to him, including a bronze Venus, just like the one supposedly gracing your drawing room at this very moment.

"I then managed some discreet inquiries at the gaming houses that you've been frequenting for so many years. You have enjoyed more than a flutter in them, Charles, most unsuccessful. You've squandered thousands of pounds, and your losses had increased alarmingly over the last few years. In short, you brought yourself to point-non-plus."

Charles rose from his chair to face Justin. "And from this flimsy fabric of supposition and coincidence you hope to persuade my colleagues at the Depot—men who have known and trusted me for decades—that I am a traitor?" He pointed a finger that trembled only slightly. "What about Bentick's reference to Mac? That seems to me a clear implication of your very good friend."

"Indeed," said Justin quietly, "I wondered about that myself until I recalled that your family originally came from Scotland. In fact, I remember at least two of your colleagues who jokingly referred to you as 'MacTavish.'"

Charles turned on his heel and walked to his desk, where he seated himself once more.

Justin steepled his fingers before him. He was finding his attitude of casual elucidation more and more difficult to maintain. "There is one more thing, Charles. I told you that Bentick had not named you in his file, but I was not being quite truthful. In the very last paragraph, he details the successful completion of the mission to get Rivenchy back to the French, and he speaks of my being blamed for the whole thing as well as a congratulatory note on my supposed death. He concludes with the words, 'I knew my man, Rutledge, would make it all right.'"

He waited for a response, but Charles, it seemed, had nothing to say.

Justin continued, his voice hard, "I shall be going to Wilkerson at the Depot tomorrow morning. Bentick, I should imagine, will be questioned shortly afterward, and I fancy it will not be difficult to persuade him to reveal all. On the other end of the situation, Robbie is probably exerting his best efforts at this moment to winkle the facts from Roger Maltby. I do not think he will fail. You are rolled up, Charles."

Charles's gaze fell to the surface of his desk, where, as if he had not heard Justin at all, as if his attention were solely directed to the work on his desk, he picked up the various papers scattered about. He gathered them into a neat pile, and, moving his ink bottle, pen, and the other small impedimenta that lay at hand, he arranged them with precision. At last, he looked up to face Justin.

"You are right," he said in a voice Justin had never heard. It was the voice of a very old man. "I have always enjoyed gambling, and after Mary died, it became my solace and my pleasure. What had once been a venial habit grew to an obsession; one that was bringing me to ruin without my even realizing it."

He smiled mirthlessly. "The clock was not the first thing to go, but it was the one that brought me the most sadness to part with. It had been a gift from Mary on the occasion of our fifth wedding anniversary.

"It was, oh, almost three years ago that I was first approached by the French. The man who contacted me was an old adversary, and our relationship had grown to one of mutual respect and even friendship. Jean asked for a specific bit of information, something quite innocuous, really. They wanted a list of ordnance depots in this country. I knew there were several other sources from which they could gather that information, and I could not see that it would be of significant benefit to them, so I passed along what I knew. I was paid an inordinate sum of money for this assistance, and in a few weeks Jean was back. Again, he wanted to know something that he could probably have found out elsewhere, and it seemed so harmless that I was able to acquiesce with a relatively clear conscience.

"The third time, however, Jean asked me about troop movements. I knew such information could have devastating consequences for Wellington, but by now I was snared. You see—" Charles picked up a letter opener and balanced it idly on his fingertips. "I had made the inexcusably stupid blunder of writing out that ordnance list in my own hand. I was thus ripe for blackmail. I could not face ruin—to say nothing of hanging—so—"

"So you sold out your country," interposed Justin, his voice a barely intelligible growl.

Charles flinched, but his gaze remained steady. "Yes."

"From there," he continued, "it was a downward spiral. I kept providing them with information—the occasional dispatches, memoranda from various conferences, a change in troop strength here or there—sometimes delivered to a courier here in London, sometimes taken by me across the Channel. Then one day, Cyrus Bentick came to me." Charles laughed, a bitter sound that hung in the room like a mourner's pall. "He was ordinarily the most obsequious of unpleasant little toads, but on this day his demeanor bordered on the insolent, and he wore a cocky smile. He virtually demanded a private meeting with me, and as we lunched at a chophouse not far from Whitehall, he informed me that he had in his possession a piece of paper that could bring about my downfall. He had found a message from one of my French contacts in a coat I had left hanging on a hook in my office. It appears the smarmy worm was in the habit of slipping his hands into other people's pockets when the opportunity presented itself."

"Behavior far beneath your standards, of course," said Justin dryly.

Charles flushed. "At any rate," he continued, "I do not know whether I was more dismayed or relieved when he told me he would not reveal what he had learned if I would allow him to be my assistant. It appears, Bentick, too, was in financial difficulties, and he saw little problem in making a profit from his position in the Depot.

"Things went smoothly for a long while. With Bentick's help, I was able to accomplish even more for my 'friends' across the Channel. They were most generous in their appreciation, and I was soon on a solid financial footing once again. However"—he looked up to gaze at Justin from anguished eyes—"once I was brought back to that condition, Justin, if you think that my conscience did not trouble me, you are mistaken. I was in an agony of remorse. Daily, I thought about confessing all and taking whatever punishment might be meted out to me."

"But you just could not bring yourself to the mark," said Justin harshly.

"No." Charles's voice was barely audible. "But I did try to draw back from the morass of deceit and lies I had created. I began providing information that was of far less value than my previous offerings. The French realized almost immediately what I was doing, and they made threats. I realized that if I were not to be exposed, I had to come up with something of real use to them. And then disaster struck." Charles tapped the letter opener on the desktop. "We learned that Rivenchy had been captured at Salamanca. I had met the man on several occasions during my forays to France with information. I knew he was cognizant of my entire operation here. If he were to reveal anything of my doings, everything would be over for me.

"I decided to try to effect his escape, for in doing so I would also redeem myself in the eyes of the French. I told Bentick to obtain false identification papers for the general. Then, rather than allow Bentick to meddle in the project, I went to Spain myself. There, disguised as a shoemaker, I made my arrangements. And meticulous arrangements they were, too. Everything was taken care of, from Rivenchy's flight through English lines, accompanied by Roger Maltby, to securing the escape route by sending an order that the bridge at Huerta be abandoned. Then I learned that Wellington, with that damnable efficiency of his, had thought to assure that the bridge remain secure."

"How very inconvenient for you, to be sure," murmured Justin.

Carefully, Charles lay the letter opener on the desk. "Yes, and then I learned that you were the officer ordered to see to that little matter. Justin, I—I truly did not wish any harm to come to you. I arranged that you would be captured but—you see, I wanted to make it seem as though I were handing an additional gift to the French—one of great value, as witnessed by the file on your background I provided for them, augmented by papers I had stolen from your tent—I also arranged that you would be allowed to escape. It was all very difficult," he said earnestly.

"Surely, you do not expect my gratitude."

"No," returned Charles shortly, "of course not. At any rate, Maltby, who had been following your progress at a distance, saw to it that you were almost dispatched on your return to camp from your imprisonment."

"It appears I owe Maltby a considerable debt," interposed Justin, his gaze slashing into Charles's. "One that I hope to address very soon. My refusal to cooperate in his scheme must have come as an unpleasant shock to him—and to you."

Once again, Charles's gaze fell. "You were the obvious choice as scapegoat for Rivenchy's escape. When you disappeared, it was imperative that you be, er, replaced."

"So you—or was it Maltby, found a ringer in the person of Private Kemp and arranged to have him killed. A little sloppy, perhaps, but not bad in such a pinch. And then I showed up here in England. You must have had a very busy time of it, Charles, making plans for my demise."

"No!" Charles almost cried out the word. "I had nothing to do with that, Justin. I promise. It was all Bentick. I wanted matters to take their own course. If you were brought to trial, you might have at least a chance of being exonerated, without my—activities—being revealed."

"Thoughtful of you."

"But Bentick insisted. He said he was going to go ahead with plans to have you—eliminated whether I cooperated or not. It was he who contacted Jasper Naismith to have you killed. I assume this Snapper Briggs was Naismith's tool. He was watching Sheffield Court when you showed up to confront St. John, and it was he who was responsible for the fire. Believe me, Justin, I had no part in any of it."

Justin stared at him levelly. "But you could have stopped it, Charles."

Charles's head sank against his breast. "Yes," he said in a low voice. "I could have stopped it."

He looked up from beneath his brows at Justin. "What do you intend to do now?"

"As I said, I intend to go to Wilkerson." As he spoke, the fleeting thought brushed through Justin's mind that, though the breeze that wafted through the study's open window was warm, he felt chilled to the core. "It is my intention to bring you to his home now. It's late, but I expect he will not mind being awakened for a matter such as this."

"There is another option," said Charles slowly. Justin said nothing, but stared at him with lifted brows. "I could leave here tonight, and by tomorrow morning I could be on my way to the West Indies to a snug plantation I own there." He stood. "I must say the latter plan holds a much greater appeal to me."

With an air of reluctance, he reached inside his waistcoat pocket and drew out a small pistol. Justin made no response, but felt his muscles tense reflexively.

"Foolish boy," said Charles with an inutterably sad smile. "Did not the fact that I was prepared to see you killed tell you that my affection for you is not strong enough to overcome my venality? I might have taken a bullet for you, Justin, were the circumstances to arise, but I cannot face disgrace and ruin for you. Did you think otherwise? I thought I had trained you better."

He raised the pistol so that it was level with Justin's breast. "I must—"

"No, you must not, Charles," said a voice from the window. Justin jerked spasmodically, and Charles spun about.

"McPherson!" Charles all but shouted.

"Robbie!" gasped Justin simultaneously. "Robbie, what are you doing here?"

"I wish everyone would stop asking me that," said Robbie pettishly, moving inside the room to stand before the windows, the pistol he held pointed at Charles. "What happened was," he said to Justin, "when I reached the coast, I hired Ben Jarvis to take me across. Before we set off, he imparted some extremely interesting information. It seems our Charles"—he waved the pistol—"hired him a couple of weeks ago to take him to Opporto on the Portuguese coast. He was wearing a black wig, and his skin was darkened—and it seems he was dressed in a most peculiar fashion. It was the sort of outfit a Spanish peasant might wear, made of homespun or some such. He was carrying a pack, and when it fell open for a moment, Ben discerned that it was apparently full of scraps of leather, some small hammers and awls, and a quantity of tiny nails. In short, Charles was got up as a shoemaker!

"Well, it hit me then. Shortly after the victory at Salamanca, I noticed a shoemaker who had set up shop in the street just outside a local cantina. He caught my eye because of his marked resemblance to Charles. At the time, I thought my wits must be addled, but when Ben finished his little tale, I realized it could only mean one thing—that Charles was the man we've been seeking. And," Robbie concluded, casting a darkling glance at Charles, "it appears I was right."

"Indeed you were, old friend," said Justin dully.

"Right, then," said Robbie, lifting the pistol again in a menacing fashion. "Let us just tie up this rascal and haul him off to the nearest magistrate."

"I don't think—" began Justin, only to be interrupted by two separate but equally startling occurrences.

First, Caliban burst through the open doors of the study. He careened immediately into Robbie, who hurtled forward, dropping his pistol. Next, in Caliban's wake, Catherine ran into the room, brandishing a large, unwieldy horse pistol, which she was obliged to clasp in both hands. With a harrowing yell that would have done credit to Boudicca, she rushed at Robbie and delivered a crushing blow to the back of his head with the pistol.

As Robbie sank to the floor like a felled oak, Charles stared, mouth agape, in understandable astonishment at the presence of upward two thousand pounds of horse in his study. His hands dropped to his side, his pistol hanging limp.

Gathering together what little presence of mind remained to

him at the moment, Justin grasped at Caliban's bridle, bringing him to an immediate and docile halt.

"Catherine!" His voice emerged in a croak.

But, Catherine ignored him. Instead she brought up her horse pistol to aim it waveringly at Robbie. "You viper!" she spat, uncaring that her victim could not hear her. She turned to Justin, and her eyes widened. "Justin, you are injured!"

As she spoke, her weapon sagged in her hand, and the next moment, a deafening report filled the room as it discharged. Since the pistol had by now faltered in its aim, the ball buried itself harmlessly in the carpet a foot or two away from where Robbie lay supine.

Catherine screamed, and scrambling over Robbie's inert form, flew to Justin's side.

"Dear Lord, Justin, I did not mean . . . I did not even think to bring a weapon with me! I found this in the carriage. What happened?" She swung fiercely back to Robbie, who was beginning to stir painfully. "Did you do this? By God, I wish I *had* killed you!" She raised the pistol again. "Perhaps I'd better try again."

Gently, Justin removed the pistol from Catherine's grip. "Not with that weapon, you won't. It only holds one shot, you know. At any rate, my dear, Robbie is not responsible for this, and I am quite all right. I'm afraid you have struck down an innocent man."

Catherine's eyes grew round with astonishment. "Robbie? Innocent? Oh, no, Justin, you do not understand. He was coming here to kill you!"

"On the contrary, my dear young woman." It was Charles who spoke from behind the desk, where he had taken refuge, still holding his pistol tight in his hand. "I am the villain of the piece. Robbie simply came to warn his friend of the danger he was—is—in from me."

"You—you are Charles Rutledge?" Catherine stammered. Charles nodded. "But I don't understand."

"It was Charles, Catherine," said Justin wearily. "It was Charles all along."

"Oh. Oh, dear God," whispered Catherine in growing comprehension. "Oh, Justin, I have been such a fool. I've ruined everything."

"It appears so," said Charles, his mouth contorted in what might have been called a smile. "As I was just informing Justin, when I was so, er, rudely interrupted, I have no intention of simply being led to my doom. It was singularly foolish of him to think I would allow him to beard me in my den, so to speak."

"Actually," said Justin, with an air of calm that went only as deep as the nerve endings that quivered beneath his skin, "I was fairly sure you would act just as you are doing. I am aware that you always carry that little pistol. However, I am banking rather heavily on the assumption that you will not use it on me."

"But why not? I did not cavil at allowing Bentick to have you snuffed."

"No, but there is a vast difference between ordering the job done and doing it oneself. Frankly, Charles, though you have stooped far lower than I would have ever thought possible of you, I do not think you have the stomach for murder, especially mine." Justin lifted his hand, palm upward. "Give me the pistol, Charles."

A very long moment ensued, during which everyone in the room seemed to cease breathing. Charles and Justin remained motionless, each staring unblinkingly into the other's eyes. At last, something inside Charles crumpled. His shoulders hunched, and he leaned against the desk as though exhausted. Justin took a step toward him, then halted abruptly. He said nothing, but simply stood motionless, his eyes questioning, as though waiting.

"I—I'm sorry, Justin," Charles whispered brokenly. "I am—so very—sorry."

"I know, Charles. I am, too." And indeed he was, thought Justin. For the whole bloody, ugly, sad mess. His gaze still held that of Charles, still waiting for what he knew was to come.

He turned slightly, toward Robbie. "Get Catherine out of here," he ordered in a desperate whisper.

But he was too late.

In a swift, odd, flicking motion, as though he had practiced it many times, Charles lifted the pistol once more, this time to his temple. In the next instant, he fired, and slumped to the floor at Justin's feet.

Chapter Twenty-two

As Justin bent over Charles, he was dimly aware of Robbie behind him, hustling a sobbing Catherine out of the door through which she had come. When he thought later of the remainder of the evening, he remembered only that, although everything occurred with bewildering speed, time itself seemed to slow, crawling in a painful blur.

A couple of footmen, wakened by the sound of gunfire, burst into the room, followed a few moments later by the neighborhood watchman, brought by the same noise. After that, there were constables and a hail of questions and the appearance not long afterward of Sir Henry Wilkerson, summoned by one of the magistrates. It was dawn before matters were sorted into a semblance of coherence and Charles's body was removed to an upstairs bedroom.

"Bless my soul!" exclaimed Sir Henry to Justin, as the two, followed by Robbie and Catherine finally left the house. Sir Henry was a tall man, rotund and ruddy, with a deceptively simple face. "I am exceedingly pleased, of course, that you are returned to us, my boy, your reputation cleansed. However, I cannot fully express my astonishment and my great sadness at the story that has unfolded here. Charles Rutledge! Who would have thought . . . ?" He trailed off into a dismal silence.

"Certainly not I," replied Justin heavily. "And now, sir, if you are through with us for the moment, I believe I must return my friends to their homes." He gestured toward Robbie, who stood with a protective arm about Catherine.

"What?" Sir Henry roused himself from his unpleasant reflection. "Oh. Yes, of course. I expect it will be a week or so before we can put an inquiry together. You will all make yourselves available, will you not? Good. Afterward"—this to Justin—"you may return to your unit, although . . ." He frowned. "It would be better, of course, if we could keep this whole matter quiet, but with all the commotion that has already attended the affair, you will be very much in the public eye. Thus, these events will certainly destroy your value to us as an undercover operative. Perhaps you will wish to sell out and rest on your laurels. Oh, yes," he said with a smile. "For you will be a hero, you know."

"What?" asked Justin blankly. He felt as though he were wrapped in a layer of thick, damp wool. Even the fact that he would now be able to take his place again among the living, and that he was free of the taint of treason did not serve to lift the fog of misery that surrounded him, penetrating his very bones.

"Why, of course," continued Sir Henry jovially. "You are an innocent man exonerated. The public loves that, and you have unmasked a traitor at considerable risk to your own person."

"Oh," Justin responded dully. Then he simply stood there, staring blindly about as though searching for something.

Robbie, at a nudge from Catherine, stepped forward.

"Right, Sir Henry," he said. "Thank you for appearing so promptly. We shall await your summons, of course, but in the meantime—it's been a very long evening."

Sir Henry sighed. "Quite right, my boy. Good-bye, then." He waved benignly as he mounted the carriage awaiting him in front of Charles's house.

Justin turned and as his gaze lighted on Catherine, he seemed to come to himself. Reaching for her hand, he clasped it tightly while Robbie hastened him toward the other carriage that waited in the street. He did not let go as he assisted Catherine into its interior, nor did he release her during the short journey to the house in Caroline Street.

Catherine exchanged a worried glance with Robbie, sitting opposite them in the carriage. Despite the chaos the events of the waning night had generated within her, her sole concern was for the man next to her. He had been through a living nightmare during the past few weeks, and now to learn that the man who had been friend, mentor, and substitute father to him was responsible for all the woes that had befallen him . . . Justin was a strong man, she told herself, but how could he possibly survive as a whole person after this upheaval in his life?

And, she wondered dismally, would there be a place for her in that life?

Responding to Justin's crushing grip on her hand, she tightened her fingers around his. Lifting her head to face Robbie, she smiled uncomfortably. "Robbie, I am so sorry for—well, you know . . ."

Robbie grinned. "For suspecting me of treason? And of trying to do away with my best friend?"

"Yes, and bludgeoning you on the back of the head. I don't know how I could have thought you guilty of such terrible things." She flushed. "And then to go peltering off to Justin's rescue, when he already had the situation well in hand." She turned to Justin, who was still staring ahead of him, unseeing. "I am so sorry for my maladroit interference, Justin. Justin?" she repeated, when he made no response.

He started, his head jerking around to look at Catherine. For the first time since they had left Charles's house, a spark of animation lit his gaze. "Actually, the memory of your rushing to my supposed rescue with no thought as to the possible consequences to yourself will be a highlight of my declining years." Disregarding Robbie's presence, he lifted her fingers to his lips. "I forgot to ask you. Were you responsible for Caliban's abrupt entrance into the proceedings?"

Catherine blushed hotly. "Well, yes. When I arrived, I thought it better not to knock on the front door, so I crept around to the side of the house. There, in the light of the window, I could see Caliban, ambling about in the garden, munching on the flowers like a duchess sampling lobster patties at an alfresco party. Then I remembered his behavior on the day you rescued Will from those ruffians. I didn't know what signal to give him, so I simply turned him about so that he faced the French doors and pushed him forward with a great slap on his rump. Caliban did the rest."

A shadow still lingered on Justin's features, but at Catherine's words, he laughed. The sound lifted Catherine's heart.

"I might have known," he murmured.

Robbie, watching interestedly, cleared his throat. "And you, Justin?" he asked awkwardly. "It is not to be wondered at that Catherine would suspect me of being the evildoer in the case. She does not know me very well, of course, and it appears that a great bit of evidence pointed in my direction." His voice became constricted. "Did you, too, believe I might be guilty of such a piece of work?"

"Not for a second, you great Scottish gowk," replied Justin instantly, suppressing the memory of the wisping, unworthy suspicions that had come to him earlier. "I knew you to be, as you've always been, my own strong right hand."

For a moment, Robbie eyed him sharply, then abruptly relaxed. "That's all right, then. I wonder, could we tell the coachman to deposit me at my lodgings? I would love to natter with you over the coffee cups, but as you said, it's been a long night."

"Of course," responded Catherine. Thumping on the roof panel, she relayed Robbie's directions to his home.

When Catherine and Justin eventually arrived at the house in Caroline Street, they were met by a worried Mariah and Lady Jane, who, not unnaturally demanded an explanation of Catherine's mysterious disappearance from her home in the middle of the night.

"My stars and garters!" exclaimed Lady Jane when they had told their story over breakfast. She and Mariah had listened, open-mouthed, with much gasping and interruptions with questions. "And it is all over now? You are exonerated, dear boy? You no longer need to pretend to be dead? Oh, I am so happy for you."

"And I," chimed Mariah, clasping Justin's hand in a speaking gesture. "But how dreadful for you to discover the perfidy of a man you had respected and admired for so long."

At this, Catherine glanced apprehensively at Justin. The blind look had left him, but his shock and grief were still apparent in his face. However, he merely replied slowly, "Yes, I am having difficulty coming to terms with his loss."

"What will you do now?" inquired Mariah.

He turned a bewildered gaze on Catherine, and her heart twisted within her.

"I don't know," he said slowly. He straightened. "I must leave here, of course."

"Leave!" cried Lady Jane. "Nonsense. I know I speak for all of us when I say you are welcome here for as long as you wish to stay."

"No." Justin's eyes were still on Catherine. "It would be much better if—" He drew a long breath. "What I think I will do is move into Sheffield House for the nonce. I do not believe St. John will mind. In fact, I shall send to him today, asking if he would consider coming to London. He will be called to the inquiry, I should imagine."

He held to this course of action through the chorus of objections raised by Mariah and Lady Jane. Catherine remained noticeably silent. At last, Mariah, with a significant glance at Lady Jane, declared her intention of departing from the breakfast room.

"I have some correspondence that I simply must attend to. And I believe, Grandmama, that you had some matters to attend to as well, did you not?"

"Eh? Oh! Yes—matters to attend to." She rose with a rustle of skirts. Pausing to drop a kiss on Justin's cheek, she exited the room on the arm of Mariah, who turned to wink at Catherine before scurrying out the door.

There was a long silence in the sunny little breakfast parlor.

Justin rose at last. "I—I suppose I'd better pack." He moved toward the door.

Catherine stood as well. "Not until you've slept for a few hours," she said with some asperity. "And after you've allowed me to look at your wounds. They don't appear to be serious, but they should be washed and bound in a real bandage." She moved to lay her hand on his arm.

He turned to her so abruptly that his eyes were brought disconcertingly close to hers.

"Catherine," he began awkwardly. "I wish—that is, I am sorry—" He sighed, running his fingers through his dark hair. "I have created such a monumental upheaval in your life."

"What?" asked Catherine, uncomprehending.

"In addition to the deception I perpetrated on you, I caused you to pull up stakes, very much against your inclination, to come to London, becoming embroiled in my difficulties—and now you must face an inquiry and a lot of poking and prying by the press. I would not have you—"

"What nonsense, Justin." Catherine smiled. "All of it was my own choice, and I would not have missed any of it for the world. It is I who should thank you, for if you had not charged into my life, I would still be cowering in the Keep, afraid to face my past and the world at large."

He was still very close to her, Catherine realized, and her heart was thundering like that of a trapped rabbit, but she made no move to distance herself.

"Are you going to be all right?" she asked at last.

It was Justin who stepped back. The smile that had begun to form on his lips faded, to be replaced by the expression of mockery that had come to be only too well-known to Catherine.

"Of course. I always land on my feet. I will admit this whole experience has been painful in the extreme, but I should have expected something of the sort. Indeed, it might be said that I have come to my just desserts. I simply was not born to become mired in tiresome relationships. I seem to have escaped, at least temporarily, the bad end predicted for me by my father, but I have learned my lesson. Other people form ties with family and friends. I enter into brief associations. I have become accustomed to that way of life, and, God knows, I deserve nothing more. No matter," he concluded softly, his gaze sinking into hers, "how much I might regret the fact from time to time."

He smiled then, briefly, but Catherine thought she had never seen such desolation as she perceived in those gun-metal eyes. Dear God, she had to do something before—She drew herself up.

"How dare you?" She fairly spat the words, and as Justin stiffened in shock, she advanced on him. "I have never heard such self-serving, self-pitying drivel in my life! Yes, you have lost a friend—more than a friend—a mentor and a man who was more a father to you than your own ever was, and you lost him in the most painful way possible, but—don't you see? You have found so much more."

"W-what?" stammered Justin, white-faced.

"For one thing, you have regained a brother—and, in a way, your own father. You and St. John may never grow close, but now you know that, deep in his heart, he cares about you, as did the old duke. You have something you can build on now. And you have affirmed your friendship with Robbie. He has proved—as he has many times before—that he is willing to risk his life for you."

She paused, and continued softly. "And you have found love."

Unthinking, Justin raised his hand to her cheek. "Catherine. you are—But, you must know—You cannot possibly consider a liaison with someone like me."

"There you go again," snapped Catherine in exasperation. "I wish you would rid yourself of this highly romantic but completely buffle-headed vision of yourself as a villain. You have shown yourself over and over again to be a man of goodness and decency. In addition," she finished triumphantly, "you are now a genuine, bona fide hero."

For a long moment, Justin simply gaped at her, until at length a mischievous smile lit his eyes. "By God, I am, aren't I?" Slowly, he lifted both hands to her shoulders.

"Of course you are, and—oh, Justin—" Catherine could feel the heat rising in her cheeks, and she could hardly speak for the knot of panic that rose in her throat. "I love you so very much."

Justin, whose head was descending slowly toward Catherine's, halted abruptly. "What did you say?" he asked in amazement.

Appalled and exhilarated by her own temerity, Catherine rushed on. "I love you, you great looby. And you love me!"

Justin's hands stilled in the delicious circles he was making on her back. He gazed at her in startled bemusement. "I do, don't I?" he murmured at last, stroking with infinite care the tendrils of hair that brushed her cheek. "I'm not so sure about all the rest—the decency and all that. On the other hand, I suppose if I tried very hard, I could achieve a certain degree of respectability. In any event—I do—love you. Dear God, I love you so!" He stepped back again, but just for a moment. "You might have told me," he said, his voice husky.

Catherine knew an urge to immolate herself in the blaze that flared in his eyes, turning them to molten silver. She laughed softly. "I might have, but you were having such a wonderful time being a scoundrel, it seemed a shame to spoil your fun."

Gently, Justin pulled her toward him. He pressed his lips against the curls he had been caressing a moment before, and Catherine settled into the lean curve of his body. She trembled as his mouth moved along her jawline, and she breathed in the wonderful, leather-and-spice smell of him. When at last his mouth covered hers, she felt the kiss down to her very toes. Everything she had thought she'd known of love vanished in the magic of his touch, and a storm of happiness washed over her in great, pulsing waves.

Justin's hands once again stroked her back, beginning with that exquisitely sensitive spot at the nape of her neck and moving along her spine. Eagerly, he pressed her to him until she thought her bones would melt into his. She uttered a tiny gasp of dismay as his mouth lifted from hers for an instant, only to feather kisses down her throat to the place where the ruffles of her neckline met the heated line of her skin.

His fingers brushed her breast, and Catherine thought she would shatter with wanting. At the small sound she made in the back of her throat, Justin stilled suddenly and drew back.

"You are going to marry me, aren't you?" His voice was a jagged rasp.

"Yes. Oh, yes, my darling, but—can't we begin now?"

A shudder passed through Justin's frame, but he dropped his hands from her shoulders.

"No. No, we cannot, you unprincipled wench. You forget, you are now talking to a pillar of propriety." He grew serious, and his gaze kindled once more into the crucible she had been drawn into a moment earlier. "The thought of making love to you has occupied my thoughts for some time now, but I—I want it to be right. You deserve more than a tumble on the breakfast room floor."

"Ah." Catherine gazed at him innocently. "Then, perhaps we should repair to your bedchamber."

"What?"

"So that I may re-bandage your wound, of course."

With hands that trembled only slightly, Catherine, reveling in her new rights, unfastened his top shirt button. Gently removing her fingers, Justin kissed her once more, slowly and lingeringly.

"I don't think that's a good idea," he whispered hoarsely.

This time it was Catherine who stepped back.

"I must say," she murmured peevishly, "I did not expect such a drastic reform so quickly. I thought I was making an offer to a declared villain—that would be you—of an unexceptionable opportunity for the ruination and despoilment of an innocent maiden—that would be me, of course—and all you do is prose on about the proprieties." The effect of this admonition was diminished somewhat by the soft kisses she feathered along his cheek.

"Hussy," said Justin unsteadily. "It was you who spoke of my innate decency and all that drivel. However," he concluded, an unmistakably anticipatory gleam flashing in his gaze, "it would not do to plunge headlong into respectability, would it? I doubt if my system could stand the shock."

He took Catherine's hand in his. "In the meantime, my wound is paining me dreadfully, Nurse. I think you had better see to it immediately."

Pausing only to press his lips to Catherine's for the briefest of kisses, Lord Justin Belforte, former spy and master of skulduggery, led his true love from the room.

Author's Note: There really *was* a bridge at Huerta. After the Battle of Salamanca, Wellington was much concerned over the problem of escaping French soldiers, and he became enraged at the news that the Spanish officer whose unit was guarding the bridge, took it upon himself to order it abandoned. Uncounted would-be prisoners of war made their way to safety over the bridge. There were no fugitive generals among them (although one did escape earlier, assisted by two British officers). Rivenchy, and the plot to help him to freedom, is solely an embroidery on the facts. The author feels this is what writers of romance fiction are for, after all.